WHAT READERS ARE ~
KAREN KINGSBURY'S BOOKS

"I've never been so moved by a novel in all my life."

—Val B.

"Karen Kingsbury's books are changing the world—one reader at a time."

—Lauren W.

"I literally cannot get enough of Karen Kingsbury's fiction. Her stories grab hold of my heart and don't let go until the very last page. Write faster, Karen!"

—Sharon A.

"Whenever I pick up a new KK book, two things are consistent: tissues and finishing the whole book in one day."

—Nel L.

"The best author in the country."

—Mary H.

"Karen's books remind me that God is real. I need that."

—Carrie F.

"Every time I read one of Karen's books I think, 'It's the best one yet.' Then the next one comes out and I think, 'No, this is the best one.'"

—April B. M.

"Novels are mini-vacations, and Karen's are my favorite destination."

—Rachel S.

Other Life-Changing Fiction™
by Karen Kingsbury

Stand-Alone Titles
Fifteen Minutes
The Chance
The Bridge
Oceans Apart
Between Sundays
When Joy Came to Stay
On Every Side
Divine
Like Dandelion Dust
Where Yesterday Lives
Shades of Blue
Unlocked
Coming Home—The Baxter Family

Angels Walking Series
Angels Walking
Chasing Sunsets
Brush of Wings

The Baxters—Redemption Series
Redemption
Remember
Return
Rejoice
Reunion

The Baxters—Firstborn Series
Fame
Forgiven
Found
Family
Forever

The Baxters—Sunrise Series
Sunrise
Summer
Someday
Sunset

The Baxters—Above the Line Series
Above the Line: Take One
Above the Line: Take Two
Above the Line: Take Three
Above the Line: Take Four

The Baxters—Bailey Flanigan Series
Leaving
Learning
Longing
Loving

Baxter Family Collection
A Baxter Family Christmas
Love Story
In This Moment
To the Moon and Back
When We Were Young
Two Weeks

9/11 Series
One Tuesday Morning
Beyond Tuesday Morning
Remember Tuesday Morning

Lost Love Series
Even Now
Ever After

Red Glove Series
Gideon's Gift
Maggie's Miracle
Sarah's Song
Hannah's Hope

e-Short Stories
The Beginning
I Can Only Imagine
*Elizabeth Baxter's 10 Secrets to
    a Happy Marriage*
Once Upon a Campus

Forever Faithful Series
Waiting for Morning
Moment of Weakness
Halfway to Forever

Women of Faith Fiction Series
A Time to Dance
A Time to Embrace

Cody Gunner Series
A Thousand Tomorrows
Just Beyond the Clouds
This Side of Heaven

**Life-Changing Bible Story
    Collections**
Family of Jesus
Friends of Jesus

Children's Titles
Let Me Hold You Longer
Let's Go on a Mommy Date
We Believe in Christmas
Let's Have a Daddy Day
*The Princess and the Three
    Knights*
The Brave Young Knight
Far Flutterby
*Go Ahead and Dream with
    Quarterback Alex Smith*
Whatever You Grow Up to Be
Always Daddy's Princess

Miracle Collections
*A Treasury of Christmas
    Miracles*
*A Treasury of Miracles for
    Women*
*A Treasury of Miracles for
    Teens*
*A Treasury of Miracles for
    Friends*
*A Treasury of Adoption
    Miracles*
Miracles—a Devotional

Gift Books
*Forever Young: Ten Gifts of
    Faith for the Graduate*
Forever My Little Boy
Forever My Little Girl
Stay Close Little Girl
Be Safe Little Boy

www.KarenKingsbury.com

KAREN KINGSBURY

TWO WEEKS

A Novel

ATRIA PAPERBACK

New York London Toronto Sydney New Delhi

ATRIA
PAPERBACK

An Imprint of Simon & Schuster, Inc.
1230 Avenue of the Americas
New York, NY 10020

This Atria trade paperback edition January 2020

ATRIA PAPERBACK and colophon are trademarks of Simon & Schuster, Inc.

For information about special discounts for bulk purchases, please contact Simon & Schuster Special Sales at 1-866-506-1949 or business@simonandschuster.com.

The Simon & Schuster Speakers Bureau can bring authors to your live event. For more information or to book an event, contact the Simon & Schuster Speakers Bureau at 1-866-248-3049 or visit our website at www.simonspeakers.com.

Designed by Davina Mock-Maniscalco

Family tree illustration by Phil Pascuzzo

Manufactured in the United States of America

1 3 5 7 9 10 8 6 4 2

Library of Congress Control Number: 2018032767

ISBN 978-1-4767-0743-3
ISBN 978-1-5011-7004-1 (pbk)
ISBN 978-1-4767-0750-1 (ebook)

To Donald:

Our family is so strong, so much closer than ever before. These are the years we dreamed about when we were raising our kids. A season when our adult kids would love God and each other, and when they would love spending a free Saturday night around the kitchen table—laughing and playing games and being best friends. These empty-nester years have been full of beautiful walks and meaningful talks, nights when we randomly jump into the car and spend an evening with Kelsey and Kyle and our adorable grandsons, Hudson and Nolan. We play tennis and Ping-Pong and hang out with our wonderful friends. And yes, we miss having our family all together every day. But when they come home the celebrating never ends. I loved raising our kids with you, and now I love this season, too. God has brought us through so many pages in our story. The Baxter family came to life while our kids were growing up. When the Baxters told stories around the family dinner table, we were doing the same. And when their kids auditioned for Christian theater, our kids were singing the same songs. Yes, our family is—and always will be—inexorably linked with the Baxters. Thank you, my love, for creating a world where our life and family and faith were so beautiful I could do nothing but write about it. So that some far-off day when we're old and the voices of our many grandchildren fill the house, we can pull out books like this one and remember. Every single beautiful moment. I love you.

To Kyle:

You will always be the young man we prayed for, the one we believed God for when it came to our precious only daughter. You love Kelsey so well, and you are such a great daddy to Hudson and Nolan. I literally thank God every day for you and for the friendship we all share. You are strong and confident, humble and kind. You lead your family in a way that is breathtaking. Thank you for bringing us constant joy. We pray and believe that the whole world will one day be changed for the better because of your music, your leadership, your love and your life.

To Kelsey:

What an amazing season this has been, watching you be the best mommy ever for precious Hudson and Nolan. Both your little boys are so happy and confident, filled with joy and innocence and a depth that goes beyond their ages. They are bright and kind and they love Jesus. I'm beyond proud of you and Kyle for the way you're parenting these angels. What a beautiful time for all of us! I'm savoring every day living so nearby to you and Kyle and the boys. As always, I believe God will continue to use your precious family as a very bright light . . . and I know that one day all the world will look to you both as an example of how to love well. Love you with all my heart, honey.

To Tyler:

I remember that long-ago day when you were ten and you said, "Mom, someday I'm going to write music and make movies. But I think I'm also going to write books in my spare time. Like you do!" And now that's exactly what you're doing. I can't believe we've just seen the release of *Best Family Ever: The Baxter Children*. It's hard to believe that we get the privilege of going back and telling the childhood stories of characters God gave me when you were a child. Really amazing, isn't it? How good God is? I always knew He had gifted you with great talent. But I never would've imagined the ways He would work it all together. You're still songwriting, still writing original screenplays and dreaming of making movies. And now you're writing books in your spare time, too. I love it! Your dad and I are beyond proud of how you serve at church and care for others. It's a privilege to be your parents. More than ever, God has great things ahead, and as always I am most thankful for this front-row seat. Oh, and for the occasional evening when you stop by for dinner and finish the night playing the piano. You are a very great blessing, Ty. Love you always.

To Sean:

I will always believe that God has great plans for you. These are the years when you choose who you'll be, the years when you will make choices that will determine your future. As you go through life, I pray you remember your loving past, your roots of faith and the way you are so very much a part of our family. God is kind to give each of us the choice, the decision to become the person we want to be—in faith, in work and in relationships. You are a beloved son, Sean. I can't wait to celebrate all that your life will be in the years to come. Stay in His word. I love you always and forever.

To Josh:

Way back when you were little, we always knew you'd grow up to be a hard worker, and you absolutely are! As our much-loved son, always remember that having a relationship with Jesus is the most important gift you will ever give your family. In the years to come, as you walk out your faith together, just know how much we love you. We always have. We believe in you. We are here for you always!

To EJ:

What a tremendous time this is for you, EJ. In just a few weeks you will walk across the stage at Liberty University, cinematic arts degree in hand! You are doing so well at school, so excited about the career in filmmaking you have chosen. And you are passionate about voice-over work! I really believe one day we'll hear you talking in a national commercial. Someone has to be the next best voice talent—it might as well be you! I've also seen you grow into a confident, communicative young man, humble and kind, but still able to speak your mind. Isn't it something how God knew—even all those years ago when you first entered our family—that you would need to be with people who loved God and loved each other . . . but also people who loved storytelling? I'm so excited about the future, and the way God will use your gifts to intersect with the gifts of so many others in our family. Maybe we should start our own studio—making movies that will change the world for God. Whatever the future holds, remember that your most powerful hour of the day is the one you give to Jesus. Stay in His word. Pray always. I love you.

To Austin:

It's hard to believe you're almost finished your junior year. One more year and you'll be a graduate! At Liberty people know you as a very bright light. The friend people turn to for a real conversation and a shoulder to cry on. Always at the center of everything fun that brings people together. You are honest and kind and your heart is deeper than the ocean. Your faith has truly become your own and it's so authentic and central to your life, it sometimes takes my breath. In addition to all that, you are a most wonderful son—always praying for us and making that random FaceTime call when you're wide awake in your apartment. I love that. You know how to invest in family and that effort always pays off. Our house is brighter when you're home. Austin, you will always be our miracle boy. Our overcomer. You are the youngest, and no question the hardest to let go. At times the quiet here is so . . . quiet. Even with your dad's jokes and little Hudson and Nolan running around. Just know that we have cherished every moment of raising you. I'm confident we will see you on the big screen one day soon! God is opening doors and making a way! We are your biggest fans and always here for you. We always will be. Love you forever, Aus.

And to God Almighty, the Author of Life,
who has—for now—blessed me with these.

THE BAXTER FAMILY

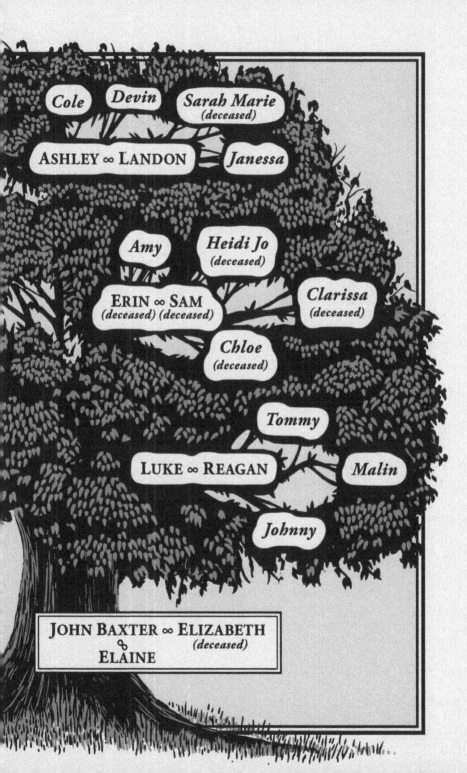

**BAXTER
FAMILY**

THIS BOOK IS part of the Baxter family collection, but it can be read as a stand-alone novel. Find out more about the Baxter family at the back of this book. Whether you've loved the Baxters for a decade, or you're finding them for the first time—*Two Weeks* is for you.

TWO
WEEKS

1

The cardboard box sat open on Elise Walker's lumpy twin bed, a note from her mother tucked inside. Three pens, half a dozen No. 2 pencils, two spiral notebooks and a pale blue binder. Under all that an old, worn red scarf. The tag was still on the frayed end. Goodwill. $2.99.

She picked up the note and read it again.

Dear Elise,

You're only eighteen, and I know you didn't want to go. But it's for the best. Randy's still mad you left. He tells everyone who'll listen. I think he would've hurt you if you'd stayed. Or worse. He's crazy, that boy. You're allowed to move on, baby. Even for a little while.

Your Bloomington school starts later this week. The least I could do is get you a few supplies and something to keep you warm. In case it snows. Plus, the scarf suits you.

Fiery red.

Don't worry about being at a new place.

You're gonna do great, baby. It's a good high school. Your aunt told me all about it. Nice part of town. Friendly kids. And they have an art club. Maybe you can join. Anyway, it's just a semester. You can come home this summer.

I miss you, Elise. Call you soon.

Love,
Mom

Elise ran her thumb over the words, her mother's writing. Why had she treated her mom so badly? Her mother wasn't exceptionally beautiful or daring or smart. She had never been married. Elise hadn't ever met the man who was her father. There had been no sign of him since Elise was born.

Still, her mama loved Jesus and she loved Elise. Loved her enough to work two jobs to pay the bills. The truth was, Elise felt treasured. Always.

You're the best thing that ever happened to me, baby. The best thing that ever happened. Elise could hear her mom's voice, hear the love in the melody of her words.

Even now. After all the ways Elise had come against her.

A sigh slipped through her lips.

Everything Elise had, her mother had scraped and saved and worked to pay for. So that when Hattie Walker came home each night at six o'clock between jobs she was exhausted. She had to be.

All for Elise.

The two of them had never been apart. Mostly because Elise hadn't had the chance to leave. In fact, last summer Elise would've done anything to get out of Leesville, Louisiana. Because for all the good Elise could say about her mother, the woman was old-fashioned and out of touch. She didn't understand real life.

Elise moved the cardboard box to the shaggy carpet and flopped down on the bed. Dinner would be ready soon, but she still had a few minutes. A sigh slipped from her lungs and she looked around. The walls were closing in. A million tiny pink roses wallpapered over every inch. Even worse were the heavy green velvet drapes that covered the only window.

As if light were forbidden here. The way it was from Elise's heart.

A week ago, on her first day in this house, Elise had dragged a clothes hamper to the window to hold back one side of the curtains. She used the desk chair for the other side. When she saw what Elise had done, her aunt had given the setup a wary look. Under her breath she whispered, "This too shall pass."

Which Elise assumed pretty much summed up how her aunt felt about having her here for the semester. Elise didn't care. She felt the same way. She was a senior. She would be out of here soon.

It's going to be a long semester. Elise relaxed into the bed. She didn't blame her aunt Carol and uncle Ken for not quite embracing the situation. Elise barely knew them, and still they were nice enough to take her in. Their two daughters—Elise's cousins—had finished college. Successful. Married. Never got in trouble.

They were nothing like Elise.

She looked out the window. Streaks of pink and blue colored the sky. What about her? What was she doing here in Bloomington, Indiana? A million miles from Leesville? This morning she'd overheard her uncle Ken talking low in the kitchen.

"Exactly how wild was she, Carol?" He was a serious man, tall and thin. Wire glasses and the same gray suit every day. He sounded like he couldn't decide if he was angry or worried. "She can get in trouble *here* just like back home."

"She won't get in trouble." Her aunt hadn't sounded quite sure. "I'll keep an eye on her."

Their words had stayed with her all day. Elise stared at the ceiling. She wasn't wild. Not really. No matter how everyone else saw her, that wasn't it. Until a year ago she'd been one of the good girls. Did her homework, stayed home Saturday night. Church on Sunday morning in the spot right next to her mama.

But two things happened midway through her junior year. Things that had changed her forever.

First, she became absolutely sure about what she wanted to do when she was older. The minute she graduated she would move to Manhattan and start classes at New York University. And she would study the only thing that stirred her soul. The one thing she wanted to spend her life doing.

Painting.

It wasn't that Elise wanted to be an artist when she grew up. She *was* an artist, born that way. She was most alive poised in front of an easel, brush in her hand. Bringing a scene to life, from her heart straight to the canvas.

Elise didn't see art as a pastime. It was her existence. Her future. Everything that mattered. And the night she figured that out, she had no choice but to tell her mother.

Midway through a dinner of grilled cheese sandwiches and tomato soup, her heart missing beats, Elise had pierced the tired silence. "So, Mama . . . I know what I want to do when I'm out of school." Her voice sounded happy, upbeat. This moment would be a time of celebration.

Her mother narrowed her weary eyes. She was between shifts cleaning floors at the hospital and working as a 911 operator for the local police department. "You're a little young." She sipped at a spoonful of soup. Her eyes looked nervous. "You know . . . to have all the answers."

"I thought I knew a long time ago what I wanted to be." She had watched for her mother's reaction. "But now I'm sure."

"Okay." Her mother's smile seemed uncertain. "What is it? You wanna be a doctor or a lawyer, baby? A school-teacher?" She stared at her still full bowl, moving her spoon through it. Anxious. A quiet, defeated laugh came from her. "Please tell me you don't want to clean hospital rooms."

"No, Mama." Elise looked at her mom for a long minute. She shook her head. "I don't want to clean anything." Her resolve grew. "I'm an artist. I want to paint." Fear tried to stop her, but she kept going. "After school, I'm moving to New York to study. Gonna enroll at NYU." She paused. "I'm good, Mama. I can make a living at it one day."

Her mother lifted her eyes and looked straight at Elise. "An artist?" The tips of her fingers began to tremble. "Baby." She shook her head. "You don't get paid to paint pictures." She didn't wait for a response. "You're smart. You can do anything you want. Be anything."

"I know. You always told me that." Her mom's disappointment ran through Elise's veins like a bad drug. "Which is why I want to be an artist."

Her mom got up and paced to the kitchen stove. When she turned and looked at Elise, her eyes filled with tears. "Baby, I can't afford New York. You know that." She hesitated. "We're simple folk. Any college would be a stretch. But NYU?"

"I can get scholarships, Mama." Panic choked off Elise's voice. "This is my dream."

Her mom was quiet for a minute. Then her expression gradually grew hard. "Tell you what, baby. Let's just settle this right now." She crossed her arms and shook her head. "You will not be an artist. Period."

"Mama!"

"No." Her lips closed tight together. "You will go to community college and be a teacher. Or a doctor. Something respectable." A final shake of her head, and her mama's eyes were cold as ice. "But you will not be an artist. Is that understood?"

And in that moment Elise felt something inside her turn to steel. No matter what her mother said, Elise would go to New York University. She would get the training she needed and she'd open her own studio. Somewhere near Manhattan's action and art scene. She'd wait tables until she could make a living selling her work. Maybe rent a flat in Chelsea, where other artists lived.

Whatever happened next in her life, Elise made herself a promise that day. She wasn't going to talk to her mother about it. No more. She would go after her dream by herself. From that moment on.

Every day her resolve grew, and with it a distance between her mom and her. Something the two of them had never known before. Elise stopped going to church, and less laughter marked their dinners. Her mother definitely noticed. She would set her fork down beside her plate and look at Elise. Just look at her.

"How was your day?" she would ask. Same question every night.

"Good." Elise would keep eating.

Images from the past dissolved and Elise stared at a patch of tiny roses on the wall of her new bedroom. She could've been nicer to her mama, should've tried harder. But her mother had no idea how serious Elise was about moving to New York. She was just a lonely single woman who talked often about how her best years were behind her. Her mama didn't seem to fathom Elise actually moving to the East Coast. Even still, Elise figured things with her mom would work themselves out eventually.

But then the second thing happened.

Elise stood and walked to the window. The sky was mostly dark now. Nighttime settling in.

"Elise, time for dinner!" Her aunt's voice carried through the small house. "Big day tomorrow!"

Yes. Elise blew at a wisp of her dark hair. Big day for sure. She was going to get straight A's here in Bloomington. No friends or guys. Not if she wanted to be serious about NYU. And she'd never been more serious about anything.

Elise turned toward the door. "Be right there." Then she looked out the window again and lifted her eyes to the sky. Things got worse with her mother after that. When the second thing happened her junior year.

She met Randy Collins.

He was the same age, a linebacker on the football team with a reputation as bad off the field as on it. Tall with tanned skin, a Hollywood face, and brown eyes that challenged everything she'd been raised to believe.

Elise knew who he was, of course, but one Friday night, the two of them wound up at the same party. Randy had a beer in his hand when he walked up to her. "Hey, pretty girl." He moved so close she could smell his breath. His lips curved into a smile, his words slurred. "Where you been all my life?"

The pickup line didn't feel like one coming from

him. She lowered her chin. Then she did something that went against everything she'd known about herself until that moment. She played along.

"Me?"

"Yeah, you." He pressed into her.

The new Elise was taking shape by the second. She didn't break eye contact. "Why . . . waiting for tonight of course." She batted her eyelashes and grinned at him. And as she did she felt something inside her shift. She was flirting, and talking close to a boy at a party. And a thought occurred to her.

She'd never felt this good before.

With Randy Collins so near she didn't need a drink. His presence was intoxicating enough.

"Elise!" Her aunt was coming for her.

She pulled away from the window and glanced at the mirror on the dresser. Randy used to say she looked like Belle in *Beauty and the Beast*. A wisp of a girl all long brown hair and big blue eyes. And he was the Beast. That's what he said.

A few blinks and Elise shook her head. "You don't look like Belle," she whispered to herself. "You look ordinary."

"Elise." Her aunt sounded beyond frustrated. "Dinner's getting cold! Please!"

"Coming." She moved away from the mirror and hurried out the door to the dining room. She wasn't Belle and she didn't believe in fairy tales. She was a bad girl, about to make good with her life.

Period.

Her aunt Carol couldn't cook, but at least she tried. Tonight was meat loaf, with ketchup and something crispy. Onions maybe. Elise wasn't sure. The green beans were cold, but that was her fault, for being late to dinner.

Uncle Ken spent most of the meal talking about a client. Someone loud and pushy. Ken wasn't sure he could handle the guy another day.

"I'm telling you, Carol, if he bursts through my door one more time with that tone, I think I'll . . . I'll tell him to leave." He shoved a forkful of beans into his mouth. One still poked out from his lips as he waved his free hand in circles. "I mean it. I don't need that kind of attitude in my office."

He caught the spare bean and chomped it. Then he poured himself a second glass of wine. Seemed the more Ken drank, the angrier he got. For the most part Aunt Carol nodded and sipped her own glass. These two drank a bottle a night. Ken kept talking, something about his boss. Carol seemed to do her best to look sympathetic. "Yes, dear," she would say every minute or so. Another sip of wine. "I understand, dear."

Elise focused on her meat loaf.

She didn't like being around so much drinking. Not now that she was away from Randy, anyway. Her mother never drank. "It's fine for some people," she would say. "But not for me." Elise understood. When she was in high school, her mama's daddy—Elise's only grandpa—died coming home from a bar. Crashed his pickup into a tree.

Anyway, the drinking made Elise uneasy. Or maybe just sad. Because the life her aunt and uncle lived felt meaningless. Empty. The walls were closing in down here, too.

When dinner was over, she helped Carol with the dishes. She'd agreed to this when she'd moved in. Take on her part of the chores. Elise didn't mind. It was the least she could do. Clearly having her stay here wasn't a part of her aunt and uncle's life plan.

Conversation with Carol wasn't easy. Not from the day Elise walked through the front door. Like her aunt wasn't sure what to make of Elise. Now though she seemed thoughtful. "Your mother must've been pretty upset to send you here." Carol was scrubbing the meat loaf pan.

Elise waited, towel ready. "I needed to leave." They'd never really talked about it before. The details about why Elise was here. Her mother had simply called her big sister over Christmas break and a week later Elise had stepped off a plane in Indiana.

Carol seemed to think about that for a minute. "She was too strict. I know my sister."

Her aunt's words were a little mumbled, directed at the soapy sink water and the meat loaf pan. Elise stared at her. "Ma'am?"

"Your mother." Carol turned to Elise. Something in her stuffy expression said she had all the answers. "She was too hard on you." A shake of her head, but she didn't look away. "All that God stuff, going to church, reading the Bible. You're young." She sighed and turned to the sink again. "Kids need freedom."

"Excuse me." Elise felt a ripple of anger work its way through her. "It's my fault I'm here." She kept her tone in check. "My mama had nothing to do with it."

Aunt Carol looked at her and raised an eyebrow. "I'm just saying." She rinsed the pan and handed it to Elise. "Anyone would have a hard time living with her. People can't measure up to the Bible. No one's that perfect. Including your mother." A small burp sounded from her lips, but her fingers got there too late to cover it up. She didn't seem to care. "How do you think you came into the world?"

That was it. Elise's heart was pounding now. How dare her aunt criticize her mama? She clenched her teeth so she wouldn't say something she'd regret. Then she dried the pan and set it on the counter. "Aunt Carol." She hesitated, choosing her words. "Please . . . don't say another word about my mama. You don't know her."

"Well." Her aunt waved a soapy hand in the air and shot Elise a disgusted look. "I wouldn't have expected you to defend her. Of all people."

Elise didn't respond to that. Ten silent minutes later and she was back in her room. Her heart was still racing, her rage in full gear. Yes, she had been a terrible daughter this past year. Her sweet mother was no match for her and the things she'd done. And no, they weren't close like they used to be.

But still, Aunt Carol had no right to talk about her

that way. Elise wanted to scream at her. None of this was her mama's fault, not at all. She glanced at the rose-papered walls. They were closing in again.

Elise closed her eyes for a few seconds. Never mind that her aunt and uncle were doing her a favor. The semester couldn't get over fast enough.

She moved to a small suitcase in the corner of the room and took a sketchbook from inside. The only way to change her mood now was to draw. She grabbed a pencil and sat on the chair near the window.

Like it had a heart of its own, her pencil began to fly across the page. This drawing wouldn't be anything original or new. She'd sketched the scene a hundred times before.

The New York City skyline.

She couldn't wait to be there, breathing in the city air, surrounded by the sounds and feels of Manhattan. And now only one thing stood between her and a move to the city. A semester in Bloomington, Indiana, at a school she'd never heard of before.

Clear Creek High.

2

Time was a thief.

That's what Cole Baxter Blake had heard his mom say before. The morning of his birthday or during some milestone for their family. It was the reason she painted. So she could capture the moments time stole.

Moments like this one.

Cole parked his car, stepped out and stared at the front of his school. His mom had reminded him earlier this morning that today—January 7—was special. Cole should take time to recognize it. Remember it. And so he would.

He breathed in and let the minute linger. Today was the first day of his last semester at Clear Creek High. A milestone. One more set of classes and midterms and final exams. One more season on the baseball team. One more prom. Then in the blink of an eye it would be May and he'd be wearing a cap and gown.

Headed to Liberty University.

His cousin Jessie was staying home to study elementary education at Indiana University. Some days Cole wanted to stay here, too. Closer to his family. But he'd visited Liberty twice and there was no turning back. God was calling him there, and not only for his undergrad degree but for medical school.

Something he'd decided over Christmas break.

Years from now, at the end of his collegiate journey, he would come back home—to Indiana—and he would work at Bloomington Hospital in the emergency room. Just like his grandpa John Baxter had done for decades.

Today, though, he was still here, still in high school. A bunch of lasts were right around the corner, but for now he would enjoy this first. He grabbed his backpack and pressed the lock button on his key chain.

The senior baseball players were meeting at lunch to talk about the season. They had a chance at the state title this year. It was only Cole's second year on the team, but he had earned a starting second base position. Practice began tomorrow afternoon. Their first game was two months away.

Across the snowy lawn a pretty blonde waved at him. Carolyn Everly. The two had been friends since freshman year. Twice they'd gone to dances together, but they'd never let things get serious. Cole was always too busy. Carolyn, too. Besides, like his dad told him—when you date things end one of two ways.

In marriage or a breakup.

Cole wasn't looking for either. Serious relationships could wait till late in college. With all the schooling he had ahead, friendships would have to do for now. He didn't have time for anything else. He grinned as Carolyn approached. "Good Christmas?"

"The best." She was a sweet girl, confident and kind. Her laughter lit up her eyes. "We got a new puppy. A golden retriever. Remy." She opened her phone and flashed a photo. "He's so cute."

Cole took a look. "He is cute. I'll have to come see him!" They kept talking as they walked toward the front doors. Ten minutes until the bell. Before they stepped inside, Cole hesitated. "Wasn't it yesterday when we were freshmen?" He looked up at the Clear Creek sign over the building. "I remember my dad dropping me off and feeling like this was the biggest school I'd ever seen."

"Yesterday." She glanced at him. "Clear Creek High. I used to think I'd never be old enough to go here."

"And now we're seniors."

"Crazy." She smiled at him. "We've had the best time, Cole. I wish we had another four years."

"Yeah." Cole didn't exactly wish that. He was excited about college and moving on with his future. But he knew what she meant. He gave her a quick hug. "I gotta get to chemistry."

"English Comp for me." They waved and parted ways.

Cole grabbed the straps of his backpack and picked up his pace. He wanted to be early. Especially on the first day. The science classes were through the main hall, out the back doors and in a separate building twenty yards to the rear of the school. This semester the class was taught by Mr. Hansen. One of Cole's favorites.

Cole walked in well before the bell, and already most

of the kids were at their desks. Front of the room was always his first choice, but that row was taken. The students in Mr. Hansen's class were serious about school. Like him, most of them were going to be premed in college. He found a spot in the second row and set his backpack on the floor.

"Hey." Her voice wasn't familiar. "Do we need composition notebooks for this class?"

Cole looked up and straight into the eyes of a girl he'd never met. Long brown hair layered around her narrow pale face. Blue eyes bigger than the ocean. He sucked in a quiet breath.

"Uh." He sat up straighter. She was the most beautiful girl he'd ever seen. "A few composition notebooks. Yes."

"Shoot." She frowned. "I knew I forgot something." Her smile was back. "I'll get them after school."

"No!" Not until he said the word did he realize it was a little too loud. Too fast. Like a command. He cleared his throat. "I mean, I have a bunch of them at home. I'll bring you a few tomorrow."

"Really?" She seemed surprised. "Thanks!" With the ease of a dancer she turned in her desk so she was facing him. "I'm Elise Walker. I'm new."

No kidding. Cole swallowed. His heart was beating so hard he half expected it to burst from his chest and land on the floor between them. "I'm Cole. Cole Blake. I'm a senior." He didn't want the conversation to end. "Where'd you transfer from?"

"Louisiana. Leesville." She wrinkled her nose, like she didn't expect him to know where that was. "One main street. Four stoplights."

Cole had a thousand questions. "Your dad got transferred here?"

"No." The light in Elise's eyes dimmed a bit. "Nothing like that."

Mr. Hansen stepped to the front of the room. "Okay, quiet down." He looked around. "I see some of Clear Creek's finest here this morning." A grin made its way up his face. "This is going to be fun."

Mr. Hansen kept talking, but Cole didn't hear a word of it. His composition notebook was open, pen ready. Occasionally he caught a phrase or a topic and scribbled it on the lined paper. But mostly he just watched Elise. The way she tossed her pretty hair over her slim shoulders, the seriousness in her big blue eyes, as if her next breath depended on whatever Mr. Hansen was talking about.

"Isn't that right, Cole?" The teacher was staring straight at him. A heavy silence followed.

"Yes, sir . . ."

"What do you think the medical community means by that?" Mr. Hansen raised his brow at Cole.

Heat filled his cheeks. *Come on, Cole. Find your way out of this.* "Absolutely." He remembered to smile. "Whatever you say, Mr. Hansen. I tell everyone you're the best teacher on campus."

Mr. Hansen appeared wary, and Cole knew he'd been

caught. He hadn't been listening even a little. But just when the man looked like he might test Cole on the fact, Elise cast him a quick look and then raised her hand.

"Yes, ma'am." Mr. Hansen's brow moved up his forehead. "You'd like to help Mr. Blake out, would you?"

"No, sir." She sat up straighter, her expression as innocent as a child's. "It's just, Cole's telling the truth. I'm new here." She glanced at a few of their classmates. "First thing he told me when I sat down was how you were the best teacher at Clear Creek." She looked at Cole like she'd known him forever. Then back to Mr. Hansen. "Just saying."

The instructor folded his arms. "All right, fine." He cast a hesitant eye at Cole. "Let's pay attention. This course moves fast. Lots to learn."

Cole nodded. "Yes, sir." He didn't dare look at Elise. Why in the world would she rescue him? Making up a story right on the spot? He had no answer, but after that he made a point of paying attention. Never mind the girl, he had a purpose for being in this class. He needed to ace the course and then pass the AP exam at the end of the semester.

He would talk to Elise later.

As it turned out, he had to wait after class to ask Mr. Hansen about the date of the AP test, and by the time he had his answer, Elise was gone. He'd see her tomorrow. Too much on his mind to worry about her today.

But it wasn't that easy.

For the first time in his life, Cole was instantly obsessed with a girl. He couldn't stop thinking about her. He caught himself looking for Elise between classes and after lunch with the senior baseball players. He didn't see her again until the end of the day, when he was walking to his car. She was maybe ten yards away.

"Elise." He jogged to her. "Wait up." She turned and smiled at him. She wore jeans and low-heeled boots. A flannel shirt the same color as her eyes. Plain navy backpack. Not a lot of makeup. Definitely more country than most of the girls he knew. It didn't matter. Elise didn't need eye shadow. Her beauty was real and raw, the kind that stood on its own.

"That Mr. Hansen." Her eyes danced into a light laugh. "Best teacher around."

Cole was a little winded. Not because of the jog but because of Elise. The way she took over his senses. "Why?" He searched her eyes. The afternoon sun shone down on the two of them, taking the chill off the January day. "You . . . didn't have to do that."

"I know." She stopped and stared at him, straight through him. "You seemed like you could use a little help."

"But . . . you barely know me."

She started walking again and he tried to keep up with her. She shot a look at him over her shoulder. "Composition notebooks." Another stop and this time she grinned and did the cutest shrug. "My mama always said one good turn deserves another."

"Yeah, well . . ." He was about to explain that he never would've asked her to lie for him, but that could wait. No reason to shift the mood. "Your car in the front lot?" His was, so he figured that's where she was headed.

Another quiet laugh. "I don't have a car." She adjusted her backpack. "I'm walking."

It was the one day Cole didn't have practice after school. This time he stayed even with her. "I'll give you a ride."

She slowed a bit and watched him. Like she was seeing him for the first time. "It's not far. Just a half a mile or so."

"I wanna hear more about you. What brought you here."

For a few seconds she seemed like she might turn him down. But then she raised one shoulder, the way she had earlier in science class. Her smile reached her eyes. "Okay. It *is* freezing here. Not like home." She shaded her eyes toward the sun. "Even with the pretty blue sky."

Because of you, Cole wanted to say. *It's only pretty because of you.* But he stopped himself. What was he thinking? No girl had made him feel like this. He kept a steady pace, one hand in his pocket. *Play it cool, Cole. Come on.* "I have an idea." He could feel a goofy grin coming over him. There wasn't a thing he could do about it. "How about coffee? You know, to celebrate. First day of the semester."

They reached his Ford Explorer and he opened the passenger door. She gave a slight shake of her head. "Not today. I have homework." Cole held the door open for her and she climbed inside.

"We won't be long. Maybe half an hour." Cole hurried around to the driver's side, slid in behind the wheel and faced her. "I think you should say yes."

"Why?" Her eyes sparkled. "Like you said, I don't even know you."

"You know Mr. Hansen is the best teacher on campus. We both agree on that." He grinned. "Also . . . I think it just might be the best decision of your life." He winced. *So much for playing it cool.* A light chuckle came from him. "Too much?"

"Definitely." She laughed. "But coffee sounds fun. If we're quick."

They went to Java on Main, one of the shops owned by his family's friends—Brandon and Bailey Paul. Sofas and rocking chairs made up the lobby. Framed Bible verses hung on the walls. Cole set his backpack on the nearest sofa and they found the back of a short line. Five minutes later they were sitting side by side, angled so they could see each other.

She sipped a steaming mint tea and he drank a hot chocolate. The longer he spent around her the dizzier he felt. He could already write her story. Good girl. Good family. Probably attended church every Sunday. He leaned his shoulder into the back of the sofa and searched her eyes. "So why here? Why Bloomington?"

Her hesitation didn't last long. "Better science department." The shine in her eyes gave her away.

"Right." Now that he was here, alone with her, Cole was willing to take his time. "That's supposed to be *my* answer."

"Yours?" She tilted her chin, clearly playing with him. "You mean you really do think Mr. Hansen is the best teacher on the planet?"

"Maybe." Cole took a deep breath. "I'm going to Liberty University in the fall. Premed. I need all A's in science and math."

She angled her head. "You're serious?"

"Yeah." It felt better every time he talked about it. He was going to be a doctor. No doubts at all. "And you? A lawyer? Those negotiating skills you impressed the class with earlier?"

Her laughter was as easy as her company. "Hardly." She paused, locking eyes with him. As if this next part might be especially important. "I'm going to NYU in August to study art." She hesitated. "At least I want to." Her expression grew deeper than before. "I mean, I know I'm only eighteen, but eventually I want to open my own studio in Manhattan. They'll be lined up around the block to get my paintings."

An artist? Just like his mom. A dawning came over Cole. "That's it." Again his voice was a little too loud. He lowered it a few notches. "I knew there was something familiar about you."

"Cole." Elise's tone fell to a whisper. "You're very loud. Anyone ever told you that?"

He liked her spunk. "I'm not usually like this. You bring it out in me."

She raised her eyebrows. "I see." Her giggle kept the moment light. "What were you going to say?"

"Right. That." *Relax*, he ordered himself. *You have to relax. And talk quieter.* "Okay . . . so you remind me of my mom. She's an artist." He brought one knee up on the sofa and surveyed her. "You even look like her."

"I do?" His statement seemed to make her uneasy. "I hope that's a good thing."

"It is." This time Cole remembered to keep his voice softer. "She's amazing. You'll have to meet her sometime."

"Sure." Elise looked down at her hands for a long moment and then at him. The idea clearly made her uncomfortable. "How long have you lived here?"

"All my life. Well, pretty much." He found a more relaxed rhythm to the conversation. "A few years in Paris, but then here since I was two."

"Paris!" A dreamy look came over her. "That's like heaven for artists. Maybe I will have to meet your mom."

"Yeah." It hadn't exactly been the best time for his mother. But that was another story. "What do you like about painting?"

"Everything." She looked like she'd just taken a breath of fresh air. "It's like . . . I become the paint. All that I see and feel and care about goes through my hand into my brush and onto the page."

"Well, you've come to the right place. My mom says there's a lot to paint here in Bloomington." He grinned at her again. "That's it, right?" He was only half teasing. "The reason your family moved here?"

"For my painting?" Her laugh died off. "Yeah, hardly."

Their eyes held for a few seconds. "It's . . . complicated."
She glanced at her knees and then up at him again. This
time fear seemed to color her expression. "We have family here." Her voice fell flat. "Everyone thought it was for
the best."

Cole nodded. He still didn't know what her dad did
for a living or how come they'd picked up in the middle
of a school year to move here. But he didn't need all the
answers now. "Whatever brought you here, it was a good
move. I'm sure about that."

"I hope so." Her smile wasn't what it had been earlier.
"We'll see." She checked the time on her phone. "I need
to go. I really do have homework."

"Okay." Cole didn't want the afternoon to end. But
she was right. He needed to pick up a new baseball bat
before practice tomorrow. They both had things to do.
He dropped her off in front of a small single-story house
with no cars out front. Whatever her parents did, they
weren't home yet.

"Thanks, Cole." She didn't linger. Instead she stepped
out and hesitated. She leaned back toward the car before
walking away. "You're my first Bloomington friend."

"Thanks." Cole wanted to think of something clever
to follow up with. But nothing came to mind. "See you
tomorrow."

Not till he was home with his new bat did it hit him.
He should've said she was his first friend from Leesville,
Louisiana. He set his things down on the kitchen counter
and spotted his mom out back. Sitting on a high stool

behind her easel in one of her favorite spots—the porch overlooking his grandma Elizabeth's rose garden.

Cole grabbed an apple and went to join her. She looked like she was just wrapping up. A person could only paint in the winter cold for so long. She lifted her eyes to his and smiled. "How was your last first day?"

"Mom." Cole raised his eyebrows. "Come on. You said you wouldn't talk about the lasts. Not all the time at least."

"Okay." She set her paintbrush down and faced him. "Just here and there." She angled her head. "It is your last semester of high school."

His heart softened at the thought. "True." He smiled. "My day was great. Amazing, actually."

"No baseball?"

"Not today. The guys got together at lunch. One of us is going to start practice every day with a Bible verse." He leaned on the nearest post and turned to her painting. A grassy field, the Baxter house in the distance, and on the front porch a gray-haired couple in rocking chairs. The people in the painting were too small to make out any real details. In the foreground were numerous children and adults. All of which seemed to be the same family at different ages. He turned to her. "Nice."

"Thanks." His mom stared at something in her work. "The older couple is the same as the one in every other part of the painting. Each of them at different points in their story."

"At first I thought it was a party on the lawn." Cole leaned closer, studying the work. "So many people."

"All the same couple. Same children." She sighed. "All of you, of course. Through the years."

"Mmm." Cole loved his mom's creativity. "What's it called?"

"*Moments Gone.*" She smiled at Cole again. "Life goes so fast. And one day you're gray and the kids have moved on and you're rocking on the front porch remembering all that ever was. A memory for every spot that makes up the land around us."

"I love it." Cole took a deep breath. He waited till his mother looked at him again. "I met a girl today."

He watched her expression brighten. "A girl, huh? Someone new?"

"Yes. She's from Louisiana." Cole tried to keep his expression casual. So this wouldn't be too big a deal. But he could feel his smile filling his face. "She's like . . . perfect."

"Wow." His mom turned a little more so she was facing him fully. "Perfect?"

"Yeah. I took her to coffee after school." He still could barely feel his feet beneath him. "She's an artist. Like you."

Warmth filled his mother's eyes. "I'd love to meet her."

Cole nodded. "You will." He took a bite of the apple. As he did he heard the sound of voices in the kitchen. The younger kids were home. Cole shot his mom a look. "Don't tell anyone, okay? I'll talk to Dad later. Like when the others are in bed."

"Okay." His mom closed up her paints and followed Cole into the house. "You can tell us both all about her."

He waited through dinner until after his siblings

turned in. Then he sat down with his parents and tried to explain Elise. What it was about her that had grabbed hold of his heart. But no matter how he tried, he couldn't put his feelings into words. Just that she was someone special, and that he couldn't stop thinking about her.

Finally, Cole stood. "I need to get to sleep." He looked from his dad to his mom. "All I know is Elise is the kind of girl I'm going to marry someday."

The slightly alarmed looks on their faces made him laugh out loud. "Don't worry. No time soon." He waved to them. "College first. But then . . . who knows?"

He left them with that thought, the same thought he took with him to bed that night. Could it happen, love at first sight? Whatever it was with Elise, no girl had affected him the way she had. All in one day.

Cole looked to the sliver of a moon in the cold dark night sky just outside his window. *Is she the one, Lord?* He heard no answer, no sense of affirmation. The idea was crazy, really. They'd known each other only one day. And they were just eighteen. But that wasn't too young, right? They were adults, after all. His mind kept spinning, replaying every minute with her. The way her blue eyes felt against his. But even as he fell asleep, one very definite thought stayed with him.

He couldn't wait till tomorrow.

• • •

ASHLEY BAXTER BLAKE watched her oldest son head up to bed, then she turned and stared at her husband. Her heart was beating in her throat. "Landon." Her voice was more laugh than cry. "What just happened?"

He was sitting across from her in the recliner. "You mean Cole?"

"Of course I mean Cole." Ashley stood and paced to the other end of the room. She raised her hands. "Our son just met this girl and he's ready to marry her."

Landon took a moment. Then he stood and came to her. When they were inches apart he put his hands on either side of her face. "Ashley. It's okay."

"Maybe not." She kept her voice low. The last thing she wanted was for Cole to hear her concern. She eased her arms around Landon's waist and leaned her forehead on his shoulder. "Cole's never like this." She looked into his eyes. "He's been the most levelheaded kid all through high school."

"Baby." Landon stared all the way to her soul. "He still is. This is infatuation. The girl's an artist. She caught Cole's attention." He kissed her cheek. "That's all."

Only then did her heart rate slow down. She studied him, the love of her life. He always knew what to say, even now. "You think so?"

"Of course." He angled his head, kindness brimming in his eyes. "At least he told us. How many kids would do that?"

"True." Ashley brushed the side of her face against Landon's and kissed him. "You always have the answers."

"Not always." He kissed her this time, and it lasted longer than before.

"Right." Ashley felt herself relax. She whispered against his skin. "Just whenever I need help."

"Which is the only time it matters." Landon took her by the hand. "Come on. Let's not borrow trouble."

Right again. Ashley exhaled. Landon was so sensible at times like this. Cole's excitement was nothing more than first-day thrills over the new girl at school.

Landon was still leading the way to the stairs that led to their room, but he stopped and took her into his arms again. This time his kiss left her breathless. He ran his thumb along her cheek. "I love you, Ashley." After a few seconds he started walking again. "Let's get our mind off Cole." He winked at her.

Ashley giggled and then at the same time she felt herself blush. Not because the kids would know what they were laughing about or even hear them at all. But because Landon had a way of making her feel like a newlywed.

Over and over and over again.

3

In the new house there was no way to avoid the room. In fact if Lucy Williams had been in charge of decorating, they wouldn't have things set up like this at all. Especially now that they'd sold the old place in Atlanta.

Bloomington was a fresh start for Aaron and her. No well-meaning friends at church asking whether they'd thought of in vitro fertilization or some special diet meant to aid fertility. No social workers calling to see if they'd foster a teenage runaway for a week in lieu of a baby. No one feeling sorry for them.

Poor Aaron and Lucy. Trying ten years to have a baby and still nothing.

Lucy crossed the upstairs hallway and stopped at the room. The nursery. Seven years ago back in Georgia they'd filled a bedroom like this one. Same crib with the pastel baby animal sheets. Same dresser with the untouched teddy bears that lined the top. Same changing table and pale gray rocking recliner. Same Winnie-the-Pooh curtains framing the windows.

Setting up the nursery again here in their new home had been Aaron's idea. A declaration of faith, he called it.

Aaron used the room for his Bible time each morning. If infertility was a boat tossed about on a stormy sea, Aaron was the one willing to step out. Willing to walk on the waves. He believed to the core of his soul that God would bring them a baby. When the two of them prayed about it, Aaron believed so completely he actually thanked God. Time and time again.

Without any signs of a child.

Lucy leaned against the doorframe and stared into the lifeless room. The Atlanta house had been a ranch. Everything on one floor. Because of the layout, she could avoid the hallway that led to the nursery. But not here.

And so every day since they'd unpacked three months ago, Lucy had to walk by this spot. Most of the time she didn't stop, didn't look in. Tried not to think about it. Especially given the job she was doing.

Pediatric nurse at Bloomington Hospital.

She stared at the crib and tried to picture it, a baby lying in the pretty bed. A nine-month-old pulling herself up and calling out for them. *Mommy . . . Daddy.*

Ghost voices that would never come to be.

A sigh made its way through her and filled the silence. God had either banned them from the child-rearing list or forgotten about them. Lucy couldn't understand why Aaron still prayed. Still believed.

The difference between the two of them was becoming a great divide. Lucy should have been angry at him for clinging to his faith after so much disappointment and heartache. But she couldn't bring herself to be upset.

Instead, she felt sorry for him.

With their views on faith and fertility growing further apart, Lucy felt more alone with every passing day. The only glimmer of hope she'd found since moving to Bloomington was a friend she'd met at the hospital. A pediatrician who made the rounds and had somehow noticed her. The sadness inside her.

A doctor named Brooke Baxter West.

Lucy turned away from the nursery and walked downstairs. Thirty minutes till her shift began, and she liked to be early. Liked to walk around the unit and smile into the faces of the babies. Where she could imagine what it would be like if one day the baby was hers.

Twenty minutes later, after a coffee stop, Lucy got off the elevator at the hospital's second-floor administrative offices. Aaron worked here, an assistant administrator. The president of the hospital was quoted as saying Aaron was one of the brightest new faces on the team, and that they expected great things from him in the future.

Lucy felt the same way about her husband's professional future.

It was their personal future that worried her.

How could she feel hopeful about their marriage when she disappointed him every twenty-eight days? All the fertility tests on the market could never determine whose fault it was. Why they couldn't get pregnant. But Lucy knew. It was her . . . it had to be. Hers was the body not making a baby. No matter how she prayed or ate or believed. No matter how often they tried.

Her period came.

She took slow steps down the hall toward Aaron's office. She wore her white nurse's scrubs, her name tag firmly in place. Her pale blond hair pulled back in a ponytail. She held both cups of coffee in her hands. A peace offering for the way her discouragement layered dark clouds over their relationship.

She used her elbow to give a quiet knock at her husband's office door, and a few seconds later she heard him approach. *God, if You're there, help me love him. Please. This isn't his fault.*

Aaron opened it and smiled at her. "Hey, beautiful." He took both coffees from her, set them down on his desk, and then gently eased her into his arms. "What a surprise."

She waited a minute in his embrace, then she shut the door behind her and nodded to the coffee. "For you."

"Mmm." His eyes found hers. "Caramel Machi-Frappiato with extra Breve Espresso?"

"Exactly." The slightest laugh came from her. "Black coffee never sounded so good."

"I try to sound like I belong." He picked up the cup with his name and breathed in the smell before setting it down again. "You know, part of the Java on Main Club."

"Right." She angled her head and looked at him. He was still blond, like her. The two of them stayed in shape so that when—if—a baby came they'd be ready. Not too old. Not yet.

He leaned against the corner of his desk and searched her face. "What's wrong?"

"My period." She took a slow breath and sank against the wall. "I got it this morning."

The familiar disappointment flashed across his face, the way it had so many times in the past. And like before he did what he could to cover it up. "Baby, that's okay." He held out his arms, a smile lifting the corners of his mouth. "We have time."

She came to him, her coffee still on the desk. *We don't have time,* she wanted to tell him. *We're getting older every month and nothing is helping. Look at all we've lost!* But like every four weeks before this, she said none of that.

Instead she moved into his arms and put her cheek against his. "You're right. We have time."

He stroked her back with one hand and cradled her head with the other. "Our baby will come to us. In God's timing, Lucy. Please." He eased away and searched her face. "Believe. Okay?"

How could she tell him she'd stopped believing years ago? Not only in having a baby of their own, but in adopting. They'd tried everything and here they were. "Sometimes . . ." Her voice was broken, barely a whisper. "I try to remember what it was like in the beginning. When just you and me was enough." She blinked back tears. "When we didn't feel this . . . this terrible emptiness . . . every month."

"Hey." He framed her face with his hands. "You're still enough. We're still enough."

Lucy lowered her gaze to the floor, to the place

where their feet touched. Not for another minute could she pretend about this. With an effort that came from the most broken place in her heart, she shook her head. "No, Aaron." She raised her eyes to him. "We're not enough. A baby . . . it's all we talk about. All we think about."

He opened his mouth, but no words came. Probably because she was right, and by now he knew it. What could he say? Instead he exhaled and finally, fully, the sadness filled his eyes as well. "I don't want you to feel that way."

"I can't help it." She lifted her hand to his face and eased her thumb over his cheek. "We both do. It's true, Aaron. You know it."

"Lucy. I still believe." He shrugged even as tears welled in his eyes. "What am I supposed to do with that?"

"I don't know." She took a few steps back and leaned against the wall again. "Maybe we could stop for a while. Give it a rest."

Confusion clouded his eyes. "What? Us?"

"No." A single tear fell on her cheek. "Of course not." She sniffed. "Like the process. The diet and fertility drugs and doctor appointments." She crossed his office and looked out his enormous picture window. All of Bloomington spread like a painting below them. After a few seconds she turned and faced him again. "Just be us. The way we used to be."

For a while, Aaron only watched her, his eyes locked

on hers. As if he wasn't sure what to say or how to move forward. But then he came to her. He took her in his arms again and held her head to his chest. "Baby, if that's what you want, then that's what we'll do." She could hear his heart beating hard. Like it was killing him to give the idea of having a baby a rest.

But maybe he would do it now. For her.

"Really?" She found his eyes once more.

"Yes." He couldn't hide the heartache in his expression, the way it narrowed his eyes and made his smile look sad. "I'll let it go, Lucy. If that's what you want."

She nodded. "It is." The desperate hurt in her heart swelled and filled her senses. Tears flooded her eyes. "I can't . . . I can't keep trying, Aaron. It's killing me."

"Shhh." He rocked her and kissed the top of her head. "I understand. We'll take a break. I promise."

"I just want to love you." Her cheeks were wet with tears, but she didn't care. She brought her lips to his and kissed him. "I don't want sex to be a science or a means to an end. I want it to be like it was in the beginning."

"Truly. Madly. Deeply." He breathed the words against the side of her face. "You and only you, Lucy."

She squeezed her eyes shut. "Yes." The words had been part of their vows. Truly. Madly. Deeply. The ones that defined them in the beginning, twelve long years ago when they stood in front of family and friends in Atlanta and promised forever to each other.

They were thirty-six now. Closer to forty than not. But still those words spoke straight to her soul. She opened her eyes and searched his. Then she kissed him again. "Thank you."

"Is it okay . . . if I still have my mornings there? In the nursery?" He looked like he would give that up, too, for her.

If she were completely honest, her answer was no. She would've liked to find a couple two-by-fours and nail the nursery door shut. For good. But if he was willing to give their desperate efforts a rest, she was willing to let him have his Bible time near the crib. "Yes." She brushed her nose against his. "If it doesn't make things too hard for you."

His look told her he understood. Praying and believing all while giving up the very efforts that might possibly make a difference. The moment grew deeper. "What happens in that room . . . that's between God and me. Not you." He kissed her. "I promise."

"Okay." She took a sharp breath and pulled away. "I have to get to work."

"Right." The rawness in his expression lingered. "Thanks for talking."

She pressed her hand against her lower stomach. Her cramps were worse than usual. "I had to, Aaron. I was feeling like . . . we were living in separate universes."

He reached for her coffee and handed it to her. Then he walked her to the door. "I'm sorry."

"It's not that I've given up." She looked at him over her shoulder. "Not completely."

"I know." He smiled. "Just for now."

"Yes." She ran her fingers beneath her eyes. "For now."

As she walked away, her heart and steps felt light for the first time in longer than she could remember. This was the break she needed.

They couldn't live life obsessed with the single goal of having a baby. She wanted real love. Love, the way it used to be. That's what this season would be. As if they'd never wanted a baby at all. She stepped onto the empty elevator and pressed the button for the sixth floor. Labor and delivery. And suddenly it was her twenty-ninth birthday and she was at the hospital in Atlanta again.

Aaron was with her and she was on a stretcher. Blood and water coming from between her legs. After every possible approach and tens of thousands of dollars the in vitro process had finally worked.

As soon as they found out the baby was a girl, they named her Sophie Grace. Every prayer had been answered, every effort had been worthwhile. Each week through her pregnancy, Aaron would read out loud about what stage the baby was at. How she was the size of a grape and then a plum and then a pear.

How her little heart and arms and legs were fully formed and how her eyelashes were growing. "Long and full like her mommy's," Aaron would say.

And Lucy was standing in the kitchen singing "Jesus Loves Me," because baby Sophie could hear. That's what the websites said. At twenty weeks she could hear everything around her, but especially Lucy's voice. So she was singing songs about Jesus whenever she could and changing the words to say, "Jesus loves you, this I know." Because the song was for Sophie. For her alone. And Lucy was drying the last pan when water suddenly gushed between her legs and splashed on the floor.

"Aaron!" She could still hear her scream, feel it deep inside her. "Aaron, come here! Hurry."

The cramps had started even as she yelled for him, and suddenly they were in the car and she was sitting on a towel and it wasn't just water. It was blood and water. And the tears wouldn't stop streaming down her face.

And they were in the elevator headed to labor and delivery, and in a blur baby Sophie was there. She was there and she was in their arms, her tiny body nowhere near ready for the world. They were holding her in a blanket and whispering to her and singing, "Jesus loves you, this I know. For the Bible tells me so."

Ten minutes. They had ten minutes with their little girl. Ten minutes to love her and sing to her and tell her how much they wanted her to live. And it was the eleventh minute and Sophie stopped breathing and the doctors weren't doing anything to help her.

"Someone! Do something!" Lucy didn't want to scream because the sound might startle her baby, her Sophie. Only the nurses and doctor in the room just bowed their heads and closed their eyes.

Before the twelfth minute, Sophie turned her tiny face toward them and her little body went still. Even now Lucy could swear she smiled. Her baby girl smiled. As if to tell them it was okay. Where she was going she'd be whole and happy and one day she'd see them again.

And like a million times before—every exhilarating moment of her pregnancy and every terrible minute after her water broke played out in the time it took Lucy to reach the sixth floor. As the doors opened she stepped out and breathed deep.

She could do this.

She could walk through the doors of the maternity ward and tend to the babies, the job she had studied for and dreamed about since she was in high school. And she could get through another shift knowing that *these* were her babies. The ones she was paid to care for and love. And later today Brooke would make her rounds and the two of them would talk. Brooke always had so much wisdom. So much concern for Lucy.

And she could do this because she and Aaron were finished trying for now. Maybe forever. From here on the memory of Sophie was all they would have. All they would need. And it would be just like it used to be at the beginning. Aaron and her. Taking walks, talking about the hospital, biking to downtown for a day of window-shopping.

Just the two of them.

Truly. Madly. Deeply.

4

This was the drive Theo Brown looked forward to every weekday. The one to Clear Creek High School, with his daughter, Vienna, at his side. By now each morning, his wife, Alma, would be headed to work where she was assistant principal of Bloomington Elementary School. Theo worked from home in pharmaceutical sales.

So since she started kindergarten, Theo got the pleasure of taking Vienna to school. Every single day.

His daughter slid into the front passenger seat, breathless. "I'm late." She dropped her backpack on the floor between her feet and fastened her seat belt. "Sorry, Daddy."

He chuckled. "You're fine, baby. You can miss a few minutes of school."

Vienna leaned her head back against the seat and exhaled. "I love when you say that. Takes away all the stress of ninth grade."

"Ninth grade can definitely be stressful." Theo flashed her a quick grin. She was such a pretty girl, just like her mother. Vienna wore her hair wavy, same as Alma. Her brown eyes shone with goodness and light, faith and possibilities. Theo stared at the road ahead of them. He couldn't be more proud of his baby girl.

Vienna was a straight-A student, the only freshman on the school's dance team, and a budding writer. A one-in-a-million girl, if ever there was one.

"Okay, Daddy." She turned in her seat and faced him. "I have an idea. I've been wanting to talk to you and Mom, but this will do."

"Thanks." He laughed. "Glad I'll do."

She giggled. "You know what I mean." Her words came quickly, in time with her enthusiasm. "Remember how you and Mom used to foster kids?"

"Of course." Theo felt his heart warm at the memory. "We stopped for you. So you'd have our full attention."

"I know." She couldn't hide the regret in her tone. "Mom keeps saying graduation will be here before I know it and y'all can foster kids after I'm in college."

"Right." Theo wasn't sure where she was going with this. Last time they'd talked about taking in foster kids, Vienna had been in agreement. This was a good time for a break. "The older kids need so many meetings and appointments. And the babies . . ."

"That's it!" Vienna's voice rang with excitement. "It's the babies, Daddy. That's what I want you and Mom to think about."

They pulled up at a red light and Theo looked at her. He raised his brow up high on his forehead. "Babies? Are you serious?"

"Yes!" She lifted her hopeful face. "Daddy, I don't

have brothers or sisters. I'd love a baby around the house. I could help, too!" She bounced in her seat. "Plus my friend Jessie said she thought it was the coolest thing that we took in foster kids and that if we ever have a baby she'd come over and take turns holding it."

Theo could feel his heart overflowing with joy. His smile, too. His wife and daughter made every day a happy one. "Hold up." He glanced at her. "Who's Jessie?"

"Jessie Taylor. She's a senior on the dance team. She's my big sister." Vienna gasped. "Wait! I didn't tell you about the big sisters! Coach said it's not easy being on the dance team and getting good grades, so she paired us younger girls with seniors, so we'd have someone looking out for us. And I got matched with Jessie Taylor. She's amazing, Dad!"

"Amazing, huh?" Sometimes Theo wondered if his daughter had a word count she had to hit each day. Not that he minded. He loved rides like this, when his only child, his little girl shared every detail of her heart with him. "Okay, then. When can we meet this new friend? Jessie Taylor?"

"Well, she's busy because her dad's the football coach at Clear Creek and she has all these aunts and uncles and cousins, but pretty soon. She wants to meet you, too. And next year she's going to Indiana University, so she'll be right here in town and she says we can still have coffee and hang out and talk about God and boys and classes. Because yeah, she believes in Jesus, too." Vienna grabbed a fast breath. "And so she can hear how my sophomore year is going."

"Your sophomore year?" Theo gave her a shocked look, teasing her the way he loved to do. "Baby, wait a minute now. I'm still getting used to you being a freshman. All old and grown up and in high school and everything."

The light changed and Theo turned his attention to the road again.

"Daddy!" She laughed the way she'd done back when she was four and he was still pushing her on the swings.

"Okay . . ." Traffic was lighter than usual. The sky bright blue. "So what you're saying is that you want Mom and me to take in a foster child." Theo glanced at her.

She made a guilty face and then smiled. "As long as it's a *baby*. Because Mom's right. Graduation really is right around the corner."

"And you want us to meet your friend Jessie."

"Exactly."

They pulled up at the school. Moments like this Theo wished they lived an hour away, so they'd have more time on the drive each morning. He reached out and patted Vienna's hand. "I'll let your mom know. About both things."

"Perfect." Vienna clapped a few times. Then she leaned over and kissed his cheek. "Oh! And Coach says parents can watch practice today after school." She grabbed her backpack and opened the door. "If you and Mom want!"

"Yes! We want! Anytime we can be there." He smiled

at her, memorizing the way her hair fell around her shoulders, the youth and hope and future in her eyes. "Praying for you, baby girl. Love you."

"Praying for *you*, Daddy. Love you!" She hopped out of the car and shut the door.

He watched her run toward the front of the school, her backpack dangling off one shoulder. "Time," Theo whispered to himself. *Where have the years gone?* He waited till she was out of sight then he pulled his car away from the curb and out of the parking lot. Her words echoed in his heart on the drive home.

Praying for you, Daddy. Love you!

Theo cracked his window and breathed in the fresh January air. *Lord, what did I ever do to deserve a daughter like Vienna?* He smiled because he knew the answer. He couldn't have done anything that good. His little girl was simply a gift from God. A child who came to them when they had given up hope of ever having a baby.

When they had already been licensed foster parents for six years.

Something about the cool breeze on his face took him back and he could see it all again. He had worked in an office back then, selling—of all things—fertility drugs to doctors. The same drugs that hadn't worked for them. But then one August day he walked through the front door and there she was.

The love of his life, his Alma.

"It happened, Theo!" She practically sang the words, her hands raised over her head. She ran to him. "I'm expecting!"

And so began the most wonderful years of their lives. Despite their struggle to get pregnant, Alma's nine months with Vienna were a dream. People talked about pregnant women glowing, but Alma actually did. She looked radiant in every way possible. And as if God wanted to complete the nine months with another gift, Alma's delivery took only four hours.

Vienna Suzanne Brown came into the world smiling and she hadn't stopped since. None of them had.

Back at home, Theo got situated at his desk. The workday flew by, marked by the idea of Vienna's plea that their family take in a foster baby. Theo had toyed with the idea all day.

Like most weekdays, just after two o'clock, Alma walked through the door. She found him in the office and grinned. "Ever have one of those days? Where everything goes right?"

He stood and closed his laptop. "You know, baby, that's what I love about you. You don't know *how* to have a bad day."

He met her at his office door and he ran his thumb along her pretty brow. "Vienna wants us to come watch her dance practice."

"Well, then, what are we waiting for?" She laughed. "Just when I thought the day couldn't get any better."

He kissed her, then flicked off the light. It was a promise he'd made to himself long ago. Twice the work in half the hours. His workday ended when Alma came home. And still he was the top sales rep for the company last year. God's blessing and the result of a happy heart. Theo believed that.

They walked into Vienna's dance practice just as it started. She must've caught a glimpse of them because she gave them a little wave and then turned to face her coach. Next to her a pretty girl with light brown hair waved, too.

"Who's that?" Alma settled in next to Theo on the short set of bleachers.

"Must be Jessie Taylor."

Alma looked at him. "Haven't heard of her."

"The younger dancers got paired up with senior girls. A big sister sort of thing." Theo watched the way Vienna and the other girl already looked like best friends. "I heard about her today on the way to school."

"That's nice." Alma faced their daughter again. After a minute she looked at Theo and a smile filled her face. "Look at our baby, Theo. She's such a beautiful dancer."

"Like her mother." Theo put his arm around his wife.

"Hardly." Alma laughed. "Vienna's twice the dancer I was."

That's when Theo remembered the other part of his conversation with Vienna. "There was one more thing we talked about on the drive this morning."

"Oh?" Alma turned to him. "Did she tell you about dance camp in Michigan this summer? Because I already told her no. That's too far away for a girl so young. Maybe when she's a junior. Because the last thing we need is—"

"Hold on." Theo stifled a laugh. The two women in his life were both talkers, but he wanted to get to the point. "I'm with you on the camp. Today it was something else."

Silence hung between the two of them for a few seconds. "Theo." With dramatic flair Alma lifted her shoulders. "Are you going to tell me or not?"

"Yes." Already Theo loved the idea. He wanted to broach the topic in such a way that Alma would love it, too. He breathed deep. "Vienna really wants us to take in a foster baby. She said it's been on her heart for a while."

"What?" His wife stayed put, her eyes locked on his, their daughter's practice forgotten. "A foster baby? Now?" She released half a laugh. "Is she serious?"

"Yes." He knew his smile looked sheepish. Like the dog Max in the cartoon Grinch movie. "I've been thinking about it and . . . Alma, I agree with her."

His wife raised her eyebrows. "That baby'll be up all night, every few hours waking up the whole house. I know what a baby's like."

"It was Vienna's idea." He leaned over his knees, and his eyes found their daughter on the dance floor. "She wants a sibling. Before she goes off to college." He looked back at his wife.

"Uh . . ." Alma shook her head and at the same time she waved her finger in the air in front of her. "Don't be telling me about before she goes off to college. That's the exact reason this idea is off the table. This season is about Vienna. The three of us." She crossed her arms, her chin tilted. "Foster babies will be there."

Theo had the feeling the topic was closed. But just in

case, he tried again. He sat up and turned to Alma. "Vienna says she'll help out. I think she really would."

"A baby?" Alma scrunched up her face and looked hard at Theo. She laughed and looked back at dance practice. "Y'all must be out of your minds."

"Okay, then." Theo did a slow nod. "So that's a no, I guess."

"Definitely."

"Meaning I shouldn't have called the social worker and put us back on the active list."

"Theo!" She spun her whole body toward him.

"I'm kidding, I'm kidding. We're still licensed but inactive. Unless we say something, of course." He put his arm around her and pulled her close. "I'll let you tell Vienna."

"My pleasure."

By then they were both laughing. Alma was right. This time belonged to Vienna. A foster child—even a baby—was a lot of work. Most of them were born drug-addicted and needed constant doctor appointments. Back when they took in foster kids before, Alma was working as a substitute teacher. Not an administrator. She had more time to care for high-needs babies.

Between their jobs and Vienna, this really wasn't the season. No matter how the idea had taken hold of Theo's heart since this morning.

When practice was over, Vienna and the other dancer, the girl who had been working beside her, skipped over to where they were standing. Both girls were laughing and breathless. Vienna bounced a few times. "Mom and Dad, this is Jessie Taylor. The senior girl I was telling you about."

"Hello, Mr. Brown, Mrs. Brown." Jessie held out her hand. She was a sweet girl with great manners.

"Hi, Jessie." Alma spoke first. "Vienna told her daddy about you this morning."

"Yes." Theo smiled at the other girl. "Apparently you two are already good friends."

"We are." Jessie grabbed a water bottle from her bag, twisted off the lid and took a sip. "Your daughter's one of the best dancers on the team. She's very special."

They talked for a minute more and then Jessie's eyes lit up. "My aunt Ashley and uncle Landon are doing a spaghetti dinner tonight. My boyfriend was going to come, but he's on the baseball team. They have late practice." She grinned. "I was wondering if Vienna could join us."

"Well . . . actually . . ." Theo heard his tone change. He never wanted Vienna to spend an evening away. Absolutely hated the idea of her missing dinner and their conversations and the chance to help her with homework.

"Please, Daddy!" Vienna clasped her hands. "I won't be late."

Alma stepped in for him. "That sounds wonderful, Jessie. Very nice of you." She patted the senior girl on the arm. "Have Vienna text me your aunt's address. We'll come get her after dinner."

"Perfect." Jessie pulled her phone from her bag and sent the text. "I'll drive her there, if that's okay? We have to stop by my house first."

Before Theo could ask if Jessie was a good driver, Alma spoke up. "Sounds fun." She pulled Vienna in for a hug and kissed the side of her face. "Be polite now, baby girl. Love you."

Theo followed his wife's actions with a similar goodbye. And like that they were back in the car driving home. Without Vienna.

"Why does she have to eat dinner with Jessie's aunt and uncle?" Theo wasn't really complaining. He gripped the steering wheel. "And we have no idea if this Jessie girl is a good driver. I mean, Vienna barely knows her. And what if her car isn't safe?" He glanced over at his wife.

"Having good friends is part of high school." Alma smiled at him, her brow raised. "Remember, Theo? We talked about that."

"Yes." He slumped a little. "I remember."

They drove in relaxed quiet for a few minutes, but at the next red light Theo cast his wife a sly-feeling smile. "Of course, if Vienna's going to have all this socializing going on, then we might as well do the other thing."

Once more she twisted her face and shook her head. Already she was laughing at him. "What other thing?"

"The foster baby."

Alma gasped and turned toward him, hands on her hips. "Theo Brown, we are not having a foster baby, end of story."

"I know." He chuckled. "I just like getting a reaction from you."

With that they were both cracking up, which led to them sharing stories from their workdays. The night was going to be a good one, it was just going to be lonelier without Vienna. Later during dinner Theo commented on the fact. "Good thing baby girl doesn't do this all the time."

"That's for sure." Alma passed the mashed potatoes to Theo.

Because if there was one thing they absolutely agreed on, it was this.

Nothing was the same with Vienna gone.

5

Cole couldn't get enough of Elise Walker.

Of course, now was too soon to talk about dating, but between baseball and school, he still found a handful of reasons each week to see her.

Snow was falling again that third Saturday since the semester began. He picked her up out front of her house. She was a vision in her navy coat and red scarf, walking to his Explorer, smiling straight at him. He climbed out, ran around the front of the car and held her door open.

"Very nice, Cole." She grinned, and her breath hung in the air. "You might not listen in chemistry class. But you're a gentleman. I'll give you that."

"Thanks." He felt his heart rate pick up speed. She had that effect on him.

When he was back in the car, and after they had their seat belts fastened and he'd pulled away from the curb, she turned to him. "I did tell you I'm a champion bowler." Her eyes sparkled, her cheeks red from the freezing air outside.

"A champion bowler?" Cole glanced at her. The teas-

ing between them was more fun than anything ahead.
"Impressive."

"Yep." She giggled. "I come from a long line of win-
ners. Bowling is our game. Always has been."

"Really." He laughed. "Can't wait to see this."

When they arrived at the bowling alley, they paid for
one game and they picked out shoes. She held up her
pair. "I used to model these. Seriously."

She was still teasing, keeping things light. But for
Cole every detail of this day would stay with him forever. He'd barely met her, but he definitely knew that
much. They got set up on a lane and she sat across from
him. No one ever looked cuter in bowling shoes.

Maybe she actually did model them. He grinned at
her. "You go first."

"No, haven't you heard?" She raised her brow and
lowered her chin, flirting with him again. "The advantage
goes to the person who starts the game."

"Okay." Cole wasn't much of a flirt. But he had no
trouble playing along now. "Right. So you go first. Champions like you need all the help they can get."

She stood and did a grand-style bow. "I defer to you, my
kind sir." Her words came in what must've been her best
British accent. "It's you who needs all the help this time."

Cole shook his head. He'd never had this much fun
with any girl, ever. He looked for the right ball and tried
to focus. A quick study of the pins and a few fast steps
and he released the ball. Just before it hit, Cole shouted,
"Strike!"

As if on cue, the ball made contact and all ten pins fell to the ground.

"Hmmm." Elise nodded. Her eyes danced as she stifled another giggle. "Impressive. You must be a champion yourself!"

The connection between them made Cole feel like he was flying. Like his ugly bowling shoes weren't quite touching the ground. "Maybe it's being in the company of someone as professional as yourself, Elise."

She smiled. "You're welcome." Then she stood and found a pink bowling ball. A few seconds to steady herself and she flew toward the lane. The ball released too quickly and shot straight for the gutter. As soon as it did, she turned to Cole, head high, and gave a casual shrug. "See! No one hits the gutters like me!"

"Wait." Cole came to her. This whole thing was the most fun ruse, and Cole had never enjoyed playing along more than he did now. "You mean you're not a champion? I'm devastated, Elise. I totally believed you."

She tilted her head back and laughed and then as impulsively as she had started the game, she threw her arms around his neck and hugged him. Nothing too long. Just a quick act of friendship that made Cole's head spin.

By the end of the game, she hadn't racked up fifty points and again she teased him on the way to the car. "Most champions let their opponents win. At least the first time."

Snow was falling and the air was bitter cold. But that didn't touch the warmth in Cole's heart. And as he dropped her off at home, he could think about only one thing.

How soon he could see her again.

• • •

THE AFTERNOON BOWLING game with Cole was still the happiest moment of the past week. But now Elise needed to focus her attention on the task ahead. The volunteer work she was doing at Bloomington Hospital. She checked in and headed to the fourth floor.

Elise found the bathroom and stared in the mirror. Her volunteer uniform was maybe the ugliest thing Elise had ever seen. She changed into the pale striped scrubs and tucked her things into a locker. Then she looked at herself again.

ELISE WALKER, her plastic name tag read. Who would've thought?

Last year she went from class good girl to one of the wildest kids at school. And now she was volunteering here, making rounds and talking to patients with organ failure. Being nice to people who didn't have long to live.

This was her fourth shift on the job.

Elise squinted at her reflection. Something was different in her eyes. More light. Whatever it was, she felt good to come here three times a week and help. Besides, being here was something she had to do if she wanted to get accepted to NYU.

By now she had the application memorized. She had the grades—even from last year, when she acted crazy with Randy. And she had extracurricular involvement from the two years she sang in her old school's choir. But she still needed community service, and now she had it for one reason.

Cole Blake.

The cute guy she couldn't stop thinking about. The one she laughed with and studied with and, yes, even pretended to be a champion bowler with. She smiled. Cole was there in her thoughts, always. She'd been having lunch at school with Cole whenever he wasn't with his baseball friends. And a few times Cole had picked her up and taken her out—bowling or for ice cream. When he didn't have practice. Not a date, exactly. They each paid for their own food. But still it was fun being with him.

Tall and strong and lanky. Blond hair that swept over his forehead. Cole was the most incredible boy she'd ever met. Elise only hoped he couldn't see how he took her breath away. He mustn't see. Elise wouldn't let herself have feelings for Cole. Because this semester wasn't about friends or boys or falling in love. It was about just one thing:

Getting accepted to NYU. Only that.

Still there was nothing she could do about this one fact: Cole was the first person she thought about when she woke up and the last person on her mind when she fell asleep. She couldn't stop herself.

In one of their first conversations, she had told him about her need for a service project. Volunteering at the hospital had been Cole's idea. His grandfather had worked here most of his adult life and even though he was retired he still taught students here a couple times a week. Three phone calls later and Elise was invited to come in for a background check.

The sorts of things she and Randy had done to get in trouble didn't show up on a fingerprint test. When she cleared, Cole's grandpa, John Baxter, called and welcomed her to the program and explained the position. Elise would come in three hours a day, three days a week for eight weeks.

That would earn her a volunteer certificate, exactly what she needed to get accepted at NYU. Already the university knew she was taking care of that requirement. Her first day at the hospital she had met up with Dr. Baxter at the fourth-floor nurses' station. The man was so nice.

He held out his hand and shook hers. "My grandson says you're very special." Dr. Baxter smiled. "I'm sure you'll be a big help around here."

"Yes, sir." Elise thought Cole looked like the older man. They had the same blue eyes. "Thank you for the opportunity."

"Cole has the biggest heart of anyone I know." Dr. Baxter crossed his arms. "If you mean a lot to him, then you mean a lot to me. And to our whole family."

Elise hadn't expected to feel so appreciated. "Thank you, sir."

Dr. Baxter gave a slow nod. "Some of our volunteers

listen to the patients' stories or pray with them. Some sing to them." He hesitated. "Just be there. The patients will let you know what they need."

Aside from that first day she'd only seen Dr. Baxter one other time, but even still she felt a connection to him. Though she didn't tell anyone, she pretended he was her grandpa. The way her grandpa might've been if she'd ever had one.

Elise looked over the sheet she'd gotten from the nurses' station. A rundown of the patients, their first names and room numbers. One woman was bad off. She wasn't expected to live long, according to the notes. Elise would visit her last. So she could spend the most time with her.

As she went to leave the bathroom, a wave of nausea came over her. She stopped and leaned against the sink. What was this? She'd felt it several times in the last few days. Out of nowhere her stomach would turn and send her straight to the toilet.

Twice she'd thrown up.

She breathed in deep through her nose, anything to keep herself from losing her lunch. It was in the guidelines. Rule No. 1: Never volunteer on a day when you feel sick. It was probably just the salad at the Clear Creek High School lunchroom. Who knew how many kids coughed or sneezed on the salad bar each day? Plus the dressing probably didn't agree with her.

Yes, that had to be it.

The wave passed and Elise looked at herself in the

mirror again. She wasn't really on speaking terms with God. But if she was, this would be a good time to pray. Not just that she would avoid getting sicker. But that whatever she was feeling wasn't something worse.

Something a person couldn't catch.

For a long moment she did the math. This was late January, and the last time she and Randy had been together was about two months ago. Just before Thanksgiving. He had taken her to his house that day, because his parents were never home. And after, when she was still in bed wondering what had happened to her life, she had caught a glimpse of her reflection in his bedroom window. Just the shadowy outline of her face. And a thought had occurred to her.

She no longer recognized herself.

Randy came back in the room, his shirt off. And he sneered at her. "Don't just lay there, Elise. Get up and get dressed. I'm hanging with the guys tonight."

And she could remember how his words made her feel. Like she was trash and he couldn't wait to get rid of her. And in that moment, she wanted just one thing—to be as far from Randy Collins as she could possibly get. She wrapped the sheet around herself and gathered her clothes from the floor.

"What are you doing?" He laughed at her. His voice sounded meaner than usual. "Like I haven't seen everything."

He was right, of course.

He'd seen her body too many times to count. But he

had never seen her soul. And Elise made a decision that afternoon that he never would. She held the sheet tight around her as she brushed by him.

"Oh. One more thing." He looked disgusted with her. "If you ever get pregnant, you're on your own. I don't want a kid." He had said things like that before. But that time Elise knew she'd remember his words forever. He raised his voice. "You hear me, Elise?"

She didn't answer him. Just stepped into the bathroom and slammed the door behind her.

Only then had it hit her what she'd been doing. How in her determination to rebel against her mother, to punish her mother for not believing in her dreams of being an artist, she had fallen victim to Randy's twisted pleasures.

Even now she couldn't bear to think about the months that had led to that single moment. But she had known one thing that afternoon. She was finished. His abusive words and actions, the way he used her whenever he wanted, all of it was over.

Ten minutes later, when she was dressed, she walked out of his house without saying a word. Just walked out and kept going.

"Elise!" She could still hear him yelling at her from his front porch. "Get back here. I told you I'd take you home."

"No." It was the last word she had ever said to him. No she wasn't going back to him. She was going to go home and tell her mother everything. Every awful detail.

Well, maybe not every detail. And then she was going to start over.

A life without Randy Collins.

Her mother had tried to be strong later that evening when Elise came clean about what had been going on with Randy. But before she fell asleep, Elise heard her mama crying against her pillow. Muffled sounds of heartbreak and regret. But at least the truth was out in the open.

Or most of it, anyway. She couldn't tell her mom the whole story. Her mama would call the police for sure. Because what Randy did to her wasn't legal. She understood that now.

Anyway, Elise had expected her mom to be upset. What she hadn't expected was how Randy wouldn't let her go. It made no sense. Randy had other girls. What did it matter if she walked away? But it mattered to Randy. And for weeks he threatened to find her and take her back. No matter how he had to make it happen. "You're mine, Elise." He cornered her near her locker one day at school. "Watch your back."

Threats like that were what had led her mama to make the decision—the only one that made sense. Elise would move to Bloomington to live with her aunt and uncle and she'd finish school there. Randy wouldn't know where she'd gone, and he could move on. Forget about her.

But as far away as all that felt, the reality was this: The last time she'd been with Randy was the Wednesday before Thanksgiving. Elise turned to the sink and ran the water. She dipped her fingers in the cool stream and pressed them to her forehead. *I don't know if You're there or not, God. But please, no. Please.*

Randy didn't always use protection, and even still she'd never gotten pregnant. Elise figured she probably couldn't have a baby. Not when she'd never been a willing party to their afternoons at his house.

Still, what was this nausea? How long could she blame it on the school cafeteria?

The cold water helped and as Elise dried her forehead a sense of normalcy came over her. It was impossible. She was already getting straight A's in her new classes and her NYU paperwork and dorm application were filled out. She'd send it in next week with a letter from Dr. Baxter about her volunteer work. NYU was a sure thing. She could feel it.

She filled her lungs and stood straight. The patients were waiting. With her work sheet in one hand, she left the bathroom and walked toward the patient hallway.

The first room she passed, a woman called out to her. "Dear, right here! Please!"

Elise stopped and looked in. The name on the door was Evelyn. A glance at her notes told her this was the woman she'd planned to save for last. The woman whose hours were numbered. Elise stepped inside and smiled. "Yes, ma'am."

"Dear, if you could please hold my hand." The woman's voice trembled. She was very old. In her nineties, probably. She reached out shaking fingers. "I'm waiting for my son to get here. But . . ." Her voice broke. "I feel so alone, dear."

There was no way Elise could leave her. She grabbed a spot of hand sanitizer and rubbed her fingers together. "I'm here. Everything's fine."

"Okay." Evelyn visibly exhaled. "That's good."

Elise pulled up a chair near the woman's bed and took hold of her hand. "Would you like to tell me your story? What life was like when you were a little girl?"

For a long moment the woman thought about that. Like maybe she might start at the beginning. But then she shook her head. "No, dear. That'll take too long."

A smile pulled on Elise's lips. Sweet woman. What lucky kids and grandkids to have a caring soul like Evelyn. Whoever they were, wherever they were, Elise hoped they'd get here soon.

"You know what I'd like?" The woman wasn't shaking as bad now. "Could you sing to me? The nurse said you're a singer."

"Well." Elise looked into Evelyn's eyes. "I wouldn't say that. I used to sing in my school choir. That's all."

"How nice." Again the woman seemed to relax a little. "There was a song my mother used to sing to me. Whenever I was sick." Her eyes filled with tears, the papery skin on her face trembling at the memory.

"Tell me." Elise doubted she would know it. But she could sing something, at least. If that's what the woman wanted.

"'Jesus Loves Me.' That's what she would sing and it always . . . always made me feel better." Evelyn shook her head. "I don't know what's wrong with me today. But I don't seem right and I thought . . . that song . . ."

Elise knew it, of course. Her own mother used to sing it to her whenever she was sick or scared. Or when she couldn't sleep. All the way through her sophomore year in high school. Only after things changed between them did her mama stop. Elise blinked back tears of her own. "Yes. I . . . I can sing that one."

The woman nodded. "Thank you. I just need to picture my mom right now."

This was a part of the job Elise hadn't expected, the idea that even very old people still wanted their parents. Still called out for their moms and dads when things felt out of control. When they needed comfort.

It made her hate herself for how she'd treated her mom.

Elise looked deep into the woman's frightened eyes. "Jesus loves me, this I know, for the Bible tells me so . . ." Gradually, she felt her voice getting stronger. If this was what the dear woman needed, then this was what she was going to do. She would deal with her feelings about her own mother later.

As the song grew and filled the room, Evelyn's fears seemed to fall away. Elise watched it happen. And by the time she was on the last line of the last chorus, the woman was asleep. Elise looked at the monitors by her bed. She didn't know how to read them, but this much was obvious. Evelyn was more peaceful now than she'd been before Elise got here.

Not only that, but Elise was feeling better. The nausea was gone. Probably just the salad dressing, like she'd thought earlier.

As Elise left the room, she checked her work sheet. The woman in the next room needed a visit, too. But before Elise was done today, she would do what she had promised herself. She would end the day back here with Evelyn. Because if anyone needed extra love this afternoon, it was her. And as Elise stepped into the next room and cleaned her hands, she told herself something else. When she got home she would do what she hadn't done all week.

She would call her mama.

6

Baseball practice was canceled because of the rain, and though there were a dozen things Cole could've done with his afternoon, there was only one place he wanted to be.

Bloomington Hospital.

Far too much time had passed without him stopping in to say hello to his aunt Brooke and uncle Peter—both doctors who did rounds at the hospital. And today happened to be a day when his papa would be there.

So it only made sense that he'd stop by on the way home from school.

True to his word, Cole went to the pediatric floor first and found his aunt and uncle in one of the offices. They talked for a minute about how excited Cole was to finish school and attend Liberty, and how sure he was that he wanted to become a doctor. Like them.

They shared how Maddie was enjoying her sophomore year in college and how Hayley was going to stay home after high school graduation next year and take classes online. She was working at a center for kids with disabilities—a job she loved.

After a while, Cole bid them goodbye and took the elevator to the emergency room. When his papa worked at the hospital it was usually in the ER. That's where he did his best training. It was also where Cole hoped to work once he finished school.

Sure enough his grandpa was busy with two interns when Cole checked in at the desk. Ten minutes, he was told. Then Dr. Baxter could be with him. Cole's heart raced. All he really wanted to do was get to the fourth floor. The place where Elise was volunteering today. But he had come to say hello to his papa and he wouldn't leave without doing so.

He sat in the waiting room and pulled his phone from his jeans pocket. No text messages, so he shot a quick one to his mom.

What's for dinner? Could I bring Elise?

As soon as he sent the message his heart beat even harder. He still hadn't brought her home. Hadn't met her parents or taken her on a real date. Like where he paid and it was more than friends. But every time he was with her he felt himself fall a little deeper. Cole had once watched a movie with his mom, a sappy film about some Christmas love story.

But one of the lines had stayed with him. The guy was talking to his friend, trying to describe how he felt about this girl. And all he could say was "She captivates me. Completely. When I'm with her I don't know anything else except her. Right there beside me. Only her."

Cole could've written the words himself. It was exactly how he felt about Elise.

The question was how to tell her. In the times he'd been out alone with her, the topic never naturally came up. He'd never had a girlfriend, so he wasn't sure what to say. Was he supposed to bring it up between talking about her classes or her love of painting? "Hey, Elise. Wanna go on a real date?"

Was that what he was supposed to say?

Or maybe first he should tell her how he felt. "Elise, here's the crazy thing. I can't think of anything but you lately. And I wondered if you felt the same way?"

Just running the phrases through his head made him sick to his stomach. There was nothing the least bit natural about any of that. So how should he do it? How was he supposed to move things from friends to . . . more than friends?

God, do you hear my crazy thoughts? He ran his fingers through his hair. Of course God heard him. God knew all things. *So, then, what should I do? This girl has my heart in her hands.*

My son, a different voice shook Cole's soul, *honor your father.*

The whispered words made Cole jump in his seat. He looked over one shoulder and then the other. Who had said that? After a few seconds he settled into the chair again and tried to catch his breath. God. That was the only possible answer.

The Lord had actually spoken to him. Cole wiped the back of his hand across his damp forehead. His mom and dad had talked about hearing from the Lord. But Cole had only experienced something like this a couple times before.

So what was it God wanted him to hear? What did He want him to know?

Honor your father.

Cole stared at the floor and slowly nodded his head. He was supposed to talk to his dad about Elise. That's how he could honor his dad. Yes, that was it. He hoped his mom would let her come over for dinner. Elise only had volunteer work till six o'clock. Then she could come home with him and meet his parents.

And after that, after he took her back to her house, Cole could talk to his dad about his feelings. That had to be what God was telling him. By talking to his dad, he would bring honor to him. Because that was a father's role—to give wisdom and instruction to his children. Lots of guys at school wouldn't dream of talking to their parents about anything—least of all the girls they liked.

But there was no one else on earth Cole would rather talk to about Elise.

The emergency room doors swung open and Cole looked up. His papa stepped into the lobby. "Cole!"

Since he was a little boy, Cole had loved this man. In his earliest years, Papa Baxter and his grandma Elizabeth used to watch him while his mom worked. Then as Cole got older, he would fish with Papa in the old pond on the Baxter house property.

The place where Cole and his family lived now.

Cole stood to meet him. There was no warmer place

than his grandfather's arms, especially after Grandma Elizabeth died of cancer when Cole was still a little guy. Now he and his papa hugged, and the two of them pulled back to look at each other. His papa grinned. "You're healthy, no injuries this season."

"No. Thankfully." Last spring Cole had pulled a muscle in his calf and had to sit out most of the season. This year, though, he was in perfect shape. He grinned. "Coach has me starting at second base."

"I knew it!" His papa put his hand on Cole's shoulder. "I told Elaine a hundred times that's where you belong. You're a born second baseman, Cole. I can't wait to come see you play."

Cole loved that his papa cared about his games. His grandma Elaine, too. She and Papa had been married for many years now and Cole loved her very much. They talked awhile longer about Cole's classes and the premed courses he'd be taking at Liberty next year. "The school of osteopathic medicine has built up quite a buzz." His grandfather's eyes shone, the way they always did. Like hope was part of his makeup.

"That's good!"

"Definitely." His papa nodded. Ever since Cole had decided he wanted to be a doctor, they had conversations like this. "In the future, medicine will treat the person, not the illness. Your school is on the cutting edge of that understanding."

Cole was glad, but he was also anxious to get going. He wanted to surprise Elise. She had no idea he was coming today. After another few minutes, Cole hugged his papa again. "Thanks for taking time."

"Are you kidding?" Papa rubbed his head. "I love when you stop by. Makes my day."

It was nearly five o'clock by the time Cole stepped off the elevator on the floor where Elise volunteered. He knew the nurse at the desk—a friend of their family's from church. "I'm here to see Elise." He smiled at the woman.

"That's fine." The nurse waved him on. "She's in one of the rooms down the hallway."

Cole knew his way around the hospital. Over the years he'd been here a number of times with his papa. In some ways medicine was an obvious calling. Long before his dad entered his life, Cole had loved and admired Papa. Cole would look up to the man as long as he lived.

He walked with quiet steps down the hall. That's when he felt the buzz of his phone. He checked his messages and saw one from his mom.

Definitely! Bring Elise to dinner. We'd love to meet her.

Cole shot back a reply.

She gets done at the hospital at 6. So sometime after that, okay?

His mom's response was quick.

That's great. We'll be ready!

Cole smiled. Perfect. This day was going exactly like he'd planned. After he'd walked past three rooms, he heard someone singing. It took only seconds for Cole to realize the voice belonged to Elise.

He peeked into the room and there she was, standing beside an old woman in a hospital bed, holding her hand. She had her back to Cole, so he stopped in the doorway.

"Are you afraid, Evelyn?" Elise's voice was warm with compassion.

"No." The woman shook her head. "Jesus knows me. And I know Him."

Elise nodded. "That's good. He's gonna throw a party when you get there."

Cole felt his heart soar. She was a Christian. They hadn't exactly talked about it in depth, but he could picture her, the good girl, sitting in church by her parents. Of course she was that girl. It was why she hadn't made friends with the party crowd. The reason she stayed home on Friday and Saturday nights.

He couldn't imagine anyone with more compassion than Elise. The way she looked and sounded right here, right now.

"Thank you for coming back, dear. Can you sing to me again?" The woman's voice was shaky. Cole wondered if she had long to live. "That same song. The one my mother used to sing to me?"

Elise seemed to know what song it was. She stayed close to the woman's bed, slightly bent over, all her attention on the woman's face. "Jesus loves me, this I know . . . for the Bible tells me so."

The ground beneath Cole's feet turned to Jell-O.

Elise was the most beautiful girl in the world. Not only did she look like a princess, but her heart was pure gold. What other high school senior was singing "Jesus Loves Me" to a dying woman this afternoon?

After a minute, the patient seemed to nod off. Elise waited awhile, and then gently released the woman's hand. As Elise turned toward the door she gasped and covered her mouth. "Cole!" The word was half whisper, half cry. A smile came over her and she hurried to him.

When they were out in the hall she led him to a quieter spot near one of the medicine carts. Cole couldn't wait to talk to her. "Elise. That was beautiful. Like beyond beautiful."

She looked nervous, like she wasn't sure he could be here. "That song . . . it was her favorite." Sadness filled her blue eyes. "Her name is Evelyn. She only has a few hours." The situation really tore at her, that much was obvious. "Her family isn't going to make it in time. Unless she gets a miracle."

"Then let's pray for that." Cole took her hands and as he did he felt her stiffen just a little. Felt her pull back. He searched her eyes. "It's okay. If we pray here."

"Right." She nodded, but she looked uneasy. Totally different than just a few minutes ago. "You pray."

Cole couldn't figure out her reaction. He hesitated for a second or two and then began. "Lord, we don't know Evelyn. But You do. Could You please let her live until her family gets here? Whoever is coming to see her? So she doesn't make the trip from here to heaven by herself?" Cole thought about that. "Of course, we know she isn't alone, Jesus. She has You and . . . for a while, anyway, she had Elise. Thank You, God, for Elise's heart for Evelyn and for all people. And thank You that she's in my life." He smiled, even with his eyes closed. "In Jesus' name, amen."

"Amen." Elise released his hands immediately. "Cole."

Something in her tone told him there was a problem. "Are you worried about me being here?" He looked back at the nurses' station. "They know me. It's fine."

"No . . . it's not that." She pressed her hand to her stomach. "I don't feel good."

What? Cole blinked a few times. She wasn't making sense. Just a few minutes ago she was standing over Evelyn's bed singing to her. And now she didn't feel good? "You mean . . . you came here sick?"

She shook her head. "Not really. I mean, I'm not sure. I thought maybe it was the school salad dressing, but—"

Without saying another word she darted down the hall and ran into a bathroom. Cole wasn't sure what to do. What could've made her get sick with no warning? He looked toward the bathroom door as he leaned against the hospital wall. Salad dressing at school? Wouldn't she have felt bad before this?

Finally she came out, her face red, eyes watery. She caught his gaze and held it as she approached him. "Cole. I need to leave. I'm not okay."

"Of course. I'll tell the nurse."

She nodded and waited while he did that. Cole's

mind raced. It still didn't make sense. How could she go from seeming so well to being so sick? In such a short time? He waited while she gathered her things from the bathroom locker and then he walked with her in silence down to the main lobby and out into the parking lot.

He led her to his Explorer and when they were both inside, the doors shut, he turned to her. "Elise. What's going on?"

"I threw up." She hung her head. "Something's wrong."

He leaned over and felt her cheek, the way his mother had done for him and his siblings over the years. It was cool. "I don't think you have a fever."

"No." She sniffed and leaned against the back of the seat. "We need to talk, Cole. Can we do that?"

"Okay." His mother was making chicken, looking forward to meeting her. But if they didn't eat until after six, there was still time. "Let's go to my house. My mom wants you to stay for dinner." He paused. "We can take a walk. There's a stream out back with this big rock. We can talk there."

She nodded, but on the drive to his house she didn't say a word. As if the girl he'd seen singing over the dying woman had disappeared in a matter of minutes. And in her place was this sick, sad person who looked like all the world was crashing in around her.

Cole didn't want Elise to have to meet his mom like this. The rain had stopped and it was just warm enough to sit outside. So he parked in the driveway and walked with her to the rock near the stream. All without going near the house. When they were seated next to each other, she lowered her head again.

Whatever this was, she clearly felt troubled by it. He put his hand on her shoulder. "Elise. I'm here." He kept his voice soft. "Talk to me."

For a while she said nothing, just sat there, looking down. Then she drew a slow breath and lifted her face, turned her eyes to him. "I haven't told you everything, Cole."

The world around him began to spin. He blinked a few times so he wouldn't get dizzy, wouldn't fall off the rock. What was she talking about? She hadn't told him everything? "Okay." He exhaled. "I'm listening."

She shook her head and closed her eyes. As if the last thing she wanted was to tell him. After another long minute she opened her eyes. "I don't live with my parents."

Cole steadied himself. "You . . . said your family was here."

"I know." She exhaled. "That's what I mean. You don't know everything about me." She looked at the stream. "When I said *family*, I meant my aunt and uncle. That's who I live with."

"But . . . your mom? You've talked about her, about how she goes to church and how you—"

"I never said *I* went to church." Her words were sharp this time. "I used to." The fight left her again. "A year ago." She pulled her knees to her chest and stared at the water again. "I've never met my dad. He left when my mom told him she was pregnant with me. We've lived alone, just the two of us, all my life. Until last month . . . when my mom sent me here."

The pieces were coming together. Cole's heart pounded, but he wasn't leaving her. She was still talking to him. Whatever this was they could get through it. Cole took a slow breath. "My mom had me before she met my dad, the one who raised me. So it was just the two of us for a long time."

Elise looked at him, like that surprised her. "When you talk about them . . . I thought you had the perfect family."

"Every family has broken parts. Sad chapters." He smiled at her, even as his heart kept racing. Something told him there was more to her story than a single mom who moved her to Bloomington to live with her aunt and uncle. "Did you think that would make me run away?"

"No." She turned to him, her eyes filled with hurt. "But you might when you hear the next part."

He reached for her hand. At first she pulled back, the way she'd done at the hospital. But then he felt her relax. Like a lost little girl who desperately needed someone to care. Just like the dying lady at the hospital. "I'm listening, Elise."

She nodded this time and lifted her eyes to the barren trees overhead. Elise started to shiver. "A year ago I started dating this guy, Randy. He was . . . nothing like you, Cole." She gave him a brief look and then turned her attention back to the sky. "He was bad. A troublemaker. I was with him until Thanksgiving and all that time I was . . . I was terrible."

Cole's heart was pounding again. "You're not terrible. You couldn't be terrible."

"I was. I stayed out super late and drank with him. I smoked pot and lied to my mama." She was still shivering, and she looked sicker, like just talking about her past might make her throw up again. "I slept with him, Cole. More times than I can count. And he never even loved me."

Cole's mind raced. She'd slept with some guy? And done drugs?

Before he could begin to process any of this, Elise shook her head. "No. That's not the truth. I didn't sleep with him." Tears filled her eyes. "Not willingly."

"Not willingly?" Cole's heart pounded hard in his chest.

"He . . ." Her voice cracked. "He forced me, Cole. All the time."

Anger became rage inside Cole, and then a desperation for revenge. All in a few seconds. The winter trees, the stream and the rock, all of it was spinning around him. "Is he . . . He's in jail, right?"

Elise shook her head. "I didn't press charges." She sniffed and closed her eyes. "I didn't really understand what he was doing. That I had a choice. I figured since I knew him, since we were dating, I couldn't go to the police. I wasn't sure they'd even believe me." She blinked and looked at him. "I couldn't tell my mom."

Cole's mouth was dry. "But . . . she must've known something."

"Enough to send me here." Elise folded her arms and pressed them against her stomach. "I don't feel good."

Two tears made their way down her face.

With everything in him, Cole felt for her, ached for her. His heart settled into a regular rhythm. He couldn't do anything about the guy or what had happened. All he had was the here and now. "Elise." He reached out and used his fingertips to wipe away her tears. "You thought telling me that would make me run?"

"Did you hear what I said, Cole?" She was crying harder now. Her eyes locked with his. "The last time I was with him was just before Thanksgiving." She stared at the rock beneath them, as if the burden of the situation was more than she could carry. "That's ten weeks ago."

Ten weeks? Cole felt like he'd known Elise all his life. Yet they'd only been friends since the semester started. He tried to imagine how she must feel. A little more than two months ago she was dating some creep? It was the most horrible story Cole had ever heard. "I'm sorry."

"Cole." Her frustration was back. "I'm not telling you so you'll feel sorry for me." She dried her cheeks with the palms of her hands. "I'm telling you because I feel sick. Every day. So nauseous I've been throwing up."

Cole wasn't sure what she was saying. Or he didn't want to know. "You . . . said it was the salad dressing."

"What if it's not?" She searched his eyes. "Cole . . . what if I'm pregnant?"

His world began to spin again, and for a few seconds

he wished for one thing. That he could wake up and everything about this conversation with Elise would be nothing more than a bad dream. She was good and golden and she sang to dying people. Her smile could light a room.

How could she be telling him she might be pregnant?

God, what am I supposed to say to her? How can I help? The prayer breezed through his soul before he could respond. And at the same time came a verse from his devotion earlier today. *Love one another. As I have loved you, so you must love one another.* Yes, love. That was the answer.

He was still holding her hand, but now he released it and put his arm around her. He pulled her close and just held her while she cried. "It's okay, Elise. God's here. Whatever's going on, He knows."

"I've made such a mess of my life." She turned and hugged him, held on to him. "You're the best thing that ever happened to me, Cole. Your friendship."

His friendship. Cole took a breath and steadied himself. In the time it had taken her to tell him about her past, she had also made something very clear. She wasn't looking for a relationship. Of course not.

She wanted to be his friend. Nothing more. And given the circumstances, Cole completely understood. He would care for her, be the friend she needed. He would love as Jesus loved—whatever it took to help her.

"My mom's been through pregnancy alone." Cole

whispered the words of comfort near her face. After another minute, she let go of him and pulled her knees up to her chest again. Her eyes on his.

"My mama, too." She closed her eyes for a second. "I wonder if they felt as scared as I do."

Cole let that sit for a moment. He couldn't speak for Elise's mother. But he knew some of his mom's struggle. "There's a crisis pregnancy center in town. My aunt Brooke and my mom volunteer there. Maybe they can get you a test." He still couldn't believe they were talking about this. An hour ago he was ready to admit his love to this girl. Now he was trying to help her find a pregnancy test. His heart broke for her. "I'll stay by you, Elise. Whatever happens."

"I . . . I can't ask that of you." She shook her head and covered her face. "It's your senior year. Oh, Cole . . . I don't know what to do."

"I told you." He felt his resolve grow. "There's nothing more important than being your friend. Helping you through this. Whatever's going on."

Suddenly Cole imagined a scenario he had never dreamed possible. He took her hand again. What if she was pregnant and what if she had nowhere to turn? Maybe God was calling him to step in the way his dad had stepped in all those years ago. His mother had been a broken, lonely single mother when Landon Blake came back into her life.

He rescued her and he rescued Cole, and in the process he became Cole's father. The only one he'd ever known.

Now here was this beautiful, wounded girl, possibly facing the same thing. An artist, no less. And in that moment—before praying about it or talking to his parents or even giving it a second thought, Cole knew this. If God was calling him to take responsibility for Elise and her child, he didn't need to think about it. He would do it. He would step up like his dad had stepped up. If she would let him, he would love her with all his heart, the rest of his days.

Even if the whole world thought he was crazy.

7

Ashley stood at the back patio window, her face pressed against the glass. If Cole thought she couldn't see him, he was wrong. She had watched him pull into the driveway and then lead Elise to the creek that ran behind their house.

So why hadn't he brought her inside?

The feelings rushing through Ashley's heart were all new. She sighed and returned to the stove. She was making an Alfredo sauce for the chicken. That and broccoli along with cauliflower rice. Already she'd called Landon and asked him to get off work early if possible. Cole had dozens of friends, people who came over in groups all the time.

But this was the first time he'd brought home a girl.

Even Carolyn, his school friend for years, had never come to the house by herself. Not unless it was a big dance or if other kids were here, too.

Ashley stirred the melted butter and added the cream. Why would Cole take the girl out back first? Were they having some serious conversation? Was he about to ask her to be his girlfriend? The thought was ridiculous. Surely not. The two just met.

Cole talked to her and Landon about everything. He

wouldn't ask Elise out unless he'd discussed it with them, right? Fear took the spot beside her and breathed against her neck. Studied her. "No." She squeezed her eyes shut. "Stop, Ashley. You're losing it."

What was there to fear? Cole had only just met this girl. But what kind of girl wouldn't want to come inside and meet a boy's mother? Before taking a walk to the stream. The order of events gave Ashley a nervous stomach.

An hour later her phone buzzed. She grabbed it and immediately saw the text from Cole.

Mom, so sorry. Elise isn't feeling well. I'm taking her home, okay? I'll be right back.

Ashley stared at his words. What was she supposed to say to that? If the girl was sick why had she come here in the first place? And what was the long conversation? She had to respond. She began moving her fingers across the phone.

Okay. I wish you would've come in first. I saw you pull up. Anyway, sorry we missed her. Tell her we hope she feels better.

She read it over and shook her head. This wasn't how she wanted to sound. Cole hadn't done anything wrong. Not that she knew about. Besides, he would tell them the whole story when he got back from dropping Elise off. She erased a few lines and read the text again.

Okay. Tell her we hope she feels better. She can come for dinner anytime.

Yes, that was better. She had made the mistake before with her kids, saying things she couldn't take back, sending text messages she should've thought about first. This was even more important because it involved a girl. One Cole clearly liked a lot. Ashley wouldn't say anything to hurt him in the midst of whatever was happening.

By the time Cole returned, the rest of the family was home and around the table, and Landon was helping her serve dinner. She felt her frustration with Cole creep back in. What had taken so long at Elise's house? What had they been doing?

Her thoughts created a slippery slope, one she didn't want to slide down. *Help me be kind here, God. He's my son and I trust him. We'll talk later.* She could feel Landon staring at her, casting her nervous glances. As if he knew what she was thinking and he didn't want her to say anything she'd regret.

She didn't. They had a wonderful dinner, and the whole time Amy talked about her eighth-grade culture fair. How she was going to make copies of favorite family photos and write a poem about each of them and let all the school see that her family actually did exist. They just lived in heaven and Amy lived with her aunt and uncle.

Ashley patted her niece's head. "Your project will be perfect." Right now she couldn't get past the situation with Cole. He hadn't said more than a few words all dinner.

Devin and Janessa joined in, talking about school and

Bloomington Little League and how this year the team was going to win State.

Most of the meal was little more than a blur. When the dishes and homework were done, and when the younger kids were in bed, Cole came back downstairs. By then, Ashley and Landon were side by side on the sofa. She'd been catching Landon up on how Cole hadn't brought Elise inside. And how it had taken so long for him to drive her home. She got about that far into the story when Cole finally joined them.

Ashley had a hundred questions battling for position in her mind. Landon gave her hand a tender squeeze. She understood. Let Cole talk first. It was a parenting motto they had adopted when Cole was in preschool.

"Have a seat, Son." Landon nodded at the chair across from them. "What's on your mind?"

"Elise." He dropped to the chair and clasped his hands. For a long time he kept his eyes fixed on his fingers. When he looked up, he said words Ashley never in all her life expected him to say. "She thinks she might be pregnant."

Instantly Ashley was on her feet. "Cole!" She felt the blood drain from her face. Her voice was louder than she intended. "Are you serious? You barely know her!"

Landon reached up and helped Ashley back to the sofa cushion. "Honey." His eyes pleaded with her. "Let him finish."

Finish? Ashley was about to pass out. They didn't

even know this girl and she was worried she was pregnant? "Cole . . . what in the world? How could you?" The words came out as muttered cries. Before she had even a chance to stop them. Cole had wanted to wait till he was married, honor his future wife and God at the same time. But now . . . now every dream she had believed for Cole was being shattered without warning. *I should've known something was off when—*

"Mom!" Now it was Cole's turn to be outraged. He stood and raked his hand through his hair. Then he turned his back on them, like he might leave without an explanation. But after a few seconds he whipped around and faced Ashley. "Are *you* serious? You think *I* got her pregnant? A girl I met three weeks ago?"

Landon put his head in his hands and sighed. "Dear God . . ."

Ashley blinked. If she could've tunneled through the floor to anywhere but here, she would've gladly done it. How in the world could she have thought Cole would've already slept with this girl?

Raw hurt darkened Cole's eyes. "You should know my character better than that." He fiddled with the Giving Key necklace he wore most days. The one custom-engraved with their last name, BLAKE, across the front. A gift for his future wife. "I'm waiting until I'm married. You know that."

He was right. Ashley did know.

She dragged herself to her feet and somehow crossed the room to where her oldest son stood. "Cole." She took his hands in hers and stared into his eyes. If only she could erase the pain there, take back her words and her reaction. "I'm so . . . so sorry." She looked down for a moment. She was the very worst possible mother.

When she looked up, it was through eyes blurred with tears. "Of course I know your character."

"I'm only telling you because she needs our help." He was still struggling with what had just happened. Clearly. "Yours and dad's and mine. All of us."

Ashley pulled Cole slowly into her arms. Because he was better than her, he came to her. Even now. She hugged him for several seconds and then looked into his eyes again. "Please . . . forgive me."

The struggle was real for him. That much was obvious. But after half a minute, Cole shook his head and managed a sound that was more frustration than laugh. "Really? I mean, I can't believe you, Mom."

Landon was watching both of them now. "Your mother didn't mean it." His tone was kind and strong. The voice of reason in the madness. "She really is sorry."

"I know." Cole sighed. He hugged Ashley this time and looked into her eyes. "I forgive you. Just, please . . . don't jump to conclusions. Expect the best of me." He led Ashley back to the sofa and then returned to the chair. "Let's start over."

Yes, that was just what Ashley wanted. "I'm listening."

Landon put his arm around her and gave her a reassuring side hug. Always patient and kind with her. What would she do without him?

"Anyway." Cole was finding the words, back to the place where he had first started. "I told her about your crisis pregnancy center. I might take her there tomorrow. For the free test."

"What makes her think she's pregnant?" The question came from Landon.

Ashley was glad. She was determined just to listen from here on out. Unless Cole needed a specific answer from her. At this point she'd said enough.

His explanation took the next ten minutes. Cole told them how Elise had gotten connected with a bad guy, someone who took advantage of her. "The two of them drank and partied and stayed out way past curfew." Cole sounded sorry for her. "She hates all of this now. The guy forced himself on her. It wasn't how she wanted things to go."

"Wow." Landon rubbed the back of his neck. "Poor girl." He sounded sincere.

Ashley nodded, but inside she was struggling. This was the girl Cole was crazy about? Someone rebellious and wild? A girl who had been with some other guy as recently as November? She was glad Cole couldn't read her mind.

Cole went on about how Elise had rebelled against her mother, and when it all came crashing down before Christmas, the decision was made to send Elise to her aunt and uncle's house in Bloomington. Mostly to get away from the guy.

Great, Ashley thought. *He'll probably come after her*

and take his wrath out on Cole. Of all people. Again she bit her tongue.

"And now she thinks she's pregnant." Landon brought the conversation back to the main point.

"Yes. She's been feeling sick and throwing up." He turned to Ashley. "Can she get a test tomorrow at the center? If I take her there?"

"Of course." Ashley felt herself begin to soften. The crisis pregnancy center was something she and her sister Brooke had started several years ago, after Ashley and Landon's first daughter was born with anencephaly and died just after birth. She'd seen the girls who came through the front doors of the place. Scared and alone. Compassion began to warm the worried places in her heart. She locked eyes with Cole. "Whatever we can do to help her."

"There." Cole smiled. "That's my mom." The hurt wasn't completely gone from his face, but he looked better. They were going to be okay. "I told Elise I'd be there for her. As her friend."

Relief flooded Ashley. It was the first reassuring thing her son had said since he sat down. He wanted to be her friend. Nothing more. She was about to tell him how smart that was, just to be a companion for a girl like Elise. But God Himself must've stopped her because she shut her mouth.

Landon ran his fingers along her shoulder. As if he could tell she was practicing restraint. "But that's not how you felt about her before." He paused. "Right?"

Understanding ran rich in Landon's words. He was such a wonderful father.

He patted the spot on the sofa beside them. "Come here. This can't be easy for you."

"No." Tears built up in Cole's eyes. He took the place next to Landon and leaned onto his shoulder. "I thought I was in love with her." He wiped at his tears and seemed to try to gain composure. "I still think that."

"What about her?" Landon turned so he could see Cole better. He put his hand on their son's knee. "What does she think?"

Ashley held her breath.

"She doesn't like me. Not like that." He clenched his jaw and shook his head. "She thinks we should just be friends."

Again, Ashley didn't say a word.

"Well . . ." Landon moved his hand to Cole's shoulder. "She's probably right. It's just two months since she was in a terrible relationship. And now she might be carrying that boy's child." He hesitated, like he was letting his words sink in. "Makes sense, right?"

Exhale, Ashley reminded herself. She breathed out, her eyes fixed on Cole.

He seemed to take Landon's words to heart. Even the look in his eyes softened. "Yeah. I can see that. She's pretty upset." A certainty welled in his expression. "But if she wants me to stand by her, I'll be there." He locked eyes with Landon. "The way you were there for Mom."

Ashley wondered if she might fall to the floor. He couldn't be serious. Cole wasn't thinking he needed to date Elise, just because that was something Landon had done with Ashley? He couldn't possibly be leaning that way. The idea shot panic through her veins and she waited. *Come on, Landon. Say something.*

"I feel like that was a little different." Landon's tone was measured. Unhurried. "I had known your mom in high school, but by the time we reconnected we were in our twenties. Finished with school. And you were a two-year-old."

Cole seemed to take that in, process it. His gaze fell off toward the window. "I guess you're right." He hesitated for a few seconds and then he looked at Landon again. "But you would've stayed by Mom. If this had happened to her."

At that, Landon was quiet. There was nothing he could say. Cole was right. Landon would've stayed by Ashley. He would've done anything for her, even if Ashley had only been eighteen and just weeks out of a terrible relationship.

"Tell you what." Landon stood and helped Cole to his feet. "Why don't we all get a good night's sleep and pray about that, what your role is supposed to be in Elise's life?" He drew Cole into a long hug. "We love you very much, Son. We're proud of you."

Cole nodded and held on to Landon, clung to him like Ashley hadn't seen him do since he was a much younger boy. "I love you, Dad. Thank you. For helping me."

Again Ashley wished she had kept herself from blurting out earlier. But that moment was past. Cole moved to her and hugged her the same way he'd hugged Landon. "I love you, Mom."

"Love you, too." He was taller than she was now. Ashley laid her head on his shoulder. "I'm sorry again."

"It's okay. You didn't mean it." He looked at her, his eyes bleary from his earlier tears. "I'll just pretend you didn't say it."

"Thank you." She put her hand alongside his face. "We'll get through this. I meant what I said about Elise. Tell us how we can help her."

Cole told them again how much he appreciated them, how he was grateful because he could tell them anything. And after that he headed up to bed. Ashley turned to Landon and collapsed in his arms. "How could I say that?"

"I knew it was coming." His smile was tender, rich with understanding. "I tried to stop you."

"I felt you." She exhaled hard. "Landon, I mean, what was I thinking? Cole's never even kissed a girl."

"Exactly." He ran his hand along the back of her head. "It'll be okay. He's over it."

She was quiet for a minute, processing. Elise could be pregnant . . . and Cole was willing to stand by her. "What does that mean?" She looked up at him. "He's going to *stand by* her?"

"I don't know." Landon's eyes saw straight to the center of her anxious heart. "He's young, but I think he means forever. Like he'd marry her and be a father to this baby the way I was for him."

"No." She whispered the word, in case somewhere in the house Cole could hear her. "I don't want that for him. He has college and med school. His whole future, and just because—"

"Ash." He brought her face to his and kissed her. So she couldn't say another word. "Only God and Cole can write his story. We can't do it for him. All we can do is pray and stand by him. And once in a while, on nights like this, give him advice."

The reality of all Landon said settled in around her like a wet blanket. She wasn't ready for what might be coming, for Cole to make decisions that carried this much weight. "So . . . I have to plan a wedding?"

This time Landon laughed out loud. "Baby, we're tired. Let's go to bed." He spoke so softly she could barely hear him. Then he put his arm around her waist and walked with her to the stairs. "I don't think we need to book the church just yet."

"True." First things first. Sometime tomorrow Cole would take Elise to the crisis pregnancy center to see if she was really expecting. And if she was, Ashley would do the most powerful thing she could. The best gift a mother could give her child. Grown or not. Now and forevermore like her life depended on it.

She would pray.

8

Lucy always had a favorite baby in the maternity ward, one who caught her attention and took hold of her heart. This week it was a little boy who weighed just over a pound. Same weight as little Sophie.

Born at the same number of weeks.

Only Nathan was a few ounces heavier and a whole lot healthier. He would spend another few months in the Neonatal Intensive Care Unit, but everyone on the floor thought he'd make it. Nathan was a fighter, the doctors said. Lucy walked from the nurses' station to the spot next to his hooded bassinet.

If Nathan could survive birth at twenty weeks, why not their Sophie? Was her death one more way God was telling them that they weren't capable of being parents? That they weren't worthy, somehow? Lucy studied the miniature newborn. His legs were the size of her fingers. But his heartbeat was strong and steady.

A miracle.

But where was the miracle for Aaron and her? When their little girl came too soon? She leaned closer to the plastic hood, the barrier that kept warmth around Na-

than's body. "Mmmm." She made the sound that com-
forted most babies in the nursery. A single note that
came close to the sound a baby heard in the womb. The
single soft hum became words. "Baby Nathan. You're
okay. Everything's going to be okay."

Lucy felt someone beside her, so she straightened
and turned. It was her new friend, Brooke. Lucy drew a
slow breath and looked back at Nathan. "Tiniest one
since I've been here."

"Yes." Brooke was one of the doctors tending to him.
"He's got strong lungs and a perfect heart." She bent
down and studied the baby. "But he's a long way from his
lungs working on their own. He'll be here a lot longer."

Lucy nodded. Of course. Babies born so little always
battled to gain weight and learn to breathe. "I'll be praying for him every day." She smiled at the infant. "That's
for sure."

"Me, too." Brooke glanced at the clock on the wall
and then looked at her. "Hey, can you take a break? I
have twenty minutes before rounds."

"I was supposed to take one an hour ago." Lucy
turned back to the nurses' station. "I'll check myself out."

They went to the second-floor coffee shop and found
a table near the window. Brooke took a long sip of her
coffee and leaned back in her chair. "I needed this."

"Definitely." Lucy felt the same way. "Thanks for
finding me." She looked at Brooke over the rim of her
paper cup. "I knew everyone at my old hospital in Atlanta. Here . . . I'd be a stranger if you hadn't reached out

my first week on the job." Brooke's husband, Peter, had met Aaron at a hospital dinner when Lucy was still back in Atlanta packing up the house. "Aaron often talks about that night when you three met."

Brooke seemed unrushed. Like she had something deeper on her mind. "Did I ever tell you that? About our talk?"

"No." Lucy set her cup down. "Not in detail."

Brooke's eyes filled with empathy. "He told me about your fertility struggles, and how the two of you were hoping." She hesitated. "You know, new location, new chances. Maybe the baby would come when you got settled here."

Heat filled Lucy's face. Aaron had said that? To complete strangers? She swallowed hard and worked to hide her embarrassment. After a few seconds, she gave a light shrug and ordered herself to smile. "That's what we thought."

"There's always a chance. I have another friend who struggled to get pregnant." Brooke went on about the friend who had been unable to have a baby for six years and then—for no reason in particular—she got pregnant.

Lucy tried to listen, but she couldn't. She'd heard some version of that story every time the topic came up. Friends, family members, medical personnel. Everyone had a success story. *After so many years, all of a sudden* . . .

They were only trying to encourage her. But what did someone else's story have to do with Aaron and her? That's what Lucy could never figure out.

Brooke was still talking. "So there's always hope." Her smile was bathed in sympathy. She reached out and briefly covered Lucy's hand with her own. "You know that. Working in this profession."

The expression on Brooke's face was identical to the one Lucy always saw sitting across from her. People looked the same when they talked to her about babies. When they asked her what she and Aaron had tried and what options they might've missed in their quest for a child.

This was why Lucy hated when Aaron told people their story, how she couldn't get pregnant and how there was still no baby in their lives. It made her feel broken and outcast. Defective. Especially here with Brooke.

But since her new friend already knew, there wasn't much Lucy could hide. Still, she could change the subject. "Tell me about your girls. You and Peter never had trouble getting pregnant?"

"No. That wasn't our problem." Brooke's voice fell some. Clearly there was some other trouble. When Lucy didn't say anything, Brooke drew a slow breath. "Our littlest, Hayley, suffered a drowning accident when she was three." Brooke tilted her head, like she was underlining the point. "She's eighteen now, but . . . it's not something we'll ever get over."

"Brooke . . ." Lucy felt her heart fall to the floor. She couldn't imagine. "I'm so sorry."

"Me, too." Brooke nodded. "I don't talk about it much anymore." She paused. "The girls were at a birthday swim party. Peter was in charge of them." Her smile looked desperately sad. "I don't say that with any accusa-tion. Not anymore."

Lucy waited, not sure how much Brooke wanted to say.

"I was called in to work at the hospital, and Peter said he would watch the girls." Brooke did a slow shrug, like even after all these years she still wasn't sure what had happened. Her expression grew distant. "Hayley had arm floaties. The rule was she had to keep them on the whole time. But the kids came in for cake and . . ."

Brooke's voice trailed off, and tears shone in her lashes. Lucy felt her own eyes well up. "Next thing any-one remembers, Hayley was missing. And they were call-ing her name and no one could find her." Brooke stared at her coffee. "Peter was the first to see her in the pool. He jumped in and pulled her out. She was basically dead at that point. No telling how long she'd been in the water."

Lucy felt sick to her stomach. Now it was her turn to reach out and put her hand over Brooke's. She had no words.

"Some days I still can't believe it happened." Brooke uttered a sad sound. "Even now." After a long pause she finished the story. "Peter gave her CPR. Saved her life, for sure. I showed up as the ambulance was arriving and they rushed her here." Brooke's eyes were clearer now. "No one thought she'd live. Or if she did, they told us she'd be blind and living in a hospital bed."

"But that didn't happen?" Lucy felt hope at the center of her soul. As if Hayley had been her own daughter. "She can see and walk, right?"

The most genuine smile took over Brooke's face. "She talks a little slower than you and me, but Hayley is perfect. She is cognitively aware of all things. She can even ride a bike. Something my dad prayed for every day."

"Wow." Lucy sat back and folded her arms. "I had no idea." She felt herself opening up a little more. If Brooke could talk like this, she could, too. "I was sitting here thinking how I hate talking about our infertility. How it makes something so intimate between Aaron and me feel like a science experiment. And how it makes me feel inadequate as a mother. Like there's something wrong with me."

Brooke allowed a single nod, her eyes never leaving Lucy's. "I thought you might be feeling that way. You've been different this past week. Quieter." She took hold of her cup with both hands and sipped her drink. "Everyone has a story. Peter and I, we nearly lost our marriage over what happened to Hayley. But we clung to God and fought through." She smiled again. "Next week is our anniversary."

Lucy never dreamed they'd have so much in common, such hurt and insecurity about raising a family. She needed to be even more transparent. "A few weeks ago Aaron and I decided . . . we decided to stop trying." The words sounded strange. Lucy set her elbows on the table and linked her fingers. "We'll still be intimate. Of course. But no more ovulation tests and cutting out sugar and chasing after in vitro fertilization. I'm exhausted."

"I get that." Brooke waited, like she was being careful in choosing her words. "Aaron said the two of you . . . have been asking God for a baby for a long time."

A sigh slipped silently through Lucy's lips. She didn't want to talk about this piece of it. How God impacted their situation. Or how He didn't. "If God's a part of all this, then He doesn't want us having kids." Lucy tried to cover up her anger, but her efforts didn't work. "We've talked to Him a thousand times, and His answer is always the same. If He's even listening."

Brooke's smile faded, but her expression filled with understanding. "I've been there." She looked out the window for a long moment and then back at Lucy. "I used to stand by Hayley's bed and beg God for her to come back. That I'd hear her little voice and laugh and see those eyes. Fully there. Fully my little girl."

Tears blurred Lucy's vision. She didn't say anything. What could she say?

"Eventually God did bring her back to me. Different, but still my little girl." A lightness lifted Brooke's sorrow. "God heard me. He was there. He carried us through those times, I have no doubt."

Sad as Brooke's story was, Lucy had heard this sort of talk about God before. Someone else's experience wasn't about to push her to believing God cared. Or even that He was real.

Their break was just about up. Brooke stood and Lucy did the same. They tossed their empty cups in the trash and walked to the elevator. "I'm glad you and Aaron agree, about taking time off from trying."

"Yes." Lucy still didn't like talking about it. But she enjoyed Brooke's friendship more than she'd known before this afternoon. "It's only February. Six months from now we might feel differently. I just need a rest. So Aaron and I can be us again."

Brooke smiled as she pushed the elevator button for labor and delivery. "Sounds like a good plan."

When they reached the nursery, they both cleaned their hands. Then Brooke made her rounds and Lucy checked on each infant in the ward. They were all well. Warm and getting whatever they needed while they were here. For the most part, healthy babies waiting to be reunited with their mothers.

This section of the nursery was the holding area for newborns who needed a little extra heat or light or medical care. Most of them stayed here less than twenty-four hours. Then they would join their moms in a regular maternity ward hospital room—at the other end of the sixth floor adjacent to labor and delivery.

But since the maternity ward also had a neonatal intensive care unit, Lucy and her peers spent most of their time with very sick babies. The NICU, as they called it, was for infants like Nathan. Children born addicted to drugs or premature or with some other sort of medical condition.

Lucy made her way to check on Nathan. His bassinet was near the front. Two other babies with difficulty breathing were in oxygen tents. But because of his gestational age, Nathan was the most critical infant in the ward.

For a few minutes Lucy put her hand on the edge of his bed and just watched him. True, his lungs were strong. But they still labored with a series of machines for every inhale. The thing with this preemie was his will to keep taking that next breath. Like he was aware of what was happening and he was determined to grab on to life. Never let go.

She would love to know who this little one was going to be when he grew up. Probably climb mountains or cure cancer or run for president. If he could get through this, he could get through anything.

Brooke's story came back to her. All this time she'd been thinking she wasn't enough, that she was incomplete because she couldn't get pregnant. And here Brooke Baxter West was carrying around the reality of her daughter's drowning. Everyone was dealing with something. Brooke was right. Everyone had a story.

But that didn't make Lucy's story with Aaron any less sad. No one had tried more to have a child than they had. She took the rocking chair next to Nathan's small bed. A dozen monitors told them whether his heart rate was at a safe level and his blood pressure was enough to sustain life. Whether he was keeping up the fight.

Lucy set the rocker in motion ever so slightly.

She and Aaron hadn't talked about having kids when they got married just out of college. They graduated from the University of Alabama and began living out their happily ever after working their way up at the local hospital. Not till they moved to Atlanta did they talk about timing.

"I'm ready if you are." Aaron had been sitting across from her at their small round kitchen table. His eyes had looked misty, like he was overwhelmed with feelings. "What do you think?"

Lucy hadn't answered right away. She was a nurse, working in the emergency room at the time. She needed to keep putting in hours if she was going to get moved to the maternity ward. Where she'd always wanted to work.

But as for babies of their own, all she had known was that it was still too soon. Lucy had reached across the table and taken hold of Aaron's hand. "Now? Really?"

"Yes." He was young, but with his master's degree he was already being groomed to work in administration. "We can handle it. Financially."

She felt butterflies in her heart and suddenly she looked ahead nine months and tried to imagine what life would be like with a baby. She would have her promotion to maternity nurse by then. And once a baby came she'd work fewer hours at the hospital, for sure. Lucy never pictured working full-time when she became a mommy. And for the first time the idea sounded not only possible.

It sounded wonderful.

That night they ditched their birth control and with everything in them they believed Lucy would be pregnant a few weeks later. When she got her period, she wasn't worried. They made a game of it. No more birth control, no more caution. They teased about how fun it would be.

Trying to get pregnant.

Lucy stared at her flat stomach. Back then they'd had no idea what they were in for. How long the journey ahead would be. It took six months of trying before Lucy began to worry. She remembered the first time she broached the topic with Aaron.

They had been on a walk in the hills near their favorite lake, and Lucy stopped. Aaron took a few more strides before he realized she wasn't with him. He turned and came back to her. "You okay?"

The words wouldn't form, not easily, anyway. She looked at the path beneath their feet for a long minute. When she lifted her eyes to his, she blinked back tears. The first of way too many. "I'm not pregnant, Aaron. What's wrong with me?"

"Honey, nothing's wrong." Disappointment fell like a shadow over his face. He tried to hide it, so almost at the same time a smile lifted his lips. "It can take a year. That's what I read." He kissed her and ran his thumb along her brow. "Practice makes perfect, right? Don't worry, Lucy. God has a baby for us. I know it."

She had been doubtful even then. Especially about Aaron's unwavering faith. "How do you know what God's going to do?"

"Because I know Him, and He's good." Her husband's smile reached his eyes. "He has a baby for us."

How Aaron had kept that same belief intact for more than a decade, Lucy would never know. Back then six months hadn't seemed that long to Aaron. He did what he could to calm her fears and help her believe.

But six months turned into one year and in the second year Aaron brought up the topic of foster care. The state had a foster-adopt program, where a baby would be placed with them and if the parents' rights were terminated, they could legally adopt the child.

Lucy had been skeptical. She still wanted a baby of their own, the traditional way. But the more she and Aaron read foster-adopt stories on the Internet the more it seemed like a viable option. At least they'd be helping.

"We'll get a baby handpicked by God," Aaron had told her the day they made their decision to go ahead with the program. "And who knows, maybe He'll surprise us and you'll get pregnant."

Over the years Lucy had researched enough to know that Aaron was right. Sometimes after a couple committed to adopt, or once a foster child was placed in their home, infertility could give way to a pregnancy.

Until then they hadn't tried shots or pills or procedures. To Aaron, two years was still not terribly long. Other couples tried that long to have a baby. And once they made their decision to adopt, even Lucy expected things to fall into place.

Their house would be full of children in no time.

After they were approved for foster care, their phone began to ring. "We have a fifteen-year-old with a drug addiction. She needs a home for the weekend until her aunt gets back from vacation."

Lucy would have a hundred questions. Why wasn't anyone helping the girl with her drug addiction? And why hadn't the aunt taken her niece on vacation and how would it help the girl to drop her off with strangers for the weekend? And the biggest question: Couldn't the social workers see what Lucy and Aaron's profile said?

They wanted a baby.

At first they took in every child the state called about. A sixteen-year-old boy who could barely speak or read or hold a conversation. His grandfather had raised him, and didn't start the boy in school until he was twelve. The placement lasted eight weeks before the boy tried to steal their car and the police had to be called. It was one case after another like that.

Finally Aaron contacted their social worker. No more, he told them. Babies or nothing. They simply weren't prepared or equipped to handle severely disturbed teenagers. But since those kids made up the bulk of the foster system, the calls practically stopped.

A few weeks later they were contacted about a drug baby, an infant born to a heroin-addicted mother. She had left the hospital after the delivery. Since then the tiny boy had been hooked to a morphine pump to help wean him off the drugs. The newborn spent every minute shaking and crying and even convulsing as his little body struggled to overcome his addiction. He was still in the hospital, no family at all.

"He's been here twenty-one days," the social worker had told Aaron and Lucy on a conference call. "The need is urgent. If you could come get him, we think you'd make the best home."

Dizziness and sorrow and elation had swept over Lucy all at once. "Twenty-one days?" The situation was horrific. The poor baby. "You're telling us this baby has been in the hospital on a morphine pump for three weeks with no mother, no one to claim him?"

"Yes." Discouragement marked the man's voice. "It's fairly common. The addiction is broken at this point, which is why he needs a home." He paused. "Anyway, I have a feeling his mother's rights will be terminated very quickly."

Lucy and Aaron didn't hesitate. This many years later she could still remember how her heart had bonded with that little drug-addicted baby boy—even before she first laid eyes on him. They left work immediately and drove by Target. A car seat, a bag of diapers, a few baby clothes, and they raced to the hospital.

The child was beautiful. Pink skin and a head full of dark hair. Since they were licensed, and since the baby was a ward of the state, the process hadn't taken long. They simply packed him up, strapped him in the new car seat and signed the papers. Just like that they had a baby in their home.

A child of their own.

Because of the drugs there were long nights with little Rio. Lucy didn't mind one minute of it. She rocked him and sang to him and together with Aaron took turns feeding him and diapering him. All the while they thanked God that He had given them a baby to love. A child to raise.

Sure there was the possibility the baby might not be allowed to stay, that the potential adoption could fall through. But Lucy and Aaron never even talked about that. How could the state give little Rio back to his mother? It wasn't possible. That's what they told themselves.

Friends from church came by and brought a portable crib and more clothes and a stroller. Each time, Lucy and Aaron admitted that no, the paperwork wasn't final. But their social worker had been sure the baby would be theirs. "It'll happen," Aaron would say. "He's ours."

But six weeks later the baby's maternal grandmother contacted Rio's social worker. She was distraught at the reality that her daughter had delivered a baby and left him at the hospital. She explained how she hadn't known her daughter was pregnant, and how her daughter hadn't been home since her raging heroin addiction began.

Their social worker had no choice but to verify the woman's claims. And every last detail checked out. Ten days later, Aaron and Lucy packed up the baby clothes and diapers and infant gear, strapped Rio into his car seat and took him to the social worker's office.

Lucy could still remember holding Rio to her chest and telling him goodbye, cradling him as her tears fell on his soft cheeks. She had made a photo album of his baby days at their house, a gift she sent on with him. So he would always know what he looked like his first two months of life. Next to her, Aaron had quietly wept. Cried harder than she had. Rio was his boy.

Neither of them knew how they'd survive saying goodbye.

The memory lifted. Lucy felt the familiar ache in her heart.

Enough.

She stood and smoothed out the wrinkles in her uniform, her eyes still on baby Nathan. As long and sad and painful as her own story was, remembering it only made things worse. She studied the tiny infant in his incubator bassinet. "It's okay, sweet boy. You're going to make it." She leaned in and cooed the words near the part of the hood where her voice could get through. "Keep fighting, Nathan." And there just for a moment—she could see baby Rio again, hear his pained little cry.

She could feel him in her arms, his warm, helpless little body pressed against hers. Little Rio. The son she would always love. The baby she hadn't told her new friend Brooke about.

And for a single instant she remembered what it felt like walking out to the car that day at the social worker's office without Rio. How she had known then that something would forever be missing. Because she had left a piece of her heart with that sick baby boy.

A piece she would never get back.

9

Elise felt like she was losing her mind. She couldn't be pregnant, couldn't have Randy's baby growing inside her. The more she thought about her ex-boyfriend, the more she knew there was nothing normal about their relationship.

Not even for the bad girl she'd become when she was with him.

Now, there was no way she wanted Randy's baby. He didn't want a child, either. He'd made that very clear.

But more than a week after telling Cole that she might be pregnant, she still didn't have her period. Her nausea and vomiting were worse, and she still hadn't told her mother about any of this. She couldn't. Her mother would be crushed.

She had avoided going with Cole to the local crisis pregnancy center. The thought of it made the entire situation too real. Still, she had to find out, so that day, after school was out, she began walking to Walgreens for a pregnancy test. Snow was falling, and Elise didn't have her warmest coat. But she didn't care. She had to know if she was pregnant or not.

She was still on the school grounds when Cole must've spotted her. He slowed his Explorer and rolled down his window. "I can give you a ride."

"No, thanks." Elise didn't want to talk to him. She'd been doing everything possible to avoid moments like this. She shook her head. "I'm just going to Walgreens. It's close."

Cole looked frustrated. "Then I'll take you there. Coach canceled practice."

"No." She kept walking. This situation was her fault and she would handle it. She had no right to involve Cole Blake. Even if all she wanted was to spend every spare minute with him.

She kept her eyes straight ahead. *Be strong, Elise. Cole deserves better. Come on.*

But no matter how strong she told herself to be, her eyes must've given her away. Because Cole pulled over, parked his SUV and jogged to her.

"Elise." He moved in front of her. Snow was sticking to his hair and jacket, and his eyes looked hurt. "What's going on?"

"Cole, don't." She turned away.

"Hey. You said we were friends." He waited until she faced him again. "You can tell me anything."

In the days since she had first brought up her possible pregnancy, she had ignored Cole's offers of coffee or study sessions. Sure, she had told him she wanted to be friends. But if she was pregnant, she didn't even want that. This wasn't his problem.

But he wouldn't give up. And the truth was she didn't want him to.

Elise kept hoping she'd get better, that the sick feeling would go away and she'd get her period. Then she and Cole could go back to sharing coffee or studying together. But not if she was pregnant.

She lowered her voice, as if she couldn't bear to hear her own words. "I . . . never got my period."

"I figured." Cole didn't seem shocked. "You never said anything, so I thought you were probably still worried." His expression was rich with compassion. "I knew you'd tell me when you were ready."

Her sigh sounded marked with fear. "I need a pregnancy test. I have the money."

"You can . . . you can get a test at the store?" Cole clearly had no idea about these things. He had no reason to know.

"Yes. At Walgreens."

Cole nodded. "Okay, then." He reached for her hand. "I'll take you."

Again, the last thing Elise wanted was to drag Cole into this mess, but she needed a friend more than she needed her next breath. She took his hand, and followed him to his car.

Ten minutes later they were walking the aisles of Walgreens looking for the test. Elise didn't know where to find one, and Cole was no help. Finally, Cole located a clerk. "Where would we find a pregnancy test?"

The woman was in her fifties, Elise guessed. She

looked at Elise's left hand and then at Cole's. Her brow raised and she practically sneered the directions. "Second aisle over, halfway down on the right." Criticism sharpened her voice. "Near the birth control."

Elise wanted to scream at her. Cole wasn't the father! The woman had no right to judge him. But before she could think of anything to say, Cole led her to the right spot. Elise picked out the least expensive test and they went to the check stand.

Again, Elise felt the eyes of the clerk watching her. All her life Elise had looked young for her age. Today was apparently no exception. They must've seemed like a couple of kids in deep trouble.

Which of course was absolutely not fair to Cole.

On their way out to the car, Elise stared at him. Who was this guy? In all the world there couldn't be a nicer boy than Cole Blake. He helped her into the passenger seat, then hurried around to his side and slid behind the wheel.

"Cole." Elise was still looking at him. She might never figure him out. "What if that woman goes to your church? Or what if she's friends with your parents?"

"So." Cole started the engine and shot her a carefree look. "You mean . . . what if people think we—"

"Yes." She tucked the brown paper bag near her feet and stared at him again. "This isn't your fault. And people are going to think you and I . . . that you had a part in this."

"Elise." A quiet laugh came from him. "Really?" He

glanced at her and then back at the road. The snow was heavier now. "I don't care what people think. You need help. So I'm helping." His tone was warm. "Where do you want to take this test?"

She already had an answer. "The restroom at Java on Main. I'll slip it into my purse."

"Do you know what to do?"

"I'll read the directions." She picked up the brown bag and held it tight in her hands. "Wait in the car, okay?"

Cole shook his head. "I'll go with you. At least to the bathroom door." He turned on Main Street. The coffee shop was a few blocks down. "So you won't be alone."

"Please." She could hear her voice rising. She couldn't stand the thought of Cole Blake outside the bathroom door while she did whatever she had to do to find out if she was pregnant. "Stay in the car. That's what I want."

As they pulled into the coffee shop parking lot, Cole cut the engine, climbed out, opened her door, and looked at her. For a long time. "You're sure?"

"Yes." Relief washed over her. She wanted to be alone. This whole thing was so awkward. "I'll be right back."

There was another girl waiting for the restroom, so Elise stood there, clutching her brown bag. When it was her turn she locked the door and ripped into the package. She opened the paper box, but inside was hardly anything. A single white stick with a little window—like a thermometer.

The directions were folded up at the bottom of the

carton. Elise read them and wrinkled her nose. She had to pee on the smaller part of the white stick. The test said results were best with urine first thing in the morning. Elise shrugged. She didn't have that option.

She followed the simple steps and then stared at the small test window. Her heart pounded in her throat and just then someone knocked on the door. She dropped the stick and gasped. "Someone's . . . in here."

Her hands shook as she picked the stick up off the floor. At the same time she turned it around and stared at the answer area. And sure enough. Two plus signs were already becoming clear.

If this test was right, Elise was pregnant.

Why, God? No! Please, no! The air felt thick and she gasped for a full breath. She had guessed she was pregnant. But that didn't mean she believed it. She didn't have to believe it.

Until now.

Her hands shook as she wadded up the bag and directions and paper box. She threw them along with the test into the trash. Then she grabbed four paper towels, scrunched them up and threw them in, too.

So no one would know what she'd been doing in here.

Another knock at the door. Harder this time.

"Just a minute," Elise yelled. She was moving as fast as she could. Especially when she couldn't feel her feet on the floor. For a few seconds she paced across the tile. What was she supposed to do next?

Impulse took over. She washed her hands and walked into the hallway past three waiting girls, through the coffee shop and outside. Cole was out of his car standing in the snow long before she reached him. He held the door for her and then took the driver's seat. When he was inside with the door shut he just sat there, looking at her. "Well?"

There was no getting around any of this. Elise folded her hands on her knees. "It's positive."

Cole took her hand again and for a while neither of them said anything. Elise closed her eyes. No way she could let her aunt and uncle know she was pregnant. They would kick her out for sure, and she wouldn't get to finish her senior year.

Which would mean NYU was out of the question.

God, please, no. This couldn't really be happening. Randy had used her and forced himself on her. There was nothing loving about it. A child couldn't come from that, right?

Cole's hand was warm against hers. "I'm here for you, Elise. I'm not going anywhere."

She nodded. "Okay." She had done nothing to deserve Cole Blake's friendship. She still didn't want to burden him with her situation. But she couldn't turn him away. Not when she needed him more with every heartbeat.

"Are you scared?" Cole's voice was quiet, filled with compassion. He rubbed her hand then let it go. He clearly was keeping to the friendship boundaries she'd requested.

Elise wanted to answer him, but she only nodded. If she tried to talk she would start crying. Already she could feel her eyes welling up. *Yes*, she wanted to say. *More than scared. I'm terrified.*

Cole seemed to understand. "I meant what I said, Elise. You won't go through this alone." He paused. "Can I pray for you?"

Could he pray for her? Whether God really cared about a teenage girl who'd messed up, Elise didn't know. But no one other than her mama had ever offered to pray for her. Again, she nodded. "Please, Cole. Please, pray."

And so he took her hands, bowed his head and closed his eyes.

Elise did the same, her heart pounding.

"God, my friend Elise needs You. She's pregnant and scared and . . . well, she doesn't know what to do." He hesitated. "I don't, either. So please, would You help her? Please let her feel Your presence and please give her wisdom about what to do next. In Jesus' name, amen." He squeezed her hands ever so slightly and released them.

She wasn't sure if it was the prayer or the way she felt safe with her hands in his, but Elise could breathe better now. Cole took her home then, and walked her up the snowy path to the front door. A quick hug and goodbye, and Elise walked inside.

Her aunt was already in the kitchen, making dinner. For the next few hours, Elise helped with the cooking and dishes, all the while pretending to be happy and carefree, a senior with her whole life ahead of her.

In her room that night, Elise began to think about the test. It was the cheapest one in the store. Plus she hadn't used first morning urine. So maybe the results were wrong. She convinced herself of the possibility and three days later, early on a Saturday morning, Cole took her to Walgreens again, and once more he stayed in his Explorer and waited while she ran into Java on Main.

The test was easier this time. More familiar. And well before the one-minute limit, the pluses showed up. Two of them again. Bold and bright, as if to mock her for thinking there could've been an error.

"It could just be me," she tried to explain to Cole. "Some people just have these positive tests even when they're not pregnant. Maybe I need a different brand or—"

"Elise." Cole put his hand on her shoulder. His voice was kind, peace laced into every word. "Maybe the tests are right. And maybe you're pregnant." He didn't wait for her to debate the possibility. "If that's what this is, I'm not leaving." His eyes pierced hers. "I'm your friend and I'm here. I told you that."

There was only one way to know for sure.

Finally it was after school on the second Wednesday in February and again snowy weather had caused baseball to be canceled. This time Cole took her to the Bloomington Crisis Pregnancy Center. Until Cole told her about his mom and aunt volunteering here, Elise hadn't known places like this existed, had never needed to know. He held her hand as they walked inside.

With his fingers wrapped around hers, again Elise felt

safe. They didn't usually hold hands but she would've fallen to the ground without his support, and he seemed to know. Her arms and legs shook as they made their way through the lobby.

On the front desk was an engraved plaque. Elise studied it.

IN LOVING MEMORY OF SARAH BLAKE. LIFE IS NOT MEASURED BY THE LENGTH OF YEARS, BUT BY LOVE. SARAH, WE LOVE YOU NOW AND ALWAYS. MOM AND DAD. After that there was a date. A single date.

She turned to Cole. "Who was Sarah?"

His eyes were instantly deep, and Elise suddenly knew. Much of Cole's heart was still unexplored no matter how close she felt to him. "My little sister."

"Cole." The truth hit Elise hard. "What happened to her?"

He slid his hands into the pockets of his jeans. The situation was obviously hard on him. "She was born with . . . problems. She only lived a few hours."

Elise couldn't imagine. "I'm sorry."

He nodded. "My mom and my aunt opened this place in honor of her life."

At that moment a woman in a white coat walked up and smiled at Cole. "Hey, there."

"Hi." He hugged her. "I brought my friend Elise."

"Yes. Your mom told me you might come in." The woman smiled. "I'm Dr. Brooke Baxter West. I volunteer here a few days a month. When I'm not at my pediatric office."

"I'm Elise." What was she supposed to say? She wanted to run out the door and keep going. All the way back to Louisiana or maybe California or New York. Anywhere but here, where the truth about her situation was about to be evident to this woman, too.

Cole took Elise's hand again. "She needs an ultrasound. If that's possible. That's what my mom said to ask for."

"Absolutely. Right this way." Dr. West led them down a hallway to the last room on the right.

The whole time all Elise could think about was Cole's mother. Another weight that hung heavy on Elise's shoulders. Cole's mama had wanted to meet her ever since that day Cole invited her over for dinner. But each time Elise found a reason to stay away. What would Cole's mom think about her? She wouldn't want a bad girl for her son.

Cole was too good. Period.

They reached the door of a small room. It looked warm and clean. A poster with a picture of an unborn baby hung on the wall. Cole's aunt was talking, something about this was where the ultrasound would take place and how the procedure wouldn't hurt. Elise couldn't take her eyes off the poster or the words underneath.

For You created my inmost being; You knit me together in my mother's womb. —Psalm 139:13

Elise shifted her eyes and looked around the room. It contained a few gray padded chairs and a white examination table and next to that a machine the size of an old-fashioned boxy computer. Cole's aunt looked at her. "What do you think?"

What had she said? Elise blinked a few times. "Ma'am?"

"The ultrasound." Dr. West looked a little confused. "Did you want the test now, Elise?" The woman smiled, patient. "I can perform the ultrasound, if you're ready."

Elise felt like she was going to be sick. What was she even doing here? At a crisis pregnancy center? She was supposed to be focusing on school. Getting the right grades so she could be accepted to NYU.

"Elise?" Cole touched her hand. "You okay?"

"Umm." She looked at Cole. "Yes. I'm . . . I'm fine." There was no way out of this disaster without doing the ultrasound. She had to know. Playing mind games with herself wasn't helping anything.

Dr. West stepped back a few feet. "I can give you a little time if you want."

"No." Elise blurted out her answer. "I'm ready."

Cole stared deep into her eyes. "You're sure?"

Elise nodded. She walked into the room and looked back at Cole's aunt. "What do I do?"

"I'll have to pull your shirt up a bit. Are you . . . ?" Dr. West nodded toward Cole. "Do you want Cole in here?"

This was the last place Elise wanted Cole to see her. Already, he'd been the best friend she could've wanted at a time like this. But that didn't mean she wanted him to watch the test. Especially if her shirt had to be up.

"Just me." She lifted her gaze to Cole's. "Okay?"

"Of course." Cole started to leave. He wore his red and white baseball shirt and cap. In case the snowy weather had let up and he'd had to get to practice. The sight of him was another reminder that her trouble shouldn't have been his. Grades and baseball. That's all Cole should've been dealing with this semester.

But just as her thoughts turned on her, he stopped and spun around, his eyes deep with concern. "I'll be in the lobby. If you need me."

Elise wanted to be strong. But tears were building in her eyes and throat. "Thanks." She watched him go and her mind formed one single thought.

Cole Blake had never looked cuter.

Dr. West closed the door behind them. She instructed Elise to lie on the table and lift her shirt. "Just a little." She took a tube and squirted gel on a white paddle. "This can get a bit messy."

"It's all right."

Cole's aunt turned on the boxy computer and the screen came to life. Elise was flat on her back, her eyes glued to the ceiling. *God, if You're there, please don't let me really be pregnant. It would ruin everything.* Her thoughts raced as fast as her heartbeat. *I can't go to NYU with a baby. I'm not ready for this. None of this. Please, God.*

"Here we go." Dr. West came closer. Elise wasn't sure what she expected, but all at once, the warm gel and the paddle were on her skin and a sound filled the room. A fast whooshing, thudding sound. Over and over and over again.

"See that?" Cole's aunt was kind. Her voice soft and certain.

Elise turned her head to the screen.

Dr. West pointed to a pea-size white dot at the bottom of a dark circle.

Please God, no. "The white thing?"

"Yes." Dr. West pointed again to the small object. "That's your baby. I'd say you're about thirteen or fourteen weeks along. Just starting your second trimester." She started talking about a due date.

But Elise couldn't hear anything she said. *My baby?* This couldn't be happening. She couldn't have a baby. She was a high school senior ready to take New York by storm. Her training and painting and the studio in Chelsea, all of it was just around the corner and . . .

Elise shook her head. "I can't . . . this isn't . . ."

Dr. West didn't seem to hear her protests. The hint of a smile came over her. Not the smile of celebration, but something deeper. A look her mama might have given her. She moved the paddle a bit and the whooshing grew louder. "Hear that?"

Fear gripped Elise, filling her heart and mind and soul. Her fingers and toes felt tingly. Like she might pass out. She nodded. "Yes."

"That's your baby's heartbeat." Cole's aunt held the wand in place for a long moment. "See in the center of your baby, that fluttering part. That's his or her heart."

Elise stared at the image on the screen. Her baby had a heartbeat? And a heart? None of this felt real. She closed her eyes again. *If this is a dream, God, wake me up. I can't take it anymore.* Nausea came over her stronger than ever before. The room began to spin. When she opened her eyes she avoided the image of the tiny baby. Instead she looked straight at Cole's aunt. "Thank you, ma'am." Elise felt sick. "I'm . . . I'm finished now. I'll come back tomorrow to . . . talk about . . . about options." She closed her eyes. "Please. I . . . I need some time."

"I understand." Dr. West turned off the machine and moved the wand back to a tray. Then she grabbed three paper towels and handed them to Elise. "For your stomach." She paused. "Can I get you anything else?"

Elise couldn't breathe. Like before, she only wanted to leave out the back door and run. Run as far and fast from here as she could. Instead she wiped the goop off her skin and pulled her shirt back into place. As she sat up, she caught her reflection in the mirror. Her full dark hair pulled back in a loose messy ponytail, stomach flat. Huge blue eyes. She still looked like Belle.

How could she be pregnant?

"Should I get Cole?" Dr. West washed her hands and dried them.

Elise felt her heart skip a beat. No, she didn't want Cole. As soon as he walked in the room she would have to tell him the truth. There was no possibility of a mistake this time. And then he wouldn't see her the same. She wouldn't be Elise the adventurous artist, the beautiful dreamer. Prettiest girl he'd ever known. The things Cole had told her.

She'd be a bad girl who got in trouble.

Dr. West was waiting. Elise had no choice, no way out. She took a deep breath. "Yes, please." That was all she could say. She felt like she might throw up.

As Cole's aunt left the room, Elise barely made it to the trash can in time. As if her body wanted to rid her of the terrible news. She vomited three times and she was still wiping her mouth when she heard a soft knock at the door.

"Just a minute." A couple quick swishes of water from the sink and she was as ready as she'd ever be. She opened the door and Cole stepped in.

"Elise." He took her in his arms and held her. The sort of strong, protective hug Elise had never known before. He leaned back and searched her face. "Was it . . . are you . . . ?"

"Yes." She might as well get it over with. "I'm pregnant." Her wobbly feet carried her across the floor to one of the padded chairs. She sat down and Cole took the seat beside her. His face was pale. Like the news was still hitting him. "We should've known. I mean . . . the tests you took. They were both positive."

And there in the silence, in the awkwardness of her not knowing what to say, an idea came to Elise. The perfect idea. Of course! Why hadn't she thought of it before? The . . . the little blob inside her wasn't really a baby, after all. It was a thing. A bit of tissue with a little fluttering in the middle.

Peace came over her. "Cole." She turned to him. Her

nausea was barely noticeable. The room wasn't spinning. "I know what I want to do."

Confusion colored Cole's face. "About the baby?"

The words came then, words she never thought she'd say. "I want an abortion." She lifted her eyes to Cole's. "As soon as possible."

Cole shook his head. "No." His voice wasn't loud, but his response couldn't have been more direct. "Elise, you can't."

"It's my choice." She was on her feet. Her cheeks felt hot, her tone grew bolder. "And it's not a baby yet. It's tissue. So this is the best thing for everyone, Cole. I need to do this!"

For a long few seconds Cole didn't say anything. He only looked at her, his eyes locked on hers. She didn't see anger or condemnation or judgment. She saw something she didn't expect at all.

Compassion.

"Do me one favor first." Cole reached for her hand. "Please, Elise."

She didn't want to make any promises, but she trusted Cole. He truly cared for her. She exhaled. "What?"

He didn't hesitate. "Talk to my mom." He waited a few seconds. "Remember how I told you she studied art in Paris? Well, maybe now's a good time for you to hear the rest of her story."

Talk to Cole's mom? Elise's heart began to race again. It was the last thing she expected him to say. The last thing she wanted to do. Her reality stood like a mountain before her. She was pregnant. It wasn't a dream or a lie, the test results weren't wrong. No matter how things had been between Randy and her, she was carrying his baby.

And the worst part was she hadn't told her mom about any of this. Every week they talked, but Elise had said nothing. Not about her sickness or her fears, and of course nothing about the positive tests from Walgreens.

Deep, dark panic worked its way through her veins and made her start to shake. Maybe Cole was onto something. Elise could talk to his mom and it would be practice for the day she finally told her own mama.

The truth was, she had no real choice now. Cole was her only friend in the world. If he wanted her to meet with his mother, if he thought somehow that would help, then she had just one choice.

She would do it.

10

Up until the minute Cole pulled into his driveway with Elise, he hadn't felt nervous about the two of them talking with his mom.

His mother was the most kindhearted, deeply compassionate person he knew. Her early days had broken her. God had redeemed her. She saw hope for every person she met. "If God can love someone like me, then He must certainly love everyone," she often said.

But between parking and opening Elise's passenger door, Cole felt clammy and light-headed. He wasn't sure where today's conversation was going. He had just one prayer. *Lord, please let her keep the baby. Please, God.* His mother was expecting them. Today Elise would learn the truth. That abortion was murder. That tissue she referred to made up a life.

Cole took a deep breath. Of course he wanted Elise to talk to his mom. Her story was personal to him. It was the reason he was alive today.

On the way to the door, Elise stopped to watch Amy and Devin building a snowman in the front yard. Cole tried to smile. "That's my brother and my cousin Amy."

He paused and looked at Elise. "She lives with us. Long story." He waved at the two. "I think they're trying to make the tallest snowman ever. *Guinness Book of World Records* stuff. Something like that."

"Wish I were doing that today." Elise sounded defeated. Like she'd given up before the meeting had even begun.

There was no time to think about all that might go wrong in the next hour. His mom opened the door before they reached it. As soon as he saw her eyes, her smile and gentle expression, Cole felt himself relax. His mom wouldn't do anything to push Elise away. Today was going to be just what he'd prayed:

A turning point for the girl he cared about.

They walked inside and once they reached the kitchen, Cole peered into the living room. It was empty. "Hey, Mom." He looked around. "Where's Dad?"

"At the store." His mom chuckled. "You know us. Always out of something."

"Okay." Cole didn't laugh. As serious as today was, it didn't feel right that his dad wasn't there. "Mom, this is Elise."

"Hello." His mother turned to Elise and smiled. Like she'd known Cole's friend for years. "Nice to meet you." She went to take Elise's hand, but then seemed to change her mind and instead she hugged her. "I've looked forward to this."

"Yes, ma'am." Elise sounded sullen, like she hadn't even heard his mother.

Panic grabbed at Cole's throat. What was Elise

doing? She could at least be nice. *Please, God, don't let this be awkward.* He looked down at his shoes and then back at Elise. "Um, yeah. I'll get you some water."

His mom hesitated, but her expression remained genuine. "I'll get it." She poured water for each of them and turned to Elise. "Can I get you anything else? A sandwich or fruit?"

"No, ma'am. No thank you." Again she sounded different. Stiff, beyond scared. Which made no sense. Cole had already told Elise that if anyone would understand her situation, his mother would. So why was Elise doing this? Her eyes looked hard. Completely closed off. When they had their water, Cole led the way to the living room. He sat next to Elise on the sofa, and his mom took the chair across from them.

He didn't want to wait for someone else to start talking. "First, thank you, Mom." Cole looked from her to Elise and back again. "For meeting with us."

"Of course." His mom leaned forward in the chair, fully engaged. Ready for whatever came next. Cole had told her just the basics. That Elise was, in fact, pregnant and not happy about it. The other details he wanted his mom to hear for herself. So she wouldn't come in with any predetermined responses. Just real, genuine conversation.

His mom's wisdom at its best.

Next to him, Elise crossed her arms and stared at her knees. Cole cared about her more than he wanted to admit. But she needed to let her walls down. He put his arm around her shoulders. "Hey."

She looked up for a brief moment, then back down again. "Cole . . ." she whispered. "I don't want to do this."

His mother must've heard her. "Elise, whatever it is, I understand." She hesitated, her tone kind. "That's why we're all here."

"Please, Elise." Cole tried to make eye contact with her. He dropped his voice to a whisper. He remembered when she had made up her mind about this visit. The words she had said. "You promised."

Something about those last words seemed to get Elise's attention, snap her out of her emotional collapse. She turned to Cole and then to his mom. "I'm sorry."

His mother waited. Cole, too.

Elise sat a little straighter and took a long breath. She faced his mom and tears filled her eyes. "I'm pregnant, Mrs. Blake. I found out for sure at the crisis pregnancy center." She sniffed and wiped her tears with the palms of her hands. Her determination seemed to build. "But I've already decided . . . I want an abortion." She paused but not long enough for Cole or his mom to say anything. "It's not really a . . . a baby yet. I'm not that far along. I found a website that said it was just an embryo, cells and tissue."

Cole looked at his mother. "Mom . . . I thought maybe if . . . if you told Elise your story . . ."

"Sure." His mother nodded, and Cole could see the past filling her expression. She wasn't smiling anymore. "Would you like that, Elise? Do you want to hear what I went through?"

Elise squirmed in her spot on the sofa and finally folded her hands in her lap. As if she was only here to keep her word. "Yes." She looked at Cole then back to his mom. "Cole says it's important. I should hear it."

His mom seemed to think for a minute. Like she was trying to decide where to start. "I moved to Paris after high school. I wanted to be an artist."

Elise's eyes lit up for the first time today. She was softening. Anyone could see that. "I'm an artist, too."

"Yes." His mother looked interested. "Cole told me. He says you're very good."

Cole had seen Elise's website. It wasn't public, but it had a dozen paintings she'd done in the last year. All of them were good enough to hang in a gallery. At least Cole thought so.

"He's kind." Elise smiled at him. "All the time." She turned to his mom. "What happened in Paris?"

"I made bad choices." His mom laced her fingers together and stared at her hands. At her wedding ring, maybe. Then she focused on Elise again. "The details aren't important, but before I knew it I was pregnant."

"And you weren't married?" Elise looked at both of them.

His mom nodded. "Not close." She took a quick breath. "And my family was this . . . God-loving group. Extraordinary people. All of them. They didn't do the things I was doing." A heaviness seemed to land on his mother.

Cole had never actually heard this part. About the

rest of the family and how his mom might have felt she didn't live up to their expectations.

"My mom's like that." Elise was definitely more engaged now. "So what did they say?"

"I didn't tell them at first." His mom hesitated. "I was a world away in France. I figured I would take care of the situation before anyone knew. So one rainy Friday morning I took a cab to an abortion clinic and paid for the operation."

Elise's eyes grew wide. "That . . ." She looked at Cole. "That was . . . ?"

"Cole. Yes." His mother folded her arms.

Her eyes were shiny, Cole thought, like right before she cried at sad movies.

She took a quick breath. "I paid the girl and an hour later I was lying on a sheet over a cold metal table. And for the first time I heard the voice of God."

"God's voice?" Elise was on the edge of her seat. "I don't understand. He talked to you?"

"I think so." His mom angled her head. "It's been a long time, but there was definitely this voice. And it told me to leave that place. Get up. Get dressed and leave. As fast as I could."

"Wow." Elise was obviously gripped. Her arms had goose bumps. "Then what?"

"I listened." His mother looked down again, like even this many years later she couldn't imagine what she'd almost done. "God was telling me it was wrong. It was murder." She shook her head. "And I couldn't kill my baby. No matter how I wound up pregnant."

For the first time Cole realized something about Elise and his mom. They were kindred spirits. Both pretty with beautiful brunette hair. Both artists. Both of them dreamers and doers and people who wouldn't give up on their passions. And both bent on finding their own way. Even in the face of great consequences.

No wonder God had brought Elise into his life.

His mom explained that she had no choice but to keep her baby. "The first time I held Cole I knew. He was mine forevermore. He had always been mine." A depth filled her voice. Cole had never heard her talk like this. His mother wasn't finished. "God hadn't only spared my little boy's life. He had spared mine. Because if I would've aborted that child . . . that gift . . . I would've hated myself for the rest of my life."

An awful realization seemed to come over Elise. "You mean, like every time it would've been his birthday?"

"And every Christmas and summer vacation." Cole's mother slid forward again. Her voice was intense. "Every time I looked out the window at the morning sun, I'd wonder where that baby was. Why I hadn't done everything in my power to *protect* him." She stopped and lifted her eyes to the window, to the sky beyond. Then she turned to Elise again. "I thank God every day for Cole. For the fact that God talked to me and because He did, Cole is alive today."

Cole looked at Elise. It was a lot for her, he could tell. She closed her eyes and hung her head. Cole wondered if she might be changing her mind. Maybe doubting her decision. Finally she looked at his mom again. "So . . . you don't think I should have an abortion?"

"Elise." His mom stood and crossed the carpet to the sofa. She took the spot on the other side of Elise. "The cells inside of you are a life. A baby."

"But I don't want a baby." Elise's answer came rapid fire. "The . . . the situation was terrible. Worse than whatever happened to you in Paris."

His mom's smile was colored in sadness. "Maybe. But it's never a good situation when you wind up pregnant and considering an abortion."

An awkward feeling came over Cole. He wasn't sure he wanted to hear many more details. But he stayed quiet, waiting.

"I volunteer at the crisis pregnancy center, Elise. Week after week I see women who've already had an abortion and now they're pregnant again." She paused, her voice filled with passion. "The truth is that when a woman goes into an abortion clinic, there are two victims. One doesn't come out. One does." She looked at Elise for a long moment. "Keep your baby, Elise. Every child is a gift from God. And if you choose, you could always place your child up for adoption."

Adoption. Cole let the word ricochet in his heart. What if his mother had done that? They wouldn't even know each other. And he would've missed out on being a Baxter. He would've never known his dad, Landon.

His mom was still talking. "Elise, I don't know if you should raise your baby or place the child in an adoptive home." Her voice grew soft again. "This will be one of the biggest decisions of your life."

"H-how am I supposed to do that?" Tears fell onto her cheeks. "I want to go to NYU. To study art."

Gently, his mother reached out and took Elise's hand in hers. "There's only one way to make a decision like that. You talk to God about it."

"It's been . . . a long time." Elise sounded ashamed. "Prayer works, though. I believe that." She looked at both of them. "Cole prayed for a patient of mine. That her family would show up before she died." Elise paused. "And they did. It was a miracle. I just found that out."

"They did?" Cole felt a surge of hope. "They showed up?"

"Yes." Elise turned to him. "It's just . . . why would God listen to me now?"

Cole's response was instant. "Because He loves you." Like it was the most natural thing, Cole covered her hands with his own. "Come on. We could pray now."

Elise hesitated. Fresh tears gathered in her eyes like all of this was a battle too great for her to fight alone. Then finally she squeezed her eyes shut and hung her head.

His mom nodded to him. "Go ahead."

"Okay." Cole hesitated. This was easily the most important prayer he'd ever spoken. *Give me the words, God. Please.* He sat up straighter and closed his eyes. "Lord, we come to you with so many emotions. And so much at stake." He paused. "Elise is going to have a baby. You know that, of course. But Elise doesn't know what to do next."

He was still for a moment. God's presence was here. Cole was sure. "Please, will You give Elise clear direction? If she is supposed to raise this child, then put that on her heart. And if she's supposed to find another home for the baby, please make that clear, too. Because right now, You're the only One who can. In Jesus' name, amen."

When they stood, Elise hugged his mom. She wasn't exactly crying, but tears kept sliding down her cheeks. Even so, it seemed the fear and uncertainty from earlier were gone. "I have a lot to think about."

"You do." His mother hugged her again. "I'll be praying for you. And believing. That God will lead you where He wants you to go."

On the ride home, Cole's conversation with Elise was limited. She reached for his hand halfway there and that was enough. What could either of them say? Elise had the decision of a lifetime ahead of her. The silence was more important than words.

When he arrived at her house, Cole hurried around and opened her door. The way he always did. Something he had learned from his dad. He was about to hug her the way he had at the clinic, but she kept her distance, her words a little too quick. "Thank you, Cole. See ya later."

Cole wasn't sure what she meant. He should be thanking her. She had followed through on her promise and gone to see his mom. Something that was obviously not easy. He took her hands in his. It was mid-February, and the temperature was below freezing. Snow still covered the ground and Cole could see his breath. He searched her eyes. "For what?"

"For making me talk to her." She smiled. Her cheeks were still red, but her eyes were dry now. "Your mother is amazing."

Peace washed over him. "You two are a lot alike. I think that's why God brought you into my life."

Elise hesitated, then she looked down. A slight nod and she pulled her hands away. "I have to go."

Cole watched her leave and on the drive back home he realized something. She hadn't exactly said she wouldn't have an abortion. But she wouldn't, right? Not after listening to his mother. Elise had definitely looked touched by his mother's story, by her encouragement. Her silence on the drive, her gratitude for the talk. She couldn't possibly go through with it now.

Or could she?

As Cole turned into his driveway, he pictured Elise sitting beside him earlier, crying, trying to figure out what to do. His heart had gone out to her the entire time. Then he imagined her website full of paintings and the song in her voice when she talked about her dreams. He saw her pretty face and waves of hair, and how she looked like a Disney princess in need of a prince.

A rescue.

That could be him, right? He had thought about it before, only now the idea was more real. His dad had stepped in and saved the day for his mother. He parked his SUV and leaned back in his seat. Look how that had turned out. Yes, it was something he could definitely do. After graduation he would get a job and take college classes online. He and Elise could get married and he would be the father her tiny baby needed. She could take art courses at the community rec center. That was possible, right?

All so her baby could live.

Suddenly all of it was clear in Cole's mind, and it didn't scare him. The idea made him smile. And that was when another thought hit him. A thought that took his breath. He not only liked Elise Walker.

He loved her.

11

Brooke Baxter West was headed down the hallway to Bloomington Hospital's pediatric unit when a man in a sharp gray suit rounded the corner and nearly ran her down. He stopped and looked straight at her. Then Brooke placed him. The father of one of her very sick patients.

Abigail Green. She had gone home from the hospital yesterday.

"Mr. Green." Brooke stopped and crossed her arms. Was the little girl sick again? "How's Abigail?"

"Call me Alan." He exhaled, as if he'd been holding it in until now. "She's so much better." He looked like he might break down. "I came here to thank you." He seemed to catch his breath. "Dr. West. You saved my daughter's life."

A warmth spread through Brooke's heart. This was why she loved being a doctor. Moments like this. "Just doing my job." She leaned against the wall. Abigail had come in with what seemed like the flu. It had been Brooke's idea to check for myocarditis. An infection of the heart.

143

"I respectfully disagree." Mr. Green's expression filled with gratitude. "Do you know how many doctors wouldn't have checked her heart?"

He was right. But there was a reason, and Brooke wouldn't miss the chance to give credit where it was due. "Well, Mr. Green. I have to be honest." Brooke felt her look deepen. "Every morning I ask God two things." She hesitated. "Give me wisdom beyond my own. And bring healing to my patients."

A soft laugh came from Abigail's father. "I knew you were a Christian. I told my wife. Because who checks a sick little girl's heart unless God's giving that doctor supernatural guidance?" He leaned against the wall opposite Brooke. "She'd only been here for an hour and you were ordering all the right tests. Before we knew what was happening she was being wheeled into surgery for the heart cath."

Brooke remembered the process with the little girl. Myocarditis had to be caught early, before the infection damaged the heart. Many people die from the illness. Others need a heart transplant after being sick for just a week or two. Abigail was going to recover completely without any lasting effects.

All because God prompted her to run specific tests. And the infection was caught in time.

Brooke smiled and straightened again. Patients just down the hall were waiting for her. "I can't imagine practicing medicine without God leading me." She held out her hand and shook his. "I'm glad she's doing well."

"Here." He pulled two business cards from his pocket. "I'm an adoption attorney. If I can ever help you in any way, let me know." He shrugged. "Not sure how that would look. But I pray about *my* work, too."

Meetings like this always felt divinely orchestrated. Brooke took the cards and shared a final handshake with the man. "Tell your wife hello for me. And let Abigail know I'm glad she's feeling better." Brooke paused. "I'm still praying for her."

"I'll tell her." The man hesitated, like he couldn't say it enough. "Thank you. Again."

"You're welcome." Brooke waved as the man headed for the elevators. She breathed deep and continued toward the pediatric unit. Her rounds that day were less eventful than some. A twelve-year-old with a broken leg from a skateboarding accident. A severe case of strep throat, and a teenager with appendicitis.

Brooke took the chair in her office and grabbed a stack of patient charts. In addition to volunteering at the crisis pregnancy center, she and her husband, Peter, ran a very successful pediatric office, a practice they'd been building for years. Long ago, after Hayley's drowning though, everyone thought Brooke and Peter were finished working together.

That wasn't all. Most thought Brooke and Peter's marriage was finished, too.

Faith wasn't a part of Peter and Brooke's life in the beginning. Brooke's family had been strong Christians, especially their doctor father—a legend at Bloomington

Hospital—Dr. John Baxter. Not Brooke. She and Peter were agnostic. They had figured they would decide about God later, if they had to decide at all.

Then Hayley drowned. And that changed everything.

They were all devastated, of course. Brooke and Peter and Maddie, their older daughter. But when Peter couldn't take the pain another day he got a bottle of pills from the pharmacy. Almost overnight he was an addict—as if a prescription could deaden the ache of all they had lost when Hayley fell into that swimming pool.

But over time Brooke and Peter realized as gut-wrenching as their suffering was, letting their marriage fall apart would only make the situation worse. Maddie and Hayley needed them. Both of them. Together.

So Peter got help with his addiction, and the two of them went to counseling at Clear Creek Community Church. And there—like Paul on the road to Damascus—Brooke and Peter felt the scales fall from their eyes. They ran to Jesus and nothing had been the same since.

That was only the beginning. Their newfound faith made them hungry for more, and in recent years both Brooke and Peter were intentional about taking Jesus with them to work.

Every single day.

No one had to tell Brooke West about the power of God's redemption. She and her family were living proof. Even Hayley, who had her eyes on a college degree. Something none of them had thought possible after her drowning injury.

Brooke smiled to herself. Every day was a challenge, an adventure. And she and Peter had never been more in love. As she helped their girls figure out their way in life, Peter was at her side.

He would be as long as he drew breath. That's what he told her.

She finished her paperwork and was on her way to the maternity ward when she spotted Aaron Williams walking toward her. The entire hospital staff loved the new young administrator and his wife. They were the kind of people the medical team needed. Dedicated, qualified, and ready to take health care at Bloomington Hospital to the next level. That wasn't all. Brooke and Peter had become very good friends with Aaron and his wife, Lucy. A friendship Brooke appreciated more all the time.

Normally Aaron was one of the brightest lights in the hospital. He stood tall with a faith and commitment that made everyone want to work harder.

But that wasn't the case today.

He approached her and slid his hands into the pockets of his suit coat. "Hey, Brooke. Is Peter here today?"

"No." She and her husband took turns doing rounds at Bloomington Hospital. "He's at the office this morning."

"Okay." Aaron nodded. He hesitated and for a few seconds he looked down. When he lifted his head and his eyes met hers, it was clear something was wrong. "Maybe you can help me." He took a quick breath. "Lucy's talked to you about our situation, right? How we've been wanting a baby. For a decade." His voice caught. "I hate talking about this."

Brooke set her clipboard on the closest counter and turned her full attention to Aaron. "Yes. We've talked about it." She focused on her friend. This was clearly a day of divine appointments. If there was a way she could help this couple, she would. Prayer. A referral. Or just being a listening ear, like now.

"She said you two were taking a break. I get the feeling she's exhausted."

"She is." Aaron put his hand to his forehead and massaged his temples. "It's scaring me, Brooke. I think . . . she's given up."

The poor guy looked nothing like the confident administrator the hospital staff knew him to be. Brooke wished Peter were here. She could only offer so much encouragement. Maybe a man-to-man conversation with Peter would be more of a help. "You're not ready to move on from the idea." She searched his eyes. "Is that it?"

"Right." He breathed in sharply and shook his head. "The nursery in our house . . . I pray there every morning. I read my Bible there. I believe." The muscles in his jaw flexed. "God's going to give us a baby. I can't stop believing that."

Brooke tended to be more matter-of-fact. Part of the job, working in medicine. At least for her. Everyone in her family knew she was pragmatic. Nowhere near as emotional as her sisters, Kari and Ashley. But in this moment her heart was filled with empathy.

"Tell you what." She offered a slight smile. "I'll have

Peter call you later. You two need to get together. You can tell him about all this, and . . . I don't know, maybe think about whether you and Lucy need another conversation. Or maybe the four of us could meet."

"Yes." Aaron looked a little more hopeful. "I keep thinking God will just allow it to happen. And we'll have a baby of our own." He thought for a minute. "Or maybe there's something else we need to look into. Something we've missed."

"I'll have Peter get with you."

"Okay." He found a slight smile. "I had to talk to someone. It's just . . . I feel like I'm alone in all this. For now, anyway."

The two said goodbye and Aaron was halfway down the hall when suddenly Brooke stopped short. She'd almost forgotten! The business cards in her white coat pocket. She spun around. "Aaron!"

He turned and started walking toward her. Other medical personnel passed on either side, but Brooke didn't see them. She could only think of the lawyer from earlier, the father of her sick little patient. When Aaron reached her, Brooke pulled out one of the business cards and handed it to him. "Here."

Aaron took it and stared at it. "Alan Green? Attorney?"

Chills ran down Brooke's arms. She couldn't see the complete picture now, but she could feel it. God was up to something. "He's an adoption attorney." Brooke remembered her conversation with the man. "He said if there was any way he could help me, to let him know."

A flicker of hope lit up Aaron's eyes. "An adoption attorney."

"Yes." Brooke's shrug matched her smile. "Might be worth a call."

She smiled as the two of them parted ways again. But it wasn't until four hours later when Brooke climbed behind the wheel of her Volvo that her breath suddenly caught in her throat. She grabbed the lawyer's other card from her pocket and looked at it. No telling why Alan Green had given her two business cards this morning. Or how he possibly could've known she'd have a reason to use them both.

All in one day.

But as Brooke drove home she could feel the pieces coming together. And all she could think about was a precious girl who was coming back to the crisis pregnancy center tomorrow afternoon. A sweet waif of a beauty who had told Brooke she couldn't imagine raising a baby.

No telling what the teenager would choose to do. Brooke had to believe the girl wouldn't get an abortion. She could definitely keep her baby and raise it. But just in case, Brooke knew exactly who should get the other card.

A girl named Elise Walker.

12

Lucy heard about the sick baby as soon as she checked into work that day. A little girl born three weeks early, addicted to heroin. Brooke Baxter West was one of the doctors on the infant's case. Her notes said it all.

It will take a miracle for this child to survive.

Every time this happened, Lucy thought the same thing. Why would God—if there was a God—let a drug addict have a baby? When she and Aaron couldn't? It was still on her mind as she headed for the NICU.

Baby Nathan was doing better, gaining precious ounces. He'd been alive in their care for nearly a month now. Lucy paused at his bassinet and checked his vitals. Then she moved across the unit to their newest patient.

The little girl was long and thin, her skin red and hot and blotchy. She was on life support, oxygen and a device to help her heart beat. On top of that a morphine drip had been started—like baby Rio had needed way back when. The pain of withdrawal was excruciating for a newborn. Morphine was the only way for a baby to survive it.

"Poor little girl." Lucy ran her finger over the tiny sock on the baby's foot. Heroin was one of the most difficult drugs in all the world to beat. The President had declared the opioid crisis a national emergency because users were dying each day, on the streets of every city in the nation.

Still, Lucy couldn't fathom taking deadly drugs while pregnant. Once in her training she had heard a former heroin dealer being interviewed. "The goal is to come as close to death as possible without dying," the man said. "That's the life of an opioid addict."

But that mind-set during a pregnancy?

Lucy sat in the chair next to the sick newborn. How could a woman feel her baby kicking inside her and then shoot up with heroin? As if the life and future of her child didn't matter at all. The fact that the drug was going to cause the baby pain and harm and possible brain damage and death—of no concern to the mother.

Of course, like other addictive drugs, heroin altered the mind. So most pregnant users had probably lost the ability to make a decision for anyone but themselves. So sad.

Lucy couldn't fathom any of it.

She closed her eyes and remembered baby Rio. He had survived those nineteen days on the morphine pump, come out of what should've been a death sentence. Maybe life with his grandmother was working out. There was a chance Rio's mother had stayed clean and had reentered her little boy's life. It was possible. But the odds were against it. Lucy had asked Aaron once if they should follow up, find out how Rio was doing. Whether he was still with his grandmother.

But in the end they had decided against it. What was the point? The state cared about the parents, not the children. At least that was how it seemed so often. Lucy would've done things differently if she ran the system. If the rules were hers, she would have much stricter guidelines for birth mothers.

A door opened and Lucy saw Brooke enter the unit. She smiled at Lucy and then checked on a few babies before joining her near the sick little girl. "Another heroin baby." Brooke sighed. Her voice was heavy with sadness. "I'm surprised she made it through the night."

The infant's chest trembled and shook with every mechanical breath. Lucy blinked back tears. "She's a fighter." She turned to Brooke. "What's her situation? If she makes it?"

"Same as always." Brooke lowered her clipboard and her shoulders sank a little. "Mom's in rehab—wants to fix things, wants her baby. Grandma's willing to help."

"Something has to change." Lucy stood and touched the baby girl's foot again. "It's not fair."

"No." Brooke checked her notes. "I've got to do some tests on Nathan." She gave Lucy a sad look. But before she turned away she hesitated. "Oh . . . I've been meaning to tell you. I gave Aaron the number of an attorney a few weeks ago. The father of a patient of mine." She paused. "He handles adoptions."

Lucy nodded. "He told me." She wasn't sure what to say, how to react. "Thanks, Brooke. We're talking about it."

For a moment, Brooke only studied her, as if she could see the deeper pain in Lucy's soul. "We'll catch up later."

"Okay." Lucy waited till she was gone. Then once more she sat down next to the sick baby girl's bed. Aaron had showed her the attorney's card last night. Lucy didn't realize he'd had it that long. But at least Aaron was honest with her.

"I've held on to this thing for a while now. In fact . . . I almost threw it away." He had looked deep into her eyes. "You asked for a break. I want you to have one—no matter how I feel." He studied the business card and then handed it to her. "But don't you think this could be a sign, Lucy? From God?"

She hadn't known what to feel. Whether she should scream or hug him and never let go. Yes, she wanted a break and she loved Aaron even more for being sensitive to the fact. But his undying genuine belief that God was still going to bring about a miracle, that He was going to give them a baby, was so heartbreaking Lucy could hardly be angry.

Their lives were a trail of broken moments and closed doors when it came to having a baby. First baby Rio, then little Sophie. And one more child, a time when it seemed certain God Himself had moved heaven and earth to give them a baby.

The news had come at ten-fifteen in the morning on

a Tuesday, just eight months ago. The last summer they were in Atlanta. Lucy had been at work, but the call came to the nurses' station.

One of the doctors had found her treating a sick baby. "Lucy, you need to come. Now!"

At first she had thought something happened to Aaron. They had worked at different hospitals at that point, his fifteen miles on the other side of the city. She could remember the blood draining from her face, her heartbeat in her throat.

She hurried to the phone, but instead of Aaron, it was a familiar voice. The woman's words came fast and excited. It was Bonnie, a nurse Lucy had worked with until the previous Christmas.

"There's a baby boy here, Lucy," the woman said. "You need to come right now. Tell Aaron."

Then the woman had done her best to explain the story. A teenage girl had given birth. Not just any girl, but the daughter of a pair of attorneys from Highcastle Royal—the wealthiest housing enclave in Atlanta. Apparently she had given birth by C-section. Something her parents insisted on so that she wouldn't hear the baby cry. Wouldn't have any possible bonding with the infant. "If you can imagine." Bonnie sounded outraged.

Lucy couldn't fathom it.

"Anyway, the poor little mama never even held her baby. She and her parents have all signed off, giving up their rights to the child. I told the attending doctor about you and Aaron. She wants the two of you and your social worker to meet us at the hospital in an hour." Her voice brimmed with elation. "And the baby's yours."

It felt like a tragedy and miracle all at once. How could parents treat their daughter that way? As if prestige and money and reputation mattered more than the girl's heart. But maybe Lucy was looking too deeply into the situation. It could be the teenage mother wasn't being pressured by her parents.

Maybe she didn't want to raise a baby.

But why not at least make an adoption plan for the child? Lucy would never understand. Still, she didn't dwell on the question for more than a few seconds. The bigger reality was exploding through her.

With no warning whatsoever, she and Aaron were going to have a baby of their own! A little boy who would never know anything but the two of them, never feel the uncertainty of foster care, never know a life other than the one he would have with them.

Lucy could barely hit the numbers as she called Aaron and explained the situation. "We have a baby boy!" she blurted out.

"What?" Aaron sounded ready to run from his office to find the child. "Where? How do we . . . What do you mean? Lucy, talk to me."

She laughed, part disbelief, part otherworldly joy. A happiness she had known only a few times in all her life. They were going to be parents! She shared the details with Aaron and they called their social worker. The plan was set.

At one that afternoon, they'd meet at the hospital with the baby's medical team. Paperwork would be signed and that night their son would be sleeping under their roof. In the nursery that had been waiting for him as far back as Lucy could remember.

Lucy didn't know what to do. She asked for the rest of the day off, drove home and ran to the baby bedroom. The crib was clean, changing table ready. A quick trip to Target and she had a car seat, a selection of newborn outfits. Diapers. Wipes. Baby bottles. Pacifiers.

Everything they needed. As she packed up the car that day, Lucy checked the time on her phone. She still had thirty minutes. That's when an idea hit her. Maybe a special blanket. Yes, that was it. Something to wrap around this little boy for the ride home. Lucy laughed out loud.

They didn't even have a name for him. Of course they didn't. She'd only just found out the baby was theirs.

Whatever his name, Lucy drove to the nearest Nordstrom and picked out the softest, most beautiful blue blanket. Something she would keep forever as a reminder of this day. He might not have been born into the world with anyone ready to care for him. But no one would love him and treasure him the way they would.

Lucy could hardly draw a breath she was so excited.

Finally, at twelve-forty-five, she parked her car in the hospital employee lot and took one bag—with an outfit and the blanket—from the passenger seat. Her hands were shaking. "We're coming, Son." She whispered the words out loud. "Mommy and Daddy are on the way."

Aaron told her later that after her call he had taken a break and gone up to the maternity ward. He was an administrator, and this had been an unconventional case, so Bonnie had let him into the unit. There, Aaron had held the little boy and cradled him to his chest. Aaron said he would never forget the way he had felt in those moments.

"I'm your daddy, little one," Aaron had told the newborn. "Me and your mommy will help you grow up big and strong. No one's ever going to hurt you." For the next hour he stayed there, holding the baby. Only when he was called back to his office for a briefing did Aaron leave.

Neither he nor Lucy could wait for one o'clock.

At 12:55, Lucy was standing in the hospital lobby when Aaron stepped off the elevator and came to her. The look of love and elation was one Lucy had never before seen in his eyes. At the same time their social worker walked through the hospital front doors.

The three of them had a quick meeting to explain the situation in greater detail and then they headed up to the maternity ward. Aaron put his arm around her and kissed her as they reached the right floor. "We're parents, Lucy," he whispered. "Can you believe it?"

The social worker gave them their space, but even she smiled. "Things like this don't just happen." She shook her head. "God must be really looking out for you two."

There wasn't a single thought that something could go wrong, that this baby wouldn't be theirs. What could mess this up? The baby was an orphan.

At least that's what they had thought.

They hurried with the social worker down a long corridor, and Aaron led the way into the nursery. He must have immediately noticed something was off, because he stopped short as soon as he entered the unit.

There a few yards away was another couple—about the same age as Lucy and Aaron. The woman was holding the newborn and next to them was a stern-looking woman in a navy blazer and business skirt.

"That's our baby." Aaron pointed, his voice low.

Lucy couldn't draw a breath. What was happening? She hadn't even met the little boy and now . . . Who were these people and why were they holding Lucy and Aaron's son? Lucy was still trying to figure it out, still trying to keep herself from falling to the floor, when Bonnie walked up.

She had clearly been crying. "Please. Follow me." She motioned to them, and Lucy and Aaron and the social worker followed her into a small room. Bonnie shut the door behind her. "I'm so sorry." She looked from Lucy to Aaron and back. "I have no words."

The room began to spin. *No,* Lucy remembered thinking. *No, this couldn't be happening. Not again. Not with another baby.* She was the first to speak. "Wh-what do we have to do? The baby is ours. You said so."

Before Bonnie could respond, the social worker

cleared her voice. "Look, I'm not sure who those people are, but we're prepared to sign paperwork. The baby is going to be adopted by my clients."

Her words turned out to mean nothing.

Bonnie shook her head. "A doctor in the unit had the same idea. His sister and brother-in-law have been trying to have a child. He made arrangements with them at the same time." Fresh tears filled her eyes. "It was miscommunication on my part." She covered her face for a moment, obviously distraught. "I'm so sorry, Lucy. Aaron. It's too late." Her next words seemed almost impossible to hear. "The papers are already signed. The baby is theirs."

Lucy dropped the bag with the blanket and new outfit. How could they lose another baby? Just when they were so close? She felt the floor fall away.

Aaron put his arm around her. His entire body was shaking. "Is . . . there anything we can do?"

The social worker looked defeated. "Have the other parents passed a background check?"

"Yes." Bonnie looked sick to her stomach. "They're licensed foster parents. Just like Lucy and Aaron." She turned to them. "I'm so sorry. I feel terrible."

The memory stopped there. It was as much as Lucy could take. She blinked and let the images fade. There had been a dozen other times when their social worker called with what seemed like certain news that a baby was about to be theirs. But always the situation didn't work out.

Still, Bonnie's baby—as they had come to call him—was right up there with Rio and Sophie. Three losses that stood like wooden crosses on the highway of infertility.

Lucy looked at the sick infant in the bassinet and then lifted her eyes to the ceiling.

You want me to believe You're there? That You see our pain and keep allowing these situations? She could actually feel her heart breaking, see the faces of all three babies that had almost belonged to them. *Did we do something wrong, God? And what about this lawyer Aaron's excited about?*

The idea of contacting the man made Lucy feel nervous and sick, exhausted and jaded. God hadn't helped them before. Why would He step in now? She sighed and the sound lasted a long time. She needed to check on the other infants. As she stood up, she heard something like a voice.

I have loved you with an everlasting love, my daughter. Trust Me. Trust My timing.

Lucy gasped. She looked over one shoulder, then the other. She grabbed hold of the chair and looked around the room. No one else was around. Who could've said that? Her breathing was faster than usual, her heart pounding. Was she losing her mind? After so long without a single answer to her prayers?

She waited for the voice to say something else, to confirm what she'd already heard. But other than the whooshing and whirring of the machines, the room was silent.

Lucy moved on from there, ready to do her job. She still had no hope of having a baby, no desire to get back into the everyday conversations about what to do next.

But what did the voice mean? *Love and trust?*

Lucy shook off the thought of it and began making her rounds. Still she couldn't quite get over the realness of the spoken words, or how they had made her feel. Even for just an instant.

What if Aaron was right? Yes, they'd had far too many disappointments. But that didn't mean the next opportunity wouldn't pan out. Maybe . . . if she held out hope just a little longer, a baby would finally be theirs.

Maybe not.

She waffled back and forth all day. If she did this, if she was really willing to consider adoption again after all they'd been through, she would do it for Aaron. Her amazing husband.

And possibly because of the voice. In case it had actually come from heaven . . . or even God.

And so by the end of her shift, Lucy had made a decision. If Aaron wanted to follow up with the adoption attorney, he could.

Even if the only thing that came from it was more heartbreak.

13

There was a reason Ashley was picking the petals off a hundred roses. The only reason that made any sense. She was a mother, and her son needed her. This time because Cole was trying to pull off a surprise for Elise, a special way to ask her to the prom.

Otherwise, Ashley would've loved to have been out on the houseboat with Landon and the kids. For early March, it was an unusually warm Saturday. But Cole had asked for her help, and she wasn't going to miss the chance to be there for him. He'd be away at college before she knew it.

The basket at the middle of the table was beginning to fill up. "How is this going down again?"

Cole laughed. "I'm going to pick up Elise and tell her I'm taking her to dinner."

"But you're not going to dinner?" Ashley was halfway teasing. She had heard the plans. She just couldn't believe how elaborate they were. Also, Cole kept changing them.

"Yes. But not till after the surprise." He kept plucking. "I added one thing. I'm going to bring her half a dozen roses."

Ashley smiled. "Half a dozen?"

"Right, and when I give them to her in my car I'm going to act like it's a mistake." He looked around the kitchen table and under it, acting out the moment yet to come. "'Where are the rest of your roses?' I'll ask her."

"Hmmm." Ashley grabbed another rose and pulled the petals one at a time. "And then you'll bring her here."

"Exactly." Cole looked giddy at the prospect. "It'll be perfect. She'll think I'm a little crazy, but we'll laugh about it and then when we get here my question will be written in rose pedals across the front porch."

"P-R-O-M?" Ashley raised her brow at him. "Right?"

"I thought about writing the whole thing. 'Elise, will you please go to the prom with me?'" He chuckled. "But I couldn't afford a thousand roses."

"Thankfully!"

"Plus, I'm pretty sure she'll say yes." He smiled and kept working.

Ashley looked up at him, her firstborn son. He was so handsome, so mature. Between his height and his confidence, no one would've known he wasn't Landon's son. But times like this she could still see the little towhead he'd been when he was three years old.

And now here they were, two months till graduation.

Her heart ached at the thought. Before they knew it he'd be driving off to Liberty University and days like this would be gone forever. She took another flower from the bundle. "What's Elise thinking these days? About the baby?"

Cole nodded. "We talk about it all the time. She's four months along now."

That's about what Ashley had figured. Ashley still remembered the moment when Cole had burst through the door and run to her with the news. Elise had decided against abortion. Ashley and Cole had prayed right there in the foyer, thanking God for her change of mind.

Ever since then Ashley had felt a special bond with the girl. But they rarely talked about what Elise was going to do once the baby was born.

"What's she thinking? Any plans?" Ashley didn't want to push. She prayed every day, asking God to lead the girl. Especially since Cole was more head over heels for her all the time, Ashley wanted to know.

"She really doesn't know yet." Cole shrugged one shoulder. "One thing for sure. She's not going to talk to her old boyfriend about the baby."

Ashley hadn't thought much about that. The guy was abusive, Cole had already told them that. But legally, she might need to tell him. "Is she sure?"

Cole's expression darkened. "Her old boyfriend was . . . a bad guy." He stopped plucking petals for a moment and looked at Ashley. "Worse than I told you before. Elise keeps letting out little details. He was abusive. In a lot of ways." He paused. "Her friends say he's made threats about finding her again."

Ashley's heart sank. She hadn't known that.

"She wants nothing to do with the father." Cole

picked up another rose. "She's open to adoption. She says it probably makes the most sense."

Ashley understood that. Still, the idea of placing a child into adoption wasn't one she had ever considered. What would her life be like without Cole? She angled her head and looked into her son's blue eyes. "What about you? What do you think?"

"I'm there for her." He stopped plucking again and let his hands settle on the table. "I told her I'd stay with her . . . help her raise the baby, Mom. If that's what she wants."

Cole had hinted about this a time or two. Ashley had even talked to Landon about the possibility, and he had convinced her that Cole wasn't really serious. Not when he had so much schooling ahead. Not when he was just eighteen. But here . . . now . . . there was no mistaking Cole's words.

He was serious.

"What . . . would that look like?" Ashley didn't want to sound panicked. Whatever his plan, Cole wasn't going to leave high school and marry Elise. Of course not. Ashley wouldn't let him. But she forced herself not to voice any of that.

"We've talked about it." He looked off. "At least I've talked about it." He took a slow breath and locked eyes with her again. "I'd help Elise after the baby is born, and sometime this summer or maybe at Christmastime, we'd get married. Then we'd find a place to live and I'd take classes online."

Ashley couldn't breathe. Was he really serious? "You . . . feel that strongly for her?"

"Yes." The resolve in Cole's expression was unwavering. "Mom, I love her. With all my heart."

If there was a way for Ashley to stop time, rewind the clocks everywhere in the world and take them back to the start of the semester, she would've made sure Cole never took science with Mr. Hansen. Made sure he had a normal last semester of his senior year and that he never would've befriended Elise Walker.

Ashley's thoughts swirled and fought for attention, even as she felt terrible for having them. But what was Cole thinking? "Where would you work?"

Cole picked up another rose and once more he looked at her. "I know you're worried, Mom. But it's what Dad would do. You know it is." He returned to the flower. "Anyway, at this point I think she'll place the baby for adoption. So . . . it's not really worth talking about."

Ashley wasn't finished. "And if someone adopts her baby, what's next? For the two of you?"

A sadness fell over Cole. This was all very real to him. Clearly he loved Elise. He sighed. "She still wants to go to NYU. And I'd probably go to Liberty, the way I planned." He stopped and a slight smile lifted his lips. "And as soon as we possibly could, we'd find a way to be together." He sat a little straighter. "Because one day I'm going to marry her, Mom. She's the one."

Questions lined up in Ashley's mind, too many to

count. How could he be so sure, and what was it that drew Cole to her? How was her faith? And what had happened back in Louisiana to make her rebel? But the gentle nudge of God told her not to say a word. This wasn't the time.

They finished the project with no more talk about Elise.

Ashley didn't want this to be a stressful conversation. This was a special moment for the two of them. "You realize, this is your last prom."

"I know." His smile softened. "I remember that poem Grandma Elizabeth wrote. About the lasts." He reached out and patted Ashley's hand. "The ones you always talk about." He looked at the bowl of rose petals and then back to her. "This is one of them. My last time to ask a girl to go to a high school dance with me. Last time to ask your help with it all."

"True." Ashley tried not to think about it. Every year it had been an adventure. Asking a girl with a message on a coffee cup or holding up a giant poster at the first baseball game last season. The girls were all just friends, and Cole always made them feel special.

They were near the end of the pile of roses when Cole shook the basket. "This should be enough." He took another rose, but his fingers moved more slowly. "Remember when I was little . . . and you asked me what I wanted to be when I grew up?"

"More than once." Ashley smiled. "You had something new every day."

"But there was one thing I said just about every time." Cole kept his eyes on her.

Ashley remembered. How could she forget? "You said you might not be a firefighter, but whatever job you did, you wanted to be just like your daddy."

"Right." Cole nodded. He paused and looked straight at her. "I still feel that way. I want to be like him."

The thought gave Ashley a peace she desperately needed. Cole wasn't going to do anything crazy. He just wanted to be like Landon. So Landon could talk to him and explain that if he'd been eighteen, even he wouldn't have given up on his dreams of being a firefighter to support Ashley and Cole.

These things happened over years. Not weeks.

The conversation shifted to his classes, tests coming up, papers he had to write. Before he left to pick up Elise, Cole gathered the rose petals and scattered them on the porch. When he was gone, Ashley moved out onto the porch to put the finishing touches on a landscape painting for a client in Indianapolis.

Not long after, she saw Cole and Elise pull into the driveway. As they got closer, she could tell they were laughing about something. The rest of the family was still at the lake, so Ashley gathered her things and slipped inside. That way Cole wouldn't know they had an audience.

From a discreet spot near the window, Ashley watched her son lead Elise to the front porch, a handkerchief tied around her eyes. She still looked young and waiflike, her stomach flat. Not at all like she was carrying a baby. She practically floated across the walkway, her hand in Cole's.

When they reached the steps, Cole took off her blindfold. From inside the house Ashley could hear the girl's gasp. Elise skipped up the steps and saw the message, the rose petals spelling out the one question Cole had for her. She squealed and put her hands over her mouth and then she turned and fell into Cole's arms.

Ashley observed as they hugged for a long time and as they turned to leave, Cole looked straight at her window. As if he'd known she'd be watching them. He smiled and waved at her. Then he put his arm around Elise and they were off.

As he walked away she could see him at eight years old again, telling her for the thousandth time that he wanted to be like his daddy when he grew up. Ashley smiled. Cole didn't need to wait until then to be like Landon.

He already was.

• • •

THEY WERE RIDING their bikes around the trail next to Clear Creek High, the wind in their hair and faces, sunshine on their shoulders. The whole afternoon Elise couldn't stop thinking one thing.

She was falling hard for Cole Blake and there was nothing she could do to stop herself.

"I'm flying," she yelled ahead to Cole.

"Me, too! I love it." His short blond hair and tan arms

made him look like a California boy—even now, more than halfway through March.

She caught up to him and grinned in his direction. This was Cole's brother's bike, and it was the perfect size for her. "Three straight wins this week in baseball and now this!"

"Yeah." Cole had on sunglasses. They both did. He turned to her and laughed. "After all that snow we finally got to play. And this might even be better than that!"

Elise had sat in the stands and cheered him on for every game. The whole school thought they were a couple now, and Elise didn't mind. They went everywhere together, did everything together. She would stay in the library and do homework during his baseball practice, and every afternoon he would drive her home.

They talked about everything, and last week his aunt Brooke connected her with an obstetrician who also volunteered with the crisis pregnancy center. The man offered to deliver Elise's baby at no cost.

She lifted her face to the sun. The most wonderful thing was she still didn't show. Her stomach was flat like always. Her new doctor said she probably wouldn't look pregnant till her sixth month. Because she was so young and small.

Which meant she could enjoy this time with Cole without thinking about what was ahead. She'd already made the most important decision. The one she easily came to after talking to Cole's mother. Her baby deserved life, of course. What happened once the baby was born, she wasn't as sure. She had time to decide.

For now she didn't want to think about any of it. These days with Cole were a chance to be free again. Maybe for the last time. Elise would pretend she'd never gotten mixed up with Randy in the first place and that Cole was her first love. Her only love. She would tell herself that this time around she would do things right. The way her mama had taught her.

No sex till she was married. Because that was God's way and because His rules were for the good of His people. That's what her mother always said, and her mama had been right. About everything.

Which made Elise's heart drop a little. She still hadn't told her mother about the baby. Every day that passed the weight of it pressed on Elise and made the truth harder to face. Cole told her all the time that she had to come clean with her mom.

Elise agreed. She would tell her mama at some point. Just not now.

They rode around the track another lap and then stopped at the bleachers. The sun was full on them, warming the metal seats. Cole parked his bike and she did the same. She followed him up six rows and they sat with their faces to the sun. For a long time they were quiet, just the sound of the wind through the trees at the far side of the football field.

"I'm going to miss this place." Cole leaned back and laced his fingers behind his head. "I can't believe how fast the semester's going."

"Me, too." Elise rested her elbows on the bench behind her and looked at Cole. "What's on your heart?"

"Really?" He took a quick breath and turned to her. A jet flew by, low and loud. He waited till it passed. "I wish you'd go to church with me. We haven't talked a lot about God. You know?"

Six months ago Cole's statement would've shut her down. She probably would've gotten up and walked away. But these days, God seemed possible again. Like maybe He loved her enough to have brought her here to Bloomington, Indiana. All so she could fall in love with Cole Blake.

"Thoughts?" Cole wasn't in a hurry. Patience seemed to be at the core of his being.

"I'd like that." She smiled at him.

"Really?" Cole sat up straight and looked at her. "You'll go to church with me? With my family?"

"I will." She sat up, too, and faced him. "You see God differently than I did. Back when I used to think I knew Him."

"Hmmm. Is that a good thing?"

"Yes." She laughed, and the sound mixed with the early springtime breeze. "I saw Him as a judge, standing over me, ready to bring the hammer down if I did something wrong." She leaned back again. "When my mom didn't want me to be an artist, I felt like that was the last straw. I couldn't be what she wanted me to be—a lawyer or a doctor." She raised her eyebrows at him. "Like you want to be."

"Yeah." He smiled, but she could tell he didn't think

it was funny. "Wait . . . So, that's why you got involved with the guy?"

"Right." Elise didn't use his name, she knew Cole wouldn't want to hear it. "If I couldn't make my mom happy, I wasn't about to make God happy. That . . . 'guy.' He was the only one who seemed okay with me. At least in the beginning."

Cole looked straight ahead, like he was thinking hard about something. "You know how I told you I'd be there for you?" He turned to her. "No matter what you decide to do? About the baby?"

Elise felt her smile fade. There was something so jarring about any mention of the baby. If only she could go back and paint the picture of her life differently. The canvas would be this moment, the two of them sitting in the bleachers, young and in love with all their lives ahead of them. And Elise never would've talked to Randy at that party. And she wouldn't be pregnant.

A sigh slipped from her lips. The baby changed everything, of course. "Yes." She looked down at her tennis shoes. "You tell me all the time."

"That's why it matters that you come to church with me." He took her hand in his. He worked his fingers gently between hers. "I can't do that if we don't have God. The two of us. First in our friendship. And later . . . in a relationship. If this goes the way I hope it does."

A dozen feelings fought for her attention. She still wasn't sure about God, not really. And she didn't want to be forced. But the way Cole said it she felt peace come over her. Like if he was going to lean on God, then she could certainly lean on Cole. "I understand." She nodded and felt a chill run down her arms. "I like that."

Cole studied her for a minute. "Good." He smiled and looked away. "Because if you want to raise this baby, I'm staying with you. I'll get a job and take classes online." For a few seconds neither of them said anything. They took off their sunglasses so they could look into each other's eyes. Then Cole stood and pulled her close. The hug lasted longer than usual and when he eased back he put his hands along either side of her face. "I love you, Elise."

She didn't hesitate. "I love you, too."

The moment grew more intense, the feelings between them clearly stronger than before. Cole moved in closer, and Elise thought for sure he was going to kiss her. But then he took a quick breath and stepped back.

He exhaled hard and walked a few steps away. When he looked at her, she could see the alarm in his face. "I'm sorry. I . . . That's not what I want to do."

Elise wanted nothing more than to kiss him. But she knew what he meant. "It's okay."

"I mean . . ." He came closer again, his eyes full of apology. "I respect you more than that other guy, Elise. I care more." He paused. "I want to be different. God wants me to love you like a sister. At least for now."

"A sister?" Hurt and confusion added to the emotions already swirling inside her. Her voice raised a little. "I don't want to be your sister, Cole. Is that what you think?" She turned away and started back down the bleachers. She had made it to their bikes when he caught up with her.

"Hey, wait." He put his hand on her shoulder. "No. That's not what I mean." The passion and heat in his eyes went way beyond friendship. He breathed hard. "I'm saying, God wants me to treat you with respect. Later . . . when we get married . . ." Passion layered his expression. "I don't want to be your brother . . . or your friend, Elise." He raked his fingers through his hair. "I want nothing more than to kiss you." He crossed his arms, like he was making a serious effort to keep control.

She felt like she was soaring, back on her bike, wind in her hair. "So you mean . . ."

"I mean we need to wait. Because you matter more to me than that, Elise." He exhaled. "And that's how I'm going to treat you. Whatever happens for us in the future."

Somehow his words actually made her feel special. He hugged her again, but this time he didn't linger. They rode their bikes to Foster's Ice Cream and then back to Cole's house. For an hour they talked about school and studying and summer vacations. The subject of the baby and marriage and forever didn't come up again, but Elise could see it. There in Cole's eyes.

That night long after Cole had taken her home, after she'd talked with Aunt Carol and Uncle Ken about school and college and the things they liked to chat about, Elise turned in early. She wasn't ready to tell her aunt and uncle about the baby. Her poor mom didn't even know.

Instead she wanted to replay everything about the day with Cole. The more she thought about it, the more she could picture keeping the baby. Not that she was ready to be a mom, but with Cole at her side anything was possible. They were young, but Cole would marry her. That's what he'd said, right?

So they would get married and Cole would work and take classes online and together they would raise this baby. Elise smiled as she lay in her bed in the dark. She could paint from home, the way Cole's mother did, and everything would turn out like a dream. Cole was the perfect gentleman. And even if they weren't official he was the best boyfriend.

So maybe she should welcome this baby. Because as wonderful as Cole was now, Elise could only imagine him in the future.

He would be the greatest daddy any child ever had.

14

Ashley heard the familiar pounding of Cole's feet running down the stairs, the way he'd done every night and day for most of his life. *Not many more months of this sound,* she told herself. She loved the way it filled her heart and reminded her that he was still here. Still living under their roof.

For now.

But this time when Ashley turned around what she saw made her heart skip a beat. Dressed in a black tux with a fitted jacket, white button-down shirt, and a pale blue bow tie, Cole looked like he'd stepped out of a bridal magazine. *Don't go there,* she told herself. *Relax.* This wasn't his wedding. Not yet. Not anytime soon if God answered her prayers.

This was Cole's prom. His very last one. She stood and met him near the base of the stairs. "Honey." She held out her hand and gently squeezed his. "You look incredible."

"The bow tie matches Elise's dress." He paused as if he could read her mind. "And no, she doesn't look pregnant. I've seen pictures of her dress. She still looks just like Belle."

"I'm sure she's stunning." Ashley smiled at him. "I'll get the corsage and boutonniere."

Ashley ignored Cole's statement about Belle. She had heard him make the comparison more than once. How Elise looked like the Disney princess. It was true, Elise was beautiful. And yes, she favored the sweet girl who befriends a beast.

But it wasn't healthy for Cole to think this was some fantasy playing out around him. Elise had stepped into his life not from a fairy tale, but from Louisiana. And her struggles were very different than those of a fictional princess.

Never mind. Tonight was a celebration. His last high school dance. "When will you pick her up?" she called back to the living room.

"Ten minutes."

Like before so many other dances, Ashley snapped a few pictures of Cole by himself near the stairs before he left. Less than half an hour later her son brought Elise by the house for more photos. By then Landon was home and he stood with Ashley while she captured the perfect few shots. Elise pinning on his boutonniere and Cole giving her a wrist corsage.

Amy and Devin and Janessa came in from outside and watched, too. "Wow." Devin had the basketball under his arm. His eyes were wide as he took in his brother and Elise. "You two look like movie stars."

Ashley took another picture. "It's true." She smiled. It was easy to pretend this was any other dance, and Elise was any other girl Cole might've asked to the prom. "You're beautiful together."

"You seem like a princess." Amy's eyes shone as she took in the sight of Elise. "You'll be the prettiest girl there."

"Thank you." Elise looked from Amy to Ashley and then to Cole. "Have I mentioned how much I love your family?"

Even Landon laughed this time. "I don't think I was dressed this nice when I married your mom," he told Cole. "Hey, have a good time, you two."

Before they left, Cole hugged Ashley and kissed her cheek. "Thanks, Mom. For understanding." He smiled at her. "You're amazing."

Amazing. She slipped her arm around Landon's waist and nodded. "Thanks, Cole. You, too."

Elise hugged Ashley, and then in a blur of goodbyes, they were gone.

When the other kids were upstairs getting ready for dinner, Ashley turned to Landon. "Please pray."

He kissed her forehead. "I already know what you're going to say. And I've been praying the whole time."

"That they won't get married?"

"Right." He pulled her into his arms, slow and tender. "Our son will make a wonderful husband and father one day. But not before he's twenty."

Ashley exhaled. She and Landon had talked about Elise and the hold she had on Cole's heart. But they hadn't specifically talked about this. Ashley didn't want to bring it up. As if by doing so she might somehow make it happen.

She looked up at Landon. "You don't think he's really considering it? Running off and getting married out of high school?" An exasperated sound came from her. "Just so he could be like you?"

"No." He kissed her lips this time. "There are a lot of ways Cole could help Elise if she raises her baby. Giving up his future career doesn't seem like a very good choice."

"Yes." Ashley nodded. "Good. That's what I needed to hear."

"Of course." Landon laughed, the quiet sort that was meant only for her. "Happy to help."

Ashley chuckled. She hated feeling anxious, especially about her kids. They were God's first and God's always. All of them were only on loan to her and Landon. Still, she would pray desperately that God would work out the details for Cole and his life in the coming months. Not only for her son.

But for the girl he loved.

• • •

SINCE HE'D PICKED her up an hour ago, every time Cole looked at Elise she took his breath. Like literally, he couldn't breathe right, couldn't think straight. His mind was spinning and his feet didn't seem to touch the floor.

He had never seen a more beautiful girl in all his life.

As he walked her down the porch steps to his car,

the sun was setting over the golden fields and the slightest breeze rustled the baby leaves in the trees that lined the far side of the driveway. The sky and her dress and her crystal blue eyes were all the same color and a truth hit him in a sudden rush.

This moment would live with him forever.

He stopped and turned to her. Then he held up his hands and formed a frame. "If I ever become an artist like you, this will be my first painting." He let his hands fall slowly to his sides. "The way you look tonight."

Her eyes lit up and she held her skirt out and twirled. "That's my dream, Cole." She stopped and her smile reached to the center of his heart. "It's always been my dream."

"For me to be an artist?" He took her hand and spun her twice more. Who needed the prom? This was the dance he would remember. "I better get an easel."

"No, silly." She laughed. "To live in a painting. To be the art instead of creating it."

"Well, then . . ." Cole drew her closer and looked deep into her eyes. "Your dream just came true, Elise. Because you are the most unforgettable work of art."

This time she grew quiet, her eyes full of a love Cole had only hoped to know one day. "You're my dream come true, Cole." Her voice was like a song on the evening air. "Only you."

Just for tonight Cole didn't want to think about Elise being pregnant. He didn't want to talk about due dates and clinic visits and how her decisions in the next few months could change both their lives forever. He only wanted to be young and free and eighteen.

In love with the prettiest girl at prom.

On the ride to school, at first neither of them said anything. The feel of her fingers between his was enough. As often as he could, Cole caught a glance at her. At every stoplight she looked more beautiful. How could she ever have been the bad girl? Running around with some jerk who didn't respect her? It was impossible to believe.

Cole leaned back, his eyes on the road. He took another glimpse at her. "You know something, Elise?"

"What?" She lowered her chin, flirting with him. Her eyes sparkled even in the dim of the car.

Cole wanted to pull over and just stare at her. Instead he forced himself to look at the road. "Every guy's going to be jealous of me tonight." Another brief glance. "You look like an angel."

"Thank you." She turned and faced him. Her corsage was positioned just so on her left wrist. The smell of his carnation and her tiny white roses filled the air between them.

He could tell she was thinking about something. "What's on your mind?" They were still a few minutes from the school. Prom was taking place in the gymnasium.

"Liberty." She sounded curious, casual. All her walls completely down. "Why do you want to go there?"

Strange, Cole thought. She had barely talked to him

about Liberty University before this. Their conversations had been so much about Elise and her pregnancy, her regrets about Randy and what she was going to do once the baby was born. And most of all how he might help her. This was the first time she'd asked about his school.

He shot her a quick look. "Now?" He didn't want to think about being a world away from Elise. Not on a night like this. "You want to talk about Liberty?"

"Yes." She smiled. Her voice was softer still. "It matters to you. So it matters to me."

"Okay." He made a right turn. The school was just two miles away. "At Liberty there's a high bar and every student wants it. Higher academics. Stronger character. Deeper faith." He smiled. "Four years later, people come out ready. For a career, for life." He looked at her again. "For a family."

"That's what I thought." Elise faced straight ahead and stared into the evening. For a minute she didn't say anything. Then she took a quick breath and turned to him again. "It sounds wonderful, Cole. And the medical school you want to attend, it's there, too?"

"It is." The wonder of the night was wearing thin. Cole didn't want to talk about this now. Not right before the dance. He wanted to be Prince Charming and she his princess. At least until midnight—when her aunt and uncle wanted her home.

These adult conversations could come later. They *would* come later.

But Elise didn't let it go. "Liberty's in Virginia, right?"

"Lynchburg. Yes." He didn't want to be upset. If talking about Liberty was important to her, then he'd go along. Maybe if he laughed a little. "So what you're say-ing is"—he winked at her—"you're thinking of going to Liberty?"

"No." She laughed. "I'm for sure about NYU. I sent in my application, my service hours." Her words came with all the confidence in the world. As if she was making more of a declaration than a response.

So where was this going? Cole turned into the Clear Creek High parking lot. "Then why all the questions?"

"I told you." She was watching him. Really watching him. "If you care about it, I care about it."

He nodded. "Okay. I get that." They found a parking spot and he cut the engine. He still had hold of her hand. "NYU, huh?"

"Yes." She didn't blink, didn't look away. A deeper meaning seemed to live in her answer.

Again, this wasn't the time, but Cole could do noth-ing to stop the conversation. "Are you trying to tell me something?"

Her expression softened and she nodded. Just the slightest move of her head. "I'm not ready for a baby, Cole." Her smile held an ocean of sadness. "You . . . you make it sound so wonderful and easy. You'll stay with me. You'll help me. And if things work out, maybe we'll get married."

"They *will* work out." Cole had no doubt. "Okay, sure we're young. And yes, I have plans to attend Liberty for the next eight years. But plans change." The passion in his voice didn't waver. "You and me, Elise, we would make it work. If we keep God at the center, if we follow His lead." He paused. "Don't you believe that?"

"I do."

He leaned back in his seat. Her response took his breath. They were the words she would say to him one day if God allowed it. But it didn't look like she picked up on the fact.

"I believe it." She took a steady breath. "But not right now, Cole."

"Why?" For the first time since she'd found out she was pregnant, Cole heard a voice loud and clear. *Because she's right. This isn't the time. You barely know her. And the plans you had before you met her were good plans.* He shut out the voice. "I told you I'm here for you." He hesitated. He wished she'd never brought the subject up. They were supposed to be heading into prom. He forced himself to sound calm. "All my life I wanted to be like my dad."

"He's a nice man." Her tone held the ring of longing. "The sort of dad I always pictured having."

"Thanks." Cole looked straight ahead and suddenly he wasn't seeing across a high school parking lot. He was seeing his dad run to him when he got home from the fire station, swinging him up onto his shoulders or sitting down at the table to hear about Cole's day. No question, Cole was who he was now because of his dad.

The man who chose to be his father.

"Your mom and dad want you to go to Liberty. Your dad, especially. He's a successful man, Cole." She exhaled. "He wouldn't have cut his career short to marry your mom." Her voice fell, and a sense of control returned to the moment. "It's what he would've done in this situation if he had been your age."

"No, it's not." Cole gripped the steering wheel and for a few seconds he looked out the driver's-side window. *Please, God, let her see how serious I am.* He turned back to her. "My dad gave up his life to love my mom and take care of me." Cole turned so he could face her fully. He pressed his shoulder into the seat. "I don't have his blood in my veins, but he'll be my father till the day I die."

Elise still looked confused. "You really think your dad would've given up his school and training, at our age, to marry your mom?"

"Of course." Finally she was getting it.

But instead she shook her head. "The timing was different." Elise's tone started to rise, but she brought it back down again. "Ask him, Cole. Ask your mom. What would they do in our situation?" She lifted her hands and let them fall into her lap. "Maybe your mom would've chosen adoption if she'd only been eighteen. And maybe your dad would've kept in touch. Been a friend to her. But I can't see him giving up his calling to be a firefighter."

Cole turned toward the windshield again. Was that what he was doing? Giving up his college career? His chance at being a doctor? Online classes were just as good. They had to be. At least for the first few years. Maybe he would talk to his papa. See if being in a classroom really mattered. He looked at her again, but he had no words. This was supposed to be the best night of his life.

He still wanted it to be.

She adjusted her position. "This baby, this pregnancy . . ." She put her free hand on her belly as her voice fell. "It's my problem to figure out." She didn't look sad or upset. But there was no wavering in her tone. "I've been so confused, Cole. Some days I think about what you're offering and it's all I want. You beside me when the baby is born, the two of us making a life for ourselves. Getting married."

"Exactly." Cole didn't feel as convinced as before. Like he was confused, also. More than he'd been willing to admit. Still, his offer stood.

Elise sighed. "No, Cole. When I'm thinking straight I know there's nothing right about that plan. We barely just met." She took hold of his hand again. "Honestly, I'm not ready to be a mom."

Cole stared straight ahead, his other hand still on the steering wheel. For a long time he said nothing, just let her words hang in his heart for a bit.

She broke the silence first. "I've made up my mind." Her voice was softer now. "I'm going to call an attorney your aunt told me about. He manages adoptions. She gave me his business card when I went back to her clinic . . ."

He wasn't sure how to feel about that. "Elise, you should give it some time. You can't undo a decision like adoption." Cole still couldn't believe they were discussing this now. He studied her and tried to understand. What could've brought this up tonight? And then it hit him. The answer was there in her eyes. Kind and tender, deeper than the ocean. Until now their relationship had spun around her. But now . . . now she loved him as much as he loved her. That was it.

And this decision, it was her way of caring for him, loving him.

She smoothed her dress and smiled at him. "I want you to be at Liberty in the fall." Her smile was as genuine as springtime. She ran her thumb along the top of his hand. "You're going to be a doctor, Cole."

He didn't respond right away. There was freedom in this new plan of hers, freedom for them to pursue their dreams. But still Cole wasn't sure. Something about marrying her by Christmastime sounded wonderful. The stuff movies were made of. He reached across the console and took her other hand. "I just want to say it again." He looked deep into her beautiful eyes. "My dad would've done whatever it took to love my mom. To love me." He had never been more sure. "And I want to be the same kind of man."

They'd each said what they needed to say. Cole checked the time on his phone and then he grinned at her. "Come on, Princess. I gotta get you to the dance."

"Yes." She giggled and the mood lifted. He opened

the door and jogged around to her side. As she stepped out she put her hand on his cheek. "Thanks for listening."

His knees trembled, and not because of the chilly late March evening air. He wanted to kiss her so bad he could barely think. *Deep breath, Cole. Get to the dance.* His silent pep talk helped him. He took a step back, grinned and took her hand. "Thanks for talking." He wove his fingers between hers. As they set out across the parking lot, he kept the pace easy. "Now . . . for the next three hours, no talking, all right?"

She laughed. "What are we going to do?"

Cole let his head fall back, the joy from earlier filling him again. "We're going to dance, Elise." The night was going to be okay, after all. "Until the very last song."

And that's just what they did. They took a break only when he and Carolyn Everly were named prom king and queen. Up onstage, as they were getting their crowns, Carolyn whispered in his direction. "I knew it would be you." Her smile was more genuine than flirty. Carolyn was aware of Elise. "I don't know any other guy like you, Cole."

Her compliment touched his heart. Being with Carolyn was as natural as breathing. The two of them had grown up together. Their classmates were clapping, cheering, and the photographer was motioning for them to get closer.

"Hold hands," he told them. "This is for the yearbook."

Cole took Carolyn's hand and they both posed for the picture. After, while they were still on the stage, they faced each other. "You look pretty, Carolyn." It was true. There was something timeless about Carolyn. She was a good girl from a good family. In the back of Cole's mind he had always pictured marrying someone like Carolyn one day.

But that was before Elise.

They shared a hug and before they parted ways, Carolyn's eyes lit up. "Wait! I forgot to tell you!" Whatever her news, happiness spilled from her. Before Cole could ask what it was, Carolyn blurted it out. "I'm going to Liberty. I got my acceptance letter yesterday!" He could tell she wasn't trying to make things awkward between them. "Looks like we'll get another four years together."

Any other day, any other time and this would've been the best news and Cole would've celebrated. But he could feel Elise watching from somewhere in the crowd, so he kept his response tame. "Wow, that's amazing!" Cole took a step back. The crowns were still on both their heads. "Let's talk later." He pointed to the dance floor. "I . . . I have to go."

If Carolyn was disappointed in his response, she didn't show it. Everyone thought she was the sweetest, prettiest, most popular girl at Clear Creek High. And besides, Carolyn didn't have feelings for Cole, that much was certain. After all, she was here with Burke Ballinger, senior quarterback. She gave Cole a quick wave and danced down the steps to the spot where her date was waiting for her. Cole watched Burke take her in his arms. Whatever he was saying, one thing was sure.

He was smitten with Carolyn Everly.

Were the two dating? Cole let his look linger a bit longer. Maybe they were. The idea would've bugged him before, but not now. Not when he was here with—

A shot of fear ran through him. Elise! Where was she?

The prom king and queen process had taken far too long. He scanned the dance floor and found her leaning against the back wall. Their eyes met, and as soon as Cole saw her understanding smile, relief flooded his heart. He hurried to her and led her to the dance floor, where they stayed until the very last song. Never mind Carolyn Everly or Liberty or his title as prom king. Years from now there was only one thing he would remember about tonight's prom.

The way it felt to have Elise Walker in his arms.

15

Elise waited till Tuesday afternoon to visit the lawyer. Cole had a baseball game in Indianapolis that day. He wouldn't be home till eight or later. Already Elise had spoken by phone with the man—Alan Green.

"I want to place my baby for adoption," Elise had said during their call. She used the wording from the lawyer's website. A girl didn't give up her baby. She placed the baby in an adoptive home. Elise liked that. It was something she could do for her baby. More intentional.

The attorney sounded kind and patient. "You'll have time to change your mind." His tone was warm, like the way she pictured the gentle waves on some distant Caribbean shore. "It's important that this is your decision, Elise. Only yours."

She explained that she had no way to get to his office. Her aunt and uncle didn't know about the baby and she had no one else. Of course she wouldn't think of having Cole or his mother take her. Like Mr. Green had said, this was a choice she had to make on her own.

So the attorney had arranged for Helen, his secretary, to pick up Elise this afternoon, at the park across the street from school. Her stomach had hurt all day. She was sure about her decision, but that didn't make it easy. Elise was waiting in the meeting spot near the park entrance when she felt something sudden and fluttery.

Like butterfly wings on the inside of her stomach.

At first she thought maybe it was hunger pains. But then it happened again and Elise gasped. It was her baby! The doctor had said she'd be feeling it move soon. So that's what this had to be. As if her baby were crying out to her, *Don't place me somewhere else. Please keep me.*

Tears stung Elise's eyes. Or maybe the baby was saying something else. *Thank you for doing this. My life will be wonderful with the right parents.*

Elise wasn't sure which to believe, but she chose the second one. Yes, that was it. Her baby was thanking her. What sort of life would she give a newborn? When all she wanted was to get to New York City and start her own life?

At the exact right time, a gray-haired woman pulled up and rolled down her window. "Elise?"

"Yes." She felt instantly comfortable. "Thank you."

Elise couldn't remember what they talked about on the ride to the lawyer's office on the other side of Bloomington. All she could think about was the life inside her. The very real life. Moving and stretching and reminding her of the truth.

Her baby would be here all too soon.

Mr. Green was younger than Elise had expected, and his whole attitude very compassionate. He and his secretary sat at a long wooden table across from Elise. Between them were four large scrapbooks. Adoptive parent profiles, the attorney had told her.

"Let's start with that one." He leaned forward and pointed to one of the books. "Those are parents waiting for a baby."

Elise opened the book. The first page held the photo of an older couple. A quick glance told her that they had raised their two children. Now they were hoping to have another baby or two. A quote beneath their photo said: *We loved being parents once, so we want to be parents again. Before we're too old.*

"Hmmm." Elise turned the page. Then she flipped through a few others. Every page held the profile of a couple waiting for a baby. "There're . . . so many." The idea of choosing one was suddenly overwhelming.

"Take your time." Mr. Green stood. "I have a phone meeting in the other room." He looked from Elise to his secretary. "Helen will stay with you. In case you have any questions." He paused. "There is one couple I'd like to recommend."

Elise was grateful. How was she supposed to pick the right parents? She could be here all week and not have time to read all the profiles. "Yes." She remembered to breathe. "I'd like that."

Mr. Green walked around the table and stood beside Elise. Then he turned to the last pages in the book. "Here." He pointed to a profile. "I have a special feeling about this couple. How about you start with them?" He stepped back and headed for his office. "I'll be back in half an hour."

"Thank you." Elise stared at the photo. The couple looked young and happy. They both had blond hair and warm blue eyes. The husband looked a little like Cole Blake, the way Cole might look ten years from now. The longer she studied them, the more they almost looked familiar. From somewhere inside her heart, Elise felt a connection take root. She looked to the top of the profile.

Aaron and Lucy Williams.

Nice, Elise thought. She'd always liked the name Lucy. She lifted her eyes to Helen. The woman was working on a file of papers. "Have you met them? This couple?" She tilted the book so the secretary could see the profile. "Aaron and Lucy?"

"Yes." Helen smiled. "They were in the other day. I like them a lot."

Elise nodded. She kept reading the couple's profile. Lucy was a nurse in a maternity ward. Elise smiled. The woman would definitely be great with babies. And Aaron was an administrator at the same hospital. Right here in town.

A thought hit Elise. Maybe she had seen them before, during her time volunteering at Bloomington Hospital. Maybe that's why they looked familiar.

She kept reading. The couple had been trying to have a baby for ten years. Praying and trusting God that one day a child would come. They were foster parents and had lost several babies who were almost theirs. And Lucy had given birth too early to a baby girl who didn't survive.

Tears stung Elise's eyes. *Why, God? Why do I get pregnant from a guy like Randy? And here this poor couple has been trying forever to have a child?* Nothing about that was fair. She looked at their picture again and ran her finger lightly over their faces. These two would take care of her baby. Elise had no doubt.

She studied their photo, their eyes. What sort of life would her baby have with them? In the side notes Lucy was quoted saying she would stop working if they had a baby. She believed in being a full-time mom—at least at first. Elise smiled. That meant the baby inside her would be loved and doted on. The best kinds of private schools and . . . Suddenly she remembered Cole's declaration the other day. The main thing her baby needed was parents who loved Jesus. At the time he'd been thinking he would be the dad. Tears blurred her eyes. But she smiled despite the sadness. She would never forget the outlandish offer of Cole Blake.

And even though he wasn't going to be her baby's father, he was right about Jesus. Her mom had raised her to know faith in Christ, to memorize Bible verses and sing songs about God. Yes, she had walked away. But she was on her way back.

Which reminded her. Later today she would call her mama and come clean about the baby. They would talk about Elise's decision to place the baby for adoption and after that her mama would cry and Elise would apologize. Then finally she would tell her the good news. She was going to Easter Sunday church with Cole's family. She was coming home to Jesus, home to what was true and right and good.

She certainly wanted the same for her baby.

Again she looked over Aaron and Lucy's profile. They wrote about their faith and trust in God. There was a quote from Aaron that read: *Sometimes it's hard to believe the Lord really hears us, that He cares if we have a baby. But even now I believe He does care. He sees us and He has a plan for us.*

He has a plan. Yes. Elise wiped the tears from her cheeks. Peace flooded her heart. She didn't need to look at the other profiles. She had found the parents for her baby. And as she made the decision, she felt the fluttering in her belly one more time. She gasped. She was actually feeling her baby move!

Helen set her paperwork aside and turned to her. "Is everything okay, dear?"

"Yes." Elise stood just as Mr. Green entered the room again. She turned to him and felt a smile fill her face. "You were right about that couple." She handed the book to the attorney. "They're the ones. Aaron and Lucy Williams."

An expression that was more joy than surprise came over the man. "This will mean a great deal to them." He seemed to force a more serious look. "Now, one thing we haven't discussed. The father."

"We're not together. I don't want him involved." She shook her head. "He doesn't want to be a father."

Mr. Green hesitated. "You're sure?"

"Yes. He . . . he was abusive. He should never be near this baby." Her resolve couldn't have been stronger. "This child is my concern."

"Very well." Mr. Green nodded. "You'll give me his contact information and I'll call him. He'll need to sign something terminating his rights before we can move forward." The man crossed his arms. "Once he does terminate his rights, you do not have to identify him on the paperwork."

Relief flooded Elise. The attorney was going to handle Randy. Perfect. She couldn't answer fast enough. "Yes, please. You can call him. That's how I want it. The father not identified."

"That's fine." Mr. Green looked through a stack of papers. "Now about Aaron and Lucy. If you decide to place your baby with them, there's something you should know. The choice is yours, even after the child is born."

Elise blinked a few times. "After? What do you mean?" She'd always thought adoption was permanent. From the first day. "For how long?"

"Two weeks." He took a slow breath. "Every state is different, but the goal is to give you time to change your mind. In case you regret your decision."

An ache took up residence in her soul. "Wouldn't that be hard for Aaron and Lucy?"

"It would." Mr. Green looked straight at her. As if he

wanted her to really understand this next part. "But it's part of the adoption process. Some birth moms make an adoption plan and think they're certain about it." He paused. "But once they hold their baby, they can't go through with it. The court allows two weeks. After that the adoption is final."

The idea of waiting those two weeks, knowing she was allowed to change her mind and that her baby's future would hang in the balance was more than Elise could imagine. She clenched her jaw and shook her head. "I won't change my mind." The baby fluttered again even as she pushed ahead. "I'm sure, Mr. Green."

"The rule is there for your protection. You don't have to think about it yet." He grabbed a file from his secretary's desk. "One day at a time. That's how the adoption process goes."

Elise liked that. One day at a time. If she looked at it that way, she could handle this. The lawyer helped her sign the appropriate papers stating that she would choose Aaron and Lucy Williams as the adoptive parents for her baby. Mr. Green said he'd contact Randy later that day, and then the man talked to her about having an open or closed adoption. He gave her information to read about which would be better.

But Elise already knew. She wanted a closed adoption. If she was handing her baby over to Aaron and Lucy, then they would be the parents. An open adoption might confuse her baby. And her. No, she wanted a clean cut. Period.

When she was done, Helen drove her home. Elise thanked her, and had the woman drop her off four doors down. She didn't want any questions from her aunt and uncle. They would know the truth eventually. But first she had to tell her mama.

When dinner and dishes were over, Elise went to her room, closed the door and dialed her mother's number. Sure they had talked at least once a week, but every time Elise had kept it short. Her mom asked about school-work and Aunt Carol and Uncle Ken. A few times she asked whether Elise was making friends.

Always Elise kept her answers vague. Yes, she had friends. No, she hadn't met anyone special. No, she hadn't heard from Randy. Yes, she still had his number blocked. No, she wasn't attending church.

Today was going to be different.

Her mom picked up on the second ring. "Elise! Hi, honey." Her mom sounded nervous, like she was trying too hard to keep Elise from running again. "This is a surprise."

Elise closed her eyes. Her mother had no idea. "Mama . . . I have something to tell you."

The pause on the other end told Elise whatever it was, her mom wasn't ready. No mother could ever be ready for news like this. She took a breath. *Give me the words. Help her not to be too hurt.* And then, as if it had a will of its own, the story spilled out.

She told her mom about meeting Cole Blake and how he was a gentleman from a wonderful family. "I'm going to church with them Easter Sunday." Elise paused. It was the only bit of good news so she wanted the fact to settle in a bit. "Mama, Cole's family, they all love Jesus. You'd like them."

"Yes." Her mom sounded cautious. "I'm sure I would."

The story kept coming. Elise explained that after she got settled in Bloomington she began to feel nauseous and how Cole took her to get a pregnancy test. Two of them. "They were both positive."

She heard her mother catch her breath. "Oh, Elise." Her words were more of a quiet cry. Not disappointment, but heartbreak. Because this couldn't have been what she wanted for her baby girl.

"I know, Mama. I couldn't believe it, either." Elise felt sick. This was the last thing she ever wanted to tell her mother. She'd been nothing but completely devoted to Elise every day of her life. Tears came over Elise all at once. Sobs gathered in her throat and for a minute she couldn't talk.

"Baby." Her mom was clearly crying, too. "Why didn't you tell me? I would've gotten in my car and come to you that very minute."

The crying felt good. It was the first time Elise had really wept about all this. She lay on her side on the still-made bed and buried her face in the pillow. So Carol and Ken wouldn't hear her. Then she let the tears come, wave after wave. Like she'd stored up an ocean of heartbreak these last few months. "I'm s-s-so sorry, Mama. I . . . I should've told you."

Elise missed her mother more than she had allowed herself to think about. How could she have just lied to her and kept the phone calls short and believed everything would be okay? "I hate that I lied to you. I hate it."

For a long time they stayed that way, the two of them crying softly into the phone. Her mom spoke first. "So . . . how far are you? Five months?"

"Yes. Almost twenty-one weeks." She sat up and took a tissue from her nightstand and blew her nose. "That's assuming I got pregnant around Thanksgiving. When everything was crazy."

Her mom was quiet again before she went to the obvious next question. "What are you going to tell Randy? About the baby?"

Elise steadied herself. "I met with an attorney. He says I don't have to tell Randy anything." Two quick breaths and she explained herself. "He'll contact Randy and handle the termination of his rights. Randy never wanted to be a daddy. He used to tell me that." She took a quick breath. "Once he signs off, I can leave the father unnamed."

"Oh." Her mama sounded relieved. "Okay. Good to hear." She sniffed. "So what about the baby? What are you going to do?"

Elise wiped the tears from her face. She felt more composed as she explained her meeting with Mr. Green today. "I even picked out a couple." The bed wasn't comfortable. She moved to the chair by the window and looked out. Darkness covered all of Bloomington. As dark as the sadness in her heart. "I already decided. I want to place the baby with them."

"Elise." Her mother didn't sound convinced. "You can keep the baby. I'll help you." Panic crept into her voice. "You can live with me and we'll figure out your schooling later. When the baby is older. Randy is moving to Oregon to work with his uncle. His mother told me he's leaving after graduation. So there'd be no reason you couldn't come home."

For the first time Elise realized that her decision wasn't going to affect only her. The baby was her mama's first grandchild. "I'm sorry, Mama. I'm just . . . I'm not ready for this." She felt the weight of all that lay ahead. Especially tonight, when all she wanted to do was find her way back to her mother's arms. Back to life before she met Randy.

"We can talk about it later." Her mother seemed content with that. "You don't have to decide now."

She was right. But Elise had no intention of changing her mind. Not now or when the baby was born. And not for the two weeks that followed. But there was no point talking about it further, since her mom clearly did not want her to take the adoption route.

Elise changed the subject. "Let me tell you about Cole." She went into great detail about the guy she had fallen so fully for, the guy she was sure would only ever be a friend. She told her mother how Cole was willing to miss going away to college so he could be with her. "He even said maybe we'd get married. Next Christmas, if God was leading us that way."

"He sounds wonderful." Her mom sounded more relaxed. Hopeful, almost. "Maybe that's what you should
do. After graduation Cole could come here with you. He
could have the guest room and—if God leads you two—
you could get married and get a place not far from
home." She took a slow breath. "But if not, it worked for
me, Elise. Being a single mom. You can do it. I'll help
you." Then as if she had to say it, "If it's what you want."

What *she* wanted? Elise closed her eyes. She wanted
to go back and never talk to Randy at that party. Wanted
to be free and young and pure again. With a faith she
had never walked away from. She had already set her
mind on placing her baby for adoption. Her mom's plan
was outrageous. They were too young to play house, she
and Cole.

Then why did her mother seem bent on convincing
her about it?

The conversation went on another hour. They talked
about her due date in mid-August and finally her mama
finished the call with a warning. "If you give this baby up,
Elise, you'll never know your own child."

Elise's heart felt heavy. "I know that. But it's still the
right thing to do. For me."

But by the time the call ended, Elise was less sure
about her decision. Were Aaron and Lucy Williams the
best parents for her baby? Or was she the best?

Gradually, as the next hour passed, her heart began to
shift again. Her mother's offer of help had made the idea
of keeping her baby a little more possible. Would she re-

gret her decision the rest of her life? Always wonder where her baby was or what had become of him or her?

Maybe she'd rushed too quickly into the adoption idea.

By the time she climbed into bed that night, she thought again about her mother's idea. Mama would help with the baby and Cole would step in, even sleeping in the guest room until he and Elise figured out if they were supposed to get married. And if they didn't get married and Cole left, then she'd be a single mom. But so what? Who better to help her than her own mother? And gradually, as she drifted off to sleep, the idea of keeping her baby didn't sound so outrageous, after all.

It sounded wonderful.

16

For Aaron alone, Lucy had gotten on board and started praying once more for a child. That God would give them a baby and specifically that somehow, some way a child might come to them through the attorney. Alan Green.

The father of Brooke Baxter West's patient.

She was headed out the door to work and this time, instead of zipping past the empty nursery down the hall from their bedroom, she stopped and stepped inside. The space felt sacred, here where her husband talked to God every morning. Where he read his Bible.

A room that had only made Lucy sad.

But if she was going to pray and believe, if she was truly intent on coming alongside Aaron and asking God for a baby, then she needed to figure out what to do with this room. She needed to hope and trust God. One last time.

With slow steps, like she was walking on holy ground, Lucy crossed the nursery to the crib. She clutched the white wooden rail and looked at the soft sheet. The pastel baby animals. On the first Saturday of every month, Aaron dusted everything in the room and washed the sheet, so the place was always clean.

A fresh smell hung in the air. Like they already had a baby and washing her bedding was a part of their normal routine. Lucy ran her hand along the edge of the small bed and closed her eyes. *God, why am I doing this? Do You see me? Do You hear us?*

Aaron thought hope permeated the room. But even now, all Lucy could feel was heartbreak. *Help me believe, Lord. Help my unbelief.* She bowed her head.

I see you, my daughter. I love you now and always.

The voice was clear and real. Chills ran down her arms and legs. The same voice she'd heard a few months ago. Was God really here, His presence all around her? And did He actually love her like the voice so clearly insisted? Whatever it was, this time Lucy knew one thing for sure.

She couldn't ignore it.

Like she'd seen Aaron do, Lucy lowered herself to her knees and then she covered her face. "I'm here, Lord." Her voice was barely a whisper. "If You're the one talking to me, then I believe. I so want to believe. Help me trust You."

Tears trickled down her cheeks as she stayed there, talking to God. Listening. Believing. Finally she stood and took another look at the baby crib. At the Winnie-the-Pooh curtains and the teddy bears on the dresser. She crossed the room and ran her hand over the still-soft fur.

A conversation came back to her, from dinner the other night with their friends Brooke and Peter West.

Brooke had brought up Alan Green. "I really think he'll get your profile to the top of the list." Brooke had leaned forward, clearly convinced. "He was ready to do whatever he could for me. Because of his little girl."

Like every other time, Lucy didn't want to get her hopes up. But after that dinner, when they were in bed, Aaron had cuddled up to her. He kissed her and softly brushed her hair from her forehead and eyes. The way he used to, before everything about their intimacy became so measured and calculated. So disappointing.

"You're beautiful." He kissed her again.

For years, when they drew close to each other like this, Lucy would feel herself tense up. What was she doing wrong? How come she couldn't get pregnant? Would this be the time, and if not how could they take the letdown?

But those days were behind them. Gradually they were trying to get back to when nights like this were about touching and loving and finding their way to being one again. Truly. Madly. Deeply.

The other night seemed like it might be one of those times, but after a few minutes of kissing, Aaron eased back on his pillow and searched her eyes. "I have something I want to ask you."

She figured his request would have something to do with a baby. She smiled. A sad smile, yes. But one she hoped would tell him she cared. She wanted to hear him. "Tell me." Her fingers ran the length of his arm. Gentleness. Tenderness. The way things used to be. She had loved him all her life. They couldn't let the empty nursery change that.

"This attorney." Aaron swallowed, like he was nervous to talk about this again. "Alan Green."

"Yes."

"I have a feeling this could be it, Lucy." His eyes glistened in the darkness. He wanted a baby so much. "I mean, I really believe it. I feel like God is saying it's time. This is it."

How often had Lucy responded with an exaggerated look or an eye roll when Aaron insisted that God was on their side, that He was certainly going to give them a baby? Lucy didn't want to think about it. Aaron was one of the most genuine, godly men she knew. He deserved better.

"Yes." It was time she support him. Time she really listen. "Brooke sounded excited."

"Exactly." Hope lit up his expression. "So what I want to ask is . . . Lucy, please, if you could pray and believe. If the two of us could trust God together about this. Even if it feels crazy after all this time." He took gentle hold of her face and kissed her again. "Please?"

His eyes looked the same as the day they'd gotten married, the way they had been lost to everyone in the church but her. Lucy slid closer and hugged him, body to body. "Yes, Aaron." She brushed the side of her face against his. "I'll believe with you. I'll pray and trust God. Yes."

So it was only right that she had wound up on her knees in the nursery this morning on her way to work.

She had promised Aaron and she would keep her word. She had known there would be moments like this, times when she opened her heart to God about the most difficult subject in all her life. It was part of Aaron's request, so she had expected this.

What she hadn't expected was the call she got as she pulled into the hospital parking lot. It was from a number Lucy didn't recognize. She still had ten minutes to check in, so she found a spot and took the call. "Hello?"

"Lucy Williams?"

"Yes." What was this? "How can I help you?"

"This is Alan Green. I have good news."

· · ·

LUCY COULD BARELY complete her shift. This was the most hopeful news they'd heard in far too long. A teenage girl in the area had chosen their profile. The attorney wanted to go over the details in person.

At four o'clock Lucy met Aaron in the hospital lobby and the two of them drove in his SUV to Mr. Green's office.

"Can you believe it?" Aaron couldn't stop smiling. "I told you. It's going to happen."

Lucy couldn't respond. Her fingers were trembling and her stomach was in knots. Every time they'd ever gotten good news it had been followed up with pain. And she wasn't sure how much more pain she could take. The whole drive, she let Aaron do the talking. In response she did just one thing.

She reached out and took her husband's hand.

When they arrived, the attorney ushered them into his office. As they sat down, the man sounded upbeat. "First the good news." He smiled at them. "The young mother wants you to raise her baby. Yours was the only profile she wanted to work with."

Next to her, Aaron squeezed her hand. He kept his eyes on Mr. Green. "What all can you tell us?"

It was hard to hear over the whoosh of her racing heart, but Lucy managed to track on the details. The birth mother's name was Elise. She had gotten pregnant by a guy in her hometown in Louisiana. In January she came to Bloomington to live with her aunt and uncle. And to get away from the guy.

"The birth father has terminated his rights, so he's out of the picture. Elise has chosen not to name him." The man went on to say that Elise had chosen a closed adoption. "She doesn't want her child confused about who the parents are. She wants it to be you two alone." He checked his notes. "Oh, and she's due August fourteenth."

So far the details couldn't be better. Lucy could feel Aaron getting excited, as thrilled as if they were hearing the news that they, themselves, were pregnant. Aaron spoke up. "You said first the good news." His smile faded a little. "What's the bad news?"

The attorney took a long breath. "In this business we look for red flags, signs that increase the birth mother's odds of changing her mind." He hesitated. "And I have to tell you we encourage that."

Lucy felt like she'd been kicked in the gut. "You encourage birth moms to walk away from adoption? Even after they've come to you to arrange one?"

"Yes." He looked unashamed about the fact. "If she's going to reverse her decision, we'd rather get that out up front. As soon as possible." His expression intensified. "Less heartache for everyone."

"If you don't mind me asking . . ." Aaron leaned forward, his forearms on the edge of Mr. Green's desk. "What do you tell the birth mothers?"

"We tell them the truth. This is their choice, their decision. No one can make it for them." He leaned back in his leather chair. "We tell them that placing a child for adoption is forever. There's no going back." He looked at both of them. "Not after the two weeks, anyway."

"Two weeks?" Aaron blinked. "What about two weeks?"

"It's a state law." The man looked very serious. Like this was part of what he needed them to understand. "If the birth mother still wants to place her child, once the baby is born, the mom has two weeks to change her mind."

Lucy stared at her lap. *Two weeks?* She could decide to keep her baby for two whole weeks after the birth? What were they supposed to do while they waited? "Would the baby stay with us during that time?"

"Every case is different." Mr. Green stood and walked to his bookshelf. "Let's not get ahead of ourselves." He pulled out a volume he was obviously familiar with. It was marked at a certain page and the attorney turned right to it. "This is what you need to hear. The signs that a birth mother will change her mind."

Lucy's fingers were shaking again and the room felt suddenly cold. The meeting was beginning to seem like cruel and unusual punishment. Elise could call off the adoption up to two weeks after giving birth, and apparently there was more?

The lawyer was studying the list, going over what were considered red flags. "Her age is one issue. She's a senior in high school." He looked up. "Younger birth mothers are more likely to keep their babies even after making an adoption plan."

Lucy tried to stop her knees from shaking.

"Also, I asked Elise about her mother, what she thought. It's typically a risk when the birth mother's mom isn't on board with the adoption."

"Is she?" Aaron didn't sound nervous. "We need to know all the flags. I agree."

"I wasn't certain until a few days ago. Elise called and told me her mom wants her to keep the baby. But, Elise was still 'pretty sure' she wanted to place the baby for adoption." He paused. "Again, specifically with the two of you. Apparently after she talked to her mother, Elise spent a day thinking maybe she'd keep her baby. Now she's back to the adoption plan." He folded his hands on his desk. "This is very normal for a pregnant teenage girl."

Pretty sure? Lucy had heard enough. Maybe they should pass until something more definite came along.

She forced herself not to mention that. "Okay. Thank you." She folded her arms. "What . . . what are we supposed to do then? With the risks and her age and all?"

"You pray." The attorney's smile was marked with empathy. "And be excited. Elise is twenty-one weeks along, and—for now—she wants you to raise her baby." He smiled, even if he looked a little weary. "That's something to celebrate. Even as we take this one day at a time."

They signed paperwork then, stating their understanding that Elise had chosen them, and agreeing to pay for her medical expenses and any legal and other fees associated with the adoption. All of which were nonrefundable. Regardless of what Elise decided in the end.

On their way out of the office, Aaron put his arm around Lucy. "It's a faith walk. Definitely not easy."

This was the first time she'd heard him sound anything but completely positive. "Yes." She loved the way they fit together, the way she felt sheltered in his arms. They reached his car and he opened the door for her. Before she climbed in, she turned to him and he eased her into his embrace.

For a while they stayed that way, his arms around her waist. She pressed her head against his chest and held on. As if the winds of the situation might blow her onto the ground otherwise.

When they were halfway home, Aaron glanced at her. "August fourteenth."

"Yes." She thought about the nursery and the clean

sheets. "Four months from now we could have a baby. Is that what you're thinking?"

"It is." Aaron reached for her hand. "We need to pray more than ever. Not just that the baby will be ours. But that Elise will reach a final decision soon. Whatever is right for her and the baby."

Lucy stared at him, in awe of him. His heart was so good, so pure. That here on the way home from the attorney's office, with the best of news and the worst of odds fighting for position in their hearts, he wouldn't only think of their desires.

But those of a confused and frightened teenager.

And the baby who had already taken up residence in Lucy's heart.

17

The dinner table was alive with the laughter of Vienna, and tonight Theo did what he often did around his only child.

He sat back and just listened.

She was talking to her mother about a dance recital coming up at the high school. And how she and her friend Jessie were choreographing an encore number for the team. "Picture it, Mom!" Vienna stood and pushed in her chair. She spread her arms out and looked one way, then the other. "All of us lined up along the stage doing the exact same moves and then at the end we break into a kick line! Isn't that amazing?"

Theo looked at his wife. Alma was nodding, eyes wide, like she could definitely picture it. Theo had to work a little harder. Especially because Vienna was talking like there was a prize for most words per minute.

She was beautiful and animated and clearly thrilled with her plan, and Theo kept wondering how they had been so blessed by God to have her as their daughter. Vienna paused only long enough to take a breath. "You know, like the Rockettes. And everyone will understand it was something we planned just for the end of the show!" She exhaled and sat down. "It was my idea."

"Wow." Alma raised both arms in victory. "The dance team must love you!"

"They do." Vienna giggled. She took a bite of her broccoli and waved her fork in the air. "And, Mom, you should hear the music! Jessie and I picked out the coolest song. It's like a mix of three songs, actually." She finished her bite and looked at him. "You, too, Daddy."

"Me?" He laughed even as he nodded, feigning seriousness. "Oh, right. For sure. I'm the music connoisseur of the family. I'll be the first on my feet that night." He paused. "When is it again?"

"Daddy!" She was still smiling, her expression a mock show of outrage. Her voice was the only song the house needed. "Please. One week, exactly. Put it on your calendar in big letters: 'Vienna is dancing tonight. First time since joining the dance team. And we will be there by six-thirty for a good seat.'" Her smile warmed his soul. "Okay?"

"All of that?" He made his eyes wide. Then he turned to Alma. "Honey, we need a bigger calendar."

They all laughed and as the meal neared an end, Vienna switched topics to foster care again. She turned to Alma. "I keep thinking about it. Did Daddy ever tell you about our conversation?"

"It's been a few months, but yes. He did." Alma tilted her head. "It's just, honey, when we took in children before, I wasn't working full-time. Remember?"

"I know. You were a substitute teacher and every-thing was perfect." Vienna's expression made her look nine again. "Can we go back to that? At some point?"

"Baby girl, you'll be in college in a blink." Theo smiled at her. "Your mother's a very important adminis-trator."

Vienna wasn't letting up. She reached out and took hold of her mother's hand. "But do you really enjoy it, Mama?" Her eyes warmed the room. Sincere. Hopeful. "Wouldn't you rather be here taking care of babies? Or watching my dance rehearsals after school?"

An easy laugh came from Alma. "You make it sound tempting." She was still holding Vienna's hand. "Let's see how the year finishes out. We can definitely talk more about it."

"Yes!" Vienna was on her feet again. She did a running-type victory move, where she turned in a circle and ended in a cheerleader pose, one hand on her hip, one in the air. "I want more kids in this house. Before I'm all grown up." She stopped and looked from Theo to Alma. "Actually, I already am all grown up."

"Oh, are you now?" Theo chuckled. "At fifteen?"

"Yes." Vienna put her hands together and raised her eyebrows. Her classic pleading pose. "Which brings me to my next question." She barely hesitated. "Jessie and Sarah Jane want to pick me up and go to Foster's. You know, to talk about the encore." She looked at Alma. "Please! We won't be late."

Theo didn't like the idea. It was Sunday and they

were in for the evening. Safe under one roof. Ready for a relaxing time together, getting set for the week ahead. "Who are these girls again?"

"From dance, Daddy. They're both seniors. It was super nice of them to include me." She looked like she might break into tears if he said no. "Please! They're my best friends on the team."

"Who's driving?" Alma stood and began clearing the table. Vienna joined in as Alma continued. "And why on a Sunday night? It's almost eight o'clock."

Something about his daughter's request didn't sit well with Theo. He helped the girls with clearing the table and tried to discern his thoughts. It was just a run to the ice cream shop. She'd be back in no time. But he didn't like it.

In the kitchen Vienna was still working the moment, looking for a yes. "Jessie's driving. She's a great girl, remember? Her dad is Coach Taylor, on the football team." She looked back at Theo. "You've talked to him before, Daddy. Remember?"

Of course Theo remembered. He worked the chains on the sidelines of every home game. His way of compensating for the fact that he'd never had a son to play the game. Vienna had been a cheerleader in the fall so it kept him involved and closer to the action. Something he loved.

"Coach Taylor's a good man." Theo couldn't shake the feeling. But then if he had his way he'd never let her drive anywhere with another teenager. "Is Jessie a careful driver?"

"Of course!" Vienna seemed to sense the win at hand. "She's a straight A student, Daddy. And she never texts while she's driving."

Alma was putting the dishes in the dishwasher. "When have you ridden with her?" She stopped and looked straight at Vienna. Not accusing their daughter, but curious.

"When she invited me over for dinner the night of rehearsal. Remember? You met her. And when we all went to get dance shoes together after school. A few weeks ago." Vienna put herself between the two of them, an arm around each of their necks. "You can trust me, Parents. I wouldn't do anything crazy. This is ice cream on a Sunday night." She giggled. "Pretty normal, don't you think?"

Teenage logic, but still his little girl was right. Theo took a deep breath and kissed Vienna's cheek. "Fine. You can go." He faced her, his hands on her shoulders. "But wear your seat belt. And if she does anything dangerous, tell her. You have to say something." Theo shot a look to his wife. "Is that okay? If she goes?"

Alma uttered a single laugh, the silliness from earlier back again. "I was wondering if anyone was going to ask my opinion." She pulled Vienna close, in a side hug. Then she did the same to Theo. A family huddle, they called it. Something they did all the time. She leaned her head against their daughter's. "Ditto. To everything your daddy said."

Vienna kissed Alma's cheek and then his. "Yes!" She jumped a few times and then rushed for her cell phone on the kitchen counter. "I'll let them know. They'll be here in ten minutes."

The three of them finished the dishes together, something else Theo liked to do. Truth was, he would've enjoyed having a full house of kids. Six or seven. That's what he and Alma had talked about after getting married. But God had given them all they would ever need when He gave them Vienna. Nights like this were proof.

A few minutes later a car pulled into their driveway. Theo and Alma were in the kitchen still, making coffee. They were talking about a student who'd won a national poetry contest at Alma's school when Vienna breezed in, her purse over her shoulder.

She went to Theo and hugged him. "I'll get you a scoop of mint chocolate chip!"

Theo smiled. "Now that's what I'm talking about."

"Nothing for me." Alma pulled their daughter close and kissed the top of her head. "See you soon."

"Okay." She hurried toward the front door. Halfway there she stopped and looked over her shoulder at them. The picture of happy. "Love you!"

"Love you." They responded to her at the same time.

And then in a blur she was gone. From where he was standing, Theo could see out the window, so he watched the car back down the driveway and pull away. He still didn't feel good about her going out. But the weather was clear and his daughter was right about her friends. They were good girls. Everything would be fine. He sighed and turned to his wife.

Alma took two mugs from the cupboard and set them on the counter. The coffee wasn't quite ready, so she faced him. Nostalgia filled her expression. "She's got a point, you know."

"About what?" Theo leaned against the kitchen island and admired his wife. Vienna was the mirror image of her. "The mint chip ice cream?"

"I love your sense of humor, Theo. I always have." Her soft laugh filled the space. "Not about the ice cream. About being grown up. I don't know where the time's gone."

Theo felt the same way. He considered telling Alma about his uneasy feeling. But what was the point? Vienna was gone and in half an hour she'd be back. He'd have his mint chip ice cream and they'd be laughing and listening to something funny that happened on the trip.

"God is good, Theo." The coffee had finished brewing so Alma poured two cups and handed one to him. "What did we ever do to deserve a daughter like her?"

"I was thinking that earlier." He shook his head. "She's one in a million." The warmth of the coffee felt good against his hands. He breathed in the smell of it. "She might be onto something with her foster care idea. At least until she goes to college." He raised one eyebrow. "Since it matters to her so much."

Alma took the cream from the fridge and poured some in her cup. "It's a lot to think about." She handed the container to him. "I like my job."

"I know." He added cream to his mug, too, and put it back in the fridge. "Just something to think about."

"Which reminds me, the principal asked me to write a grant the other day. For new playground equipment." She set her coffee down. "I'll get my laptop. I want you to read it."

"I'm sure it's brilliant." He smiled as she left the room. Their marriage was as real and beautiful and fulfilling as it had been when they said their vows twenty-five years ago. Alma was a go-getter, as full of faith and life and possibility as Vienna.

When she returned they sat down at the table and he read her work. Just like he thought, it was perfect. "You should be an author." He shook his head and glanced over the grant again. "This makes *me* want to buy you the equipment. I practically cried reading it."

Alma laughed. "I'm becoming the school grant writer." Her eyes sparkled. "I'm working on another one." She clicked her computer keyboard a few times and a second document filled the screen. "This one's for the school library. We haven't had new books in twelve years."

He was halfway through reading it when he caught the time on the screen: 8:53. The number seemed to jump out at him. His heart skipped a beat and he looked at Alma. "Why isn't she back yet?"

Fear gripped her face even before he finished his question. "I should've asked for the girls' numbers. Jessie and Sarah Jane."

"They probably ran into friends at Foster's." Theo's

voice was trembling. "Or they got caught in a conversation about dance." Anything to convince himself this was normal. That she would take twice as long as she had told them and not call to say she was running late.

But the truth was something different, and they both knew it. Vienna would never be late without calling or texting.

Theo stood and walked fast to the counter. "Where's my phone? I can never find it."

By then Alma was right behind him. She found her phone on the desk in the adjacent den and called Vienna. After ten seconds, she clicked the screen. "Nothing." She stared at him. "Do you have Coach Taylor's number?"

"Maybe." He was moving faster now, trying to keep up with his racing heart. "Can you call my phone? I can't find it."

Alma was pacing, her heels clicking across the kitchen floor. "It's ringing."

The sound was coming from their bedroom. Theo ran to get it and then returned to Alma. They faced each other, Alma waiting while Theo searched his contacts. "Here it is. Coach Taylor."

But before he could tap the man's name, before the call could go through, there was the sound of a car pulling into the driveway. Theo set the phone on the counter and exhaled long and loud. "Thank You, God."

"She should have texted." Alma's irritation was masked with relief.

The two of them went to the front door, but when

Theo opened it he didn't see Vienna skipping up the driveway, waving back at her friends.

He saw a police car.

And in that moment his world stopped turning. Two officers got out of the vehicle and started up the sidewalk. Long before they uttered their apology, the words were written on their faces.

"No!" Alma doubled over, dropping to the floor. "Please, God, no!" Her screams shattered the calm of the night. "Not Vienna! Noooo."

Theo caught her and pulled her into his arms even while she was still shouting. *What happened to our baby girl? Why, God? Why our Vienna?* Theo felt the ground shift and as the officers reached the door he and Alma both fell to their knees, crying out, clinging to each other, desperate for this all to be a bad dream.

That was it. Theo held his breath. None of this was real. It was all a terrible nightmare. Vienna was fine. She was just here, dancing in the kitchen and laughing about the encore. Hugging them and kissing their cheeks.

Theo squeezed his eyes shut and held on to his wife, held her with every bit of strength he had. As if by doing so they could somehow turn back the clock. He would heed the bad feeling and tell Vienna not tonight. No one needed ice cream tonight.

And a thought occurred to him. If Vienna was gone, if something had happened to her, then Theo's life was over, too.

No matter how long his traitor heart kept beating.

• • •

ELISE COULDN'T STOP shaking as she stepped out of Cole's car that Monday morning. The news was too tragic to take in. And as she and Cole walked onto campus it was clear something was terribly wrong. Groups of students gathered near lockers and on the stairs. Many of them were crying.

Lately Cole had been picking her up, and this morning on the ride to school he had shared the saddest news with her. Two girls from their school had been killed in a car accident last night. They were on a five-minute drive to get ice cream when a drunk driver crossed all four lanes and hit them head-on.

At seventy-five miles an hour.

Elise and Cole stopped near the science building and three other kids came and stood with them. One boy put his hand on Cole's shoulder. "Last night everyone thought Jessie was killed, too. Your cousin was supposed to be with them."

Cole nodded. "We all thought that." His mom had heard from Jessie's mother, Aunt Kari, last night. "But at the last minute she didn't go with them. Too much homework."

The kid shook his head. "Saved her life."

A heaviness came over Elise. How could this happen? She knew the girls who were killed. Sarah Jane was in her English class and Vienna sat at the table next to Elise's during lunch. And of course Elise knew Jessie Taylor because of Cole. Apparently on the dance team Jessie was a special friend to Vienna. Like a mentor.

Something caught Elise's attention and she turned just as Jessie walked up. Her eyes were red and swollen, empty, like she was still in shock. She set her backpack down as Cole came to her. Jessie stepped into his arms and started crying again. "Cole . . . they're gone."

"Aww, Jessie." He held her for a long time.

There was nothing to say. The group of kids around them grew until fifteen students stood there, silently supporting Jessie Taylor and sharing the pain of what had happened.

Finally Jessie drew back and someone handed her a tissue. She wiped her face and blew her nose, but her tears didn't stop. She looked at Cole. "I keep thinking about their parents, how awful it must be."

Elise listened, trying to imagine. She could hear the missing in her own mama's voice the last time they'd talked. Jessie was right. This would be almost impossible for the girls' parents.

Like always, Cole was patient. He had no easy response, no promises or explanations. He only kept his hand on Jessie's shoulder and listened.

This wasn't the first time Jessie and Cole had suffered a loss like this. Years ago their aunt and uncle and their four girls had been coming to Bloomington for a family reunion when they were hit from behind by a semitruck. The whole family was killed except for Amy, Cole's cousin. The one who lived with him.

And now this.

Jessie used the tissue again. "I hate drunk drivers." A sad sort of rage filled her voice. "No parent should have to lose a child. Not ever."

Her last words landed directly on Elise's heart. No parent should have to lose a child. No parent. Without thinking, she put her hand on her flat stomach and as she did the baby inside her moved. Stronger than Elise had ever felt it. Truths began shouting at her soul, warring in her mind.

No parent should ever lose a child.

So then what was she doing, placing her baby for adoption? She was a parent, right? And her child was depending on her, bonding with her. The attorney had told her that Randy easily agreed to have his rights terminated. So he was out of the picture. The baby would be hers alone. How could she even think about giving this baby up? It would be a tragedy as great as the one rippling through Clear Creek High today.

Two sets of parents had lost their baby girls.

And in a few months Elise was about to lose her child. Her only child.

Jessie was struggling to talk again. She leaned into Cole and shook her head. "Every parent lives to see their daughter's dance recital and help her with finals. To be there for her at graduation. And now . . ." Her voice broke. She buried her face in Cole's shoulder.

"I'm here, Jessie." Cole ran his hand along her back. "I'm here."

Elise took in the scene and realized more than ever before that Cole wasn't only a friend helping her through a hard time. He was the most amazing, most caring guy she knew. She loved him as much as he loved her.

All at once a preview of moments flashed in her mind. Her baby's first steps and first words, the first day of kindergarten. Walks to the park and sports moments, Elise in the stands cheering at the top of her lungs. High school and dances and yes, one day graduation.

And through it all she could see one person next to her, helping her, holding her, laughing with her.

Cole Blake.

She watched him still hugging his cousin, still comforting her in the midst of this awful morning. She would talk to him later, tell him how this tragedy had changed her. She would tell him how the image of a drunk driver plowing into the girls' car had made her protective of her unborn baby. Fiercely protective.

Then she would do what she had to do, what her baby needed her to do. She would call Mr. Green and tell him she had changed her mind. She was going to keep her baby.

Because no parent should ever lose a child.

18

They had come to sit and listen, and that's what they did. Ashley took the spot next to her sister Kari on the sofa across from Theo and Alma Brown while they cried and remembered. At times, they all simply sat there in silence.

The visit had been Kari's idea. Her daughter Jessie was Vienna's big sister in dance. She would've been driving that night if her homework hadn't gotten the best of her. The pain hit close to home and Ashley had spent all morning at Kari's house.

Remembering a different car accident. One that had changed their family forever. And thanking God that this time around they were spared another heartbreak.

But that didn't make the situation any less tragic for Vienna's and Sarah Jane's families. Ashley was thankful friends had gone to sit with Sarah Jane's parents as well.

Ashley and Kari had arrived at Vienna's home at two this afternoon and simply knocked on the door. When the Browns realized who they were and that Kari was Jessie's mother, they welcomed them inside. The couple was still in shock, talking in short sentences, their expressions and voices almost trancelike.

Ashley knew exactly how they felt. There was no easy way to walk through a time like this, no formula. She and Kari had no plan or agenda. They would simply be there, ready and available.

Alma Brown held a framed photo of their daughter's freshman class picture. The girl's long dark hair hung past her shoulders, her brown eyes alive with hope and possibility for the future.

"You should've seen her light up a room." Theo, her father, put his arm around his wife. He was staring at the photograph. As if he could still talk to her, his precious daughter. "Vienna was the happiest girl. She never stopped laughing."

"Even last night." Alma nodded and leaned against Theo. "Isn't that right?"

He looked off. "Just laughing and laughing."

Ashley was sitting so close to Kari she could feel her sister breathing, feel the way the sorrow of this moment brought to the surface their own past heartache. One from not that long ago.

Everyone in Bloomington knew about the accident that took the lives of Erin and Sam and their family. Theo and Alma had lived here all their lives. So it was no surprise when Theo looked straight at Kari and then at Ashley. "How?"

Tears stung at Ashley's eyes. The man didn't have to explain himself. "One day at a time."

Kari nodded. "At first you think time will stop." Her voice was soft, marked by her intimate understanding of tragedy. "You can't believe the sun can set and rise again the next morning. Or that people are going about their days like nothing happened."

"Completely unaware that your whole world just stopped turning." Ashley took hold of her sister's hand. She felt sick at the thought of that time right after her sister's car accident, what it had felt like sitting at the hospital while the news went from bad to worse.

"I . . . can't imagine another hour of this." Alma took a tissue and pressed it to her eyes. "Let alone a lifetime."

Ashley wasn't sure of the family's faith, or what they believed about life after death. But if God would give her the opportunity, she wanted to talk about it. Heaven was the only hope at a time like this.

The opening came ten minutes later. Theo leaned back, his hand on Alma's shoulder. "Our family, we love Jesus. Always have."

New tears spilled from Alma's eyes. "I just can't understand why He'd take our Vienna now. When . . ." She couldn't finish her sentence.

"When she had so much life ahead." Theo pinched the bridge of his nose and shook his head. "I miss her so much. Dear God, I miss her."

Alma moved her hand around in the space in front of her. "She was just here. She was dancing and talking about an encore and how it was going to surprise everyone."

Ashley waited, choosing the right moment. After another bit of silence, she sat up a little straighter. "My nieces loved to dance. All of them."

Theo lifted his eyes to hers. "I keep thinking about something. Since we got the news." He sniffed and shook his head, like he was trying to find control but couldn't. His face scrunched up, like the sobs were pushing in from his heart. "Do you think . . . my little girl can dance in heaven?"

Here was her moment. Ashley stood and took the spot on the other side of Theo. Kari did the same, sitting next to Alma. For a while they sat like that, Ashley and Kari surrounding the devastated parents with a physical reminder of God's presence. The way His people were supposed to do.

"Yes, Theo." Ashley shifted so she could see the man's eyes. "There's dancing in heaven. Vienna is dancing right now. I believe that."

The man covered his face with his hand and pulled his wife closer. "She is. I can see her."

And in a rush Ashley could feel the imitation leather seat beneath her, smell the mix of medicine and bleach in the hospital waiting room that summer day when Erin was killed. "You asked us how."

Kari handed Theo and Alma each another tissue. Alma was still holding the framed photo of Vienna. It took a few seconds, but eventually the Browns turned to Ashley, waiting. As if they were desperate for anything that might keep them going.

"The answer is Jesus." Ashley took a slow breath. "Because of Jesus, this isn't the end. It's farewell for now. But it's never goodbye."

On the other side of Alma, Kari nodded. "My dad always says Erin and her family are still alive. They just live in heaven now."

The statement seemed to spark something in Theo. "I gave my life to Jesus a long time ago." He smiled at Alma through his tears. "We both did, isn't that right, baby?"

"Yes." Alma dabbed the tissue at her eyes and nose. "Do you remember what the pastor said that day?"

"Of course." Theo seemed a little stronger. Talk of eternity was clearly helping. "He said the odds were simple. Every one of us is going to die. Every single person. But the people who choose faith in Jesus would live forever in heaven."

Ashley couldn't see through the tears blurring her eyes. "You'll see her again."

"Yes." Theo was still crying, still broken. "I just wish . . . it wasn't so long. I . . ." He covered his face with his hand again. "I wanted to see that dance recital so bad."

Kari put her arm around Alma and waited. Finally she looked at the Browns. "I believe she'll have a window. And she'll be dancing right along with her team that day."

A minute later the pastor from Mt. Zion Church arrived. The man explained to Ashley and Kari that he'd known Vienna since she was born. Ashley and Kari chatted with him and then used the moment to say goodbye.

Out front near their cars, Ashley hugged her sister. The tears they'd held back when they were inside came now. "A hundred years goes by in a blink." Ashley took a tissue from her purse and held it to her cheek. "But days like this, earth feels like eternity."

Kari was shaking, her shoulders trembling despite the warm April afternoon. "What if Jessie hadn't had homework? What if . . ."

"Shhh. Kari, don't." Ashley stepped back a bit and searched her sister's eyes. "We can't. The Lord gives and the Lord takes away. It wasn't Jessie's time."

"I know." Kari looked straight at her, all the way to her heart. "I just wish it hadn't been Vienna's time. Or Sarah Jane's." She closed her eyes for a long moment and then looked at Ashley again. "Sometimes it's so hard."

"Yes. It is." Ashley could still picture their youngest sister, the light in her eyes and the way she loved her family.

"You were right what you said." Kari stepped back and seemed to compose herself a little. "Only Jesus. Him on the cross. Him here with us now. So that death doesn't have the final word."

"Not for those who believe." Ashley hugged her once more.

They stood outside their cars and made plans for later that night. Everyone was getting together for dinner at Ashley and Landon's. They were all feeling a connection to the accident. Dinner had been Landon's idea.

Because every minute of life was precious.

· · ·

BASEBALL PRACTICE WAS called off because of the accident, so Cole had spent those two hours sitting with
Elise in the bleachers, the sun on their faces. He wasn't
surprised at how the tragedy had affected her.

She wanted to keep her baby and she wanted Cole to
stay with her through the process. It was something he
had offered from the beginning and he would keep his
promise. Just like his dad would if he were in this situation.

The problem was he had no idea how he would tell
his parents.

In the week since Elise made the decision to have a
young couple adopt her child, Cole's plans had really
started taking shape. The baseball coach at Liberty had
contacted him about a walk-on tryout the third week of
August, right before school started. Cole wasn't sure he
was talented enough to make the team.

But since the man wanted him to try, Cole had given
his word. It would be a dream to play for Liberty. He
had his classes picked out, his dorm in the Commons
Two building reserved, and a plan that would take him
through the next eight years.

Until today.

Now it was five o'clock and his family would arrive
for dinner in the next half hour. His papa and Grandma
Elaine, Aunt Brooke and Uncle Peter and their daughter
Hayley, Aunt Kari and Uncle Ryan and their kids.

Including Jessie, who was still not okay.

Cole figured the love from everyone tonight would

be good for her and sure enough, it was. They talked in quiet voices over dinner, sharing their thoughts about the two girls who had been killed. And remembering back when the disaster had been their own.

Amy, the only one of his aunt Erin's kids who had survived, was more like a sister to Cole now. She finished her lasagna and looked at the others. "Maybe someday I can go visit Vienna's parents."

Cole's mom smiled at Amy from across the table. "I think that would be very nice, sweetie."

"Yes." Amy nodded. The light in her eyes remained, even when everyone else seemed sad. "There's a trick to getting through this."

"A trick?" Their papa sat at the other end. He angled his head, all his attention on Amy.

"Yes." She looked at him and then around the room. "I never think of them as dead." Her eyes grew softer. "They're alive. They just have a new address in heaven."

Their papa nodded, slow and sure. He squinted, like Amy's words had really made him think. "I like that. Just a new address."

When the dinner was over, when everyone had hugged each other and promised to do an even better job of calling and texting and getting together, and when his siblings were upstairs getting ready for bed, Cole found his mom and dad in the kitchen.

"Mom . . . Dad?" He hesitated. How was he going to do this? He grabbed a quick breath. "Can . . . I talk to you for a minute?"

"Sure, honey." His mother didn't look too surprised. Today had been a lot. For all of them. She dried her hands on a towel and his dad did the same. They followed him to the living room and his parents took the sofa. Cole sat across from them in the recliner.

"What's on your mind?" His dad turned so his back was against the sofa arm. "I bet today was hard."

"It was." Cole's heart picked up speed, the sound of it louder than jet engines. Cole swallowed. "So . . . I talked to Elise for a few hours after school today."

His mom was the first to show a flicker of concern. "How is she? Everything okay with the baby?"

"It is. Yes." Cole linked his hands together and stared at them. He tried to imagine a wedding ring on his left hand before the end of the year and he could feel his palms getting damp. "Anyway. We talked about the accident, what happened to the two girls."

They nodded, waiting.

"The thing is, everyone was talking about the girls' mom and dad, and how no parent should have to say goodbye to their child so soon. So early." He looked from his mom to his dad. "And . . . yeah, Elise's mind started spinning."

"About?" His mom looked a bit paler than before.

"Well . . . keeping the baby. Like she thought about what they said. How no parent should have to say goodbye to their child, and sometime today that became her. And she made a new decision."

His mom and dad seemed to both hold their breath.

"Elise . . . she talked to her mom back in Louisiana and, well, after graduation her mom wants her to come back home and have the baby. Raise the baby." The conversation felt like something from a dream. Like he could see himself talking, but nothing about it seemed real. He pushed on. "Her mom said I could have the guest room. That way I could help her with the baby and be there. Be a father for her child. But also be praying about whether Elise and I should get married this Christmas."

There. He'd said it.

His dad slid to the edge of the sofa so he could look right into Cole's eyes. At least it seemed that's why he did it. "Are you saying that's what Elise wants to do?"

Nothing about this felt logical. He was just a kid. Who was he fooling that this would be a good time to forget college and live in the guest room of a person he'd never met? Cole narrowed his eyes and tried to find the right words. "I'm saying . . . that's what we both decided. That she can't give up her baby, and I said I'd be there for her."

"Cole." His mother's voice rose and she put her hand to her mouth. Like she was trying to quiet herself. But her tone was still louder than before. "If Elise is going home to have her baby, then she'll be with her mother. She'll have plenty of help." She shook her head, like she couldn't make sense of the situation. "How does that involve you?"

"Because." Cole felt his own frustration rising. "Her baby has no father, so I'll step in. That's what I said I'd do." He looked at his dad, then his mom. "Children need both parents."

The silence was as awkward as anything Cole could remember. His dad cleared his throat. "Son . . . I deeply respect your heart on this issue. And I know you care about Elise."

"I love her." Cole thought maybe his answer came a little too quickly. Being defensive would only make him sound like a kid.

His mom shaded her eyes with her hand. She looked like she wasn't sure whether to break down and cry or send him to his room. Cole turned to his dad and steeled himself for what was coming.

"Yes." His dad's voice was nothing but calm. "Okay, you love her. But, Son, that doesn't make you a parent. It doesn't mean you're ready for marriage." This wasn't a lecture. The way his father spoke, Cole couldn't help but listen with his head and his heart.

"Yes, sir."

Next to him, his mother lowered her hand. She still didn't say anything.

A long sigh came from his dad. "You and Elise have only known each other a few months. You've never even met her mother." He leaned forward, elbows on his knees. "My advice? Stay in touch, visit her. Let her mom step into the helping role." His father paused, not a stitch of judgment in his tone. "Take time to see if this is where God is leading or if it's just you and Elise trying to make sense of a rough situation."

Cole agreed with every detail, but there was something his dad didn't seem to understand. "You're right, Dad. Everything you said." Cole worked the muscles in his jaw, frustrated. "But maybe all the logic in the world doesn't stand up against doing the right thing. I offered to be there for her, and now that's what she wants. She needs me." He looked from his dad to his mother and back again. "You know?"

Again it was his dad who took the lead. "The right thing comes from God, not from us. No matter how it seems." He breathed deep, stood and helped Cole to his feet. His dad hugged him and then looked into his eyes. "That's all I have, Cole. Can we pray for you?"

Cole turned to his mom. "You want to pray?"

"Yes." It was the first word she'd said in a while. She joined them and they formed a tight circle, arms around each other.

His dad led the prayer, asking for God's wisdom and for Elise to know the right decision for the baby. Cole hugged each of his parents and then he went to his room. He had no choice but to take Elise's side. After all, he had offered to skip school to be there for her and the baby. Today on the bleachers she'd made it clear. She was taking him up on his offer. And he would keep his promise.

Like he'd told his dad, staying with Elise was the right thing to do. He would be a man of honor, like his father. But the truth was building and growing inside him. What was he about to commit to? He must be crazy to think he should miss out on school and becoming a doctor. And the more he thought about it, the more he agreed completely with his dad. He understood his mom's discouragement. The way she looked terrified about his future.

Because deep inside, Cole felt exactly the same way.

19

Lucy and Aaron were sitting in the attorney's office again. It was clear from the expression on the man's face the news wasn't good.

Alan Green sighed as he took the seat across from them. "I told you teenage mothers are known to change their minds." He opened a file in front of him. "I got a call from Elise yesterday. She says she's sorry, but she wants to keep her baby."

This moment had played out in Lucy's nightmares since they'd heard about the child. Each time she wondered how she would react, whether she would start crying or run to the bathroom or just sit there. Numb to the entire process.

What she hadn't expected was the freezing cold feeling working its way through her veins. Her arms and legs began to shiver and even with the sun streaming in from outside the lawyer's office window, Lucy couldn't seem to get warm.

Aaron must've noticed because he put his arm around her. "Okay . . . so she changed her mind." His voice still held a fraction of hope. "What if she changes it again?"

"She could." The attorney folded his hands and looked at them. "That's why I called you in today." He paused. "I have an idea."

Lucy tried to focus while he explained his thoughts. First, he wanted them to sign a document acknowledging that they'd been informed about Elise changing her mind. "But we're still the adoptive parents, if she decides to go through with it?" Aaron slid the signed paperwork back across the desk.

"Yes." Mr. Green pulled another paper from the file. "Sign this and it will be noted that if she chooses to place her child after all, you still want to be the baby's parents."

It all felt like the worst possible scenario. Lucy's head hurt. Why were they doing this? Taking time off work only to get their hearts broken? She looked at Aaron, and she knew what he was thinking. They'd already talked about this possibility. Even if Elise changed her mind, they wanted to be the adoptive parents on record until the last possible moment.

Even though it meant no other birth mother could choose their profile in the meantime.

Lucy hated the pain in Aaron's expression. All this time he'd been the strong one, the guy praying in the nursery and counting on God to bring them a baby. But now he looked sick, like this final loss was too much for him. Lucy turned to the lawyer. She stopped shivering. *God, let me be strong for my husband. This one time. Please.*

She took a deep breath. "Mr. Green, my husband and

I have discussed this. We are certain about this baby." She forced a smile. "We still believe the child is supposed to be ours." There. She'd done something positive. Which was only right after all the times Aaron had been strong for her.

The attorney's countenance lifted some. "I like that attitude." He sat a little higher in his chair. "It's very possible." He hesitated, as if he hadn't planned on telling them what was coming. "She changed her mind because of the car accident the other day. The one where the two high school girls were killed. She thought maybe she was supposed to keep her baby because of that."

"Hmmm." Aaron looked upset. Again, his eyes told her he was struggling here, grasping to find the faith he'd come through the door with.

So the accident changed her mind? The reasoning made no sense to Lucy. But it didn't have to. Ultimately this was Elise's choice, no matter what prompted her decision. The wreck was tragic. Both girls had died on the scene.

Mr. Green was talking about the other part of his idea, how they needed a way to protect everyone if Elise did, in fact, choose adoption again.

Lucy liked this. A positive plan. Something the attorney wouldn't have done if he didn't believe there was at least a hope the adoption could still go through.

The attorney explained the situation. The process was simple. If Elise chose to place her baby with Aaron and Lucy, then she would still have the two-week window in which she could change her mind. "What we do in cases like this is pay the state for the baby to be placed in foster care. Just for the fourteen days."

On the roller coaster that was infertility this was another drop. "So . . . even if Elise wants us to adopt her child"—Lucy heard the frustration in her voice—"we can't bring the baby home until after two weeks?"

"It's the best option for everyone." Empathy colored the lawyer's face. "I know it's not ideal. But it gives legal protection to us all. It's typical protocol when a birth mom changes her mind at some point in the process."

Aaron looked pensive. "You're saying you don't want our hearts broken." He sat a little straighter. "What if we're willing to take the risk?"

"It isn't just for you." The attorney clearly wasn't budging. "You have several parties at risk. You two, certainly. But also Elise and the baby. If her little one is placed with you from birth, she'll feel pressured to go with the adoption. Or she could say she was forced into her decision." He raised his brow. "When a birth mother feels backed into a corner, a judge could reverse the adoption. Even a year or two later." He nodded. "It's happened before."

Another blow. Lucy folded her arms tight against her stomach. "So we don't want her to have a reason to feel coerced. Is that it?"

"Exactly." Mr. Green frowned. "Another party at risk is me. I have to do everything in my power to give the birth mother room to make the best decision for her and the baby. Those two weeks absolutely belong to the birth mother. Foster parents give the baby a neutral location, so whatever choice Elise makes will be binding."

"Couldn't she still try to get the baby back?" Aaron's face looked pale.

Lucy stared at her hands. Neither of them had any idea about these possibilities. Private adoption was new to them. Even still, it wasn't so different from the foster-adopt program in Atlanta, the one that had placed baby Rio with them and then taken him away again. Either way the pain was real.

Mr. Green seemed to think about Aaron's question. "She could try to get the baby back, but she wouldn't win. No lawyer would take her case." He sighed. "As long as we place the baby in foster care during the waiting period."

It was a lot to consider. Mr. Green gave them a few minutes to talk about their wishes, whether they would be okay with the two-week foster care, or whether they'd rather back out and make their profile open to another birth mother.

In the end the decision was an easy one. Aaron still believed God had led them here, still thought this baby was supposed to be theirs. Still trusted that Elise would change her mind again and want the two of them to raise her child. If that happened, then they couldn't let two weeks of foster care scare them.

They signed the final papers acknowledging they approved this newest plan. The meeting had taken their lunch hour plus some, and now they had to get back to the hospital.

In the attorney's parking lot Aaron took Lucy in his arms. "Thank you."

"For what?" She gave him a tired smile.

"I was losing it." He searched her eyes. "And you were there for me." He kissed her forehead. "You'll never know how much that meant to me."

His compliment felt wonderful. She was glad he'd noticed. "All this time, you've never wavered." She stepped back and took his hands in hers. "You believed God would do this, and you still believe. It's time I have that sort of attitude. Especially now."

"Yes." He looked serious, troubled again. "But what if God's will is for Elise to keep this baby?"

"Then He has a different child for us." Her strength had to be coming from heaven. It certainly wasn't her own. "I really believe that, Aaron."

"Amazing." He hugged her again. "I love you."

"Love you, too." They held each other for another minute before climbing in the car and heading to the hospital. There they took the elevator to their separate floors. Lucy signed in to the maternity ward and checked the charts. She was needed in the NICU again. The heroin-addicted baby had somehow survived, but she was sicker. Pneumonia. Probably from the weeks of morphine. The painkiller meant the infant wasn't moving much, and the stillness had most likely caused fluid to build up in the baby's lungs.

Poor thing.

But there was good news, too. Baby Nathan, the preemie born at twenty weeks—just like their little Sophie—was going home today. He had finally reached five pounds! He would need oxygen at night and a monitor to make sure he didn't stop breathing. But they all agreed Nathan was going to be fine.

Later that afternoon the baby's parents came with his grandma and grandpa, aunts and uncles. The whole family was crying as they loaded Nathan into his car seat and thanked the nursing staff.

Lucy watched them go, smiling through eyes blurred with tears. God had given Nathan's family a miracle.

Now she could only pray along with Aaron that God would give them one, too.

• • •

THEO COULDN'T REMEMBER the last time they'd had music in their house.

When Vienna was alive, there was always a song playing in the background. Theo had talked to Alma about it the other day. Neither of them had noticed how often their daughter had a playlist on. Dance beats coming from her bedroom or Christian songs from the computer in the den. Sometimes it was just a pop list on her phone.

But their daughter loved music. Most of the time it wasn't just the song playing, it was Vienna singing along. And Theo and Alma had figured the melodies would last forever. Not for a minute did they think there would be a time when their home would be silent.

The way it was now.

Vienna had only been gone a week but everything about their lives was utterly different. Alma had taken a leave of absence through the end of the school year and Theo had asked for time from his company.

They gave him just three weeks. As if a man could recover from losing his daughter in less than a month.

Theo and Alma had somehow survived two memorials. One at the church and one at Clear Creek High. Alma had found a dozen photos of Vienna—some from dance, some from cheer. One of her just sitting at the dinner table smiling. Her eyes bright and innocent and brimming with a limitless future.

In the days after the accident, Alma had worked on those photos like her life depended on it. She had several of the pictures turned into ten-by-fourteen prints, framed in white vintage wood. At each of the memorials, she set them up on a long table covered with lace. Sarah Jane's mother did the same thing for her.

Theo remembered watching his wife work, seeing her comb through photos on the computer and on Vienna's phone, which had been recovered from the accident scene. He caught himself thinking that his wife wasn't supposed to be doing this until Vienna was a senior. The pictures were supposed to be part of a video they'd play at her high school graduation.

Not her funeral.

A thousand people must've hugged them and prayed for them and cried with them in the days after Vienna died. They spilled out the back door of the church and into the hallways at the school. Most of them signed the guest books set out on each of the girls' tables.

Theo wished he could remember everything they said about his little girl, the compliments and anecdotes and declarations of her sweet spirit and bright light at Clear Creek High. But looking back at the memorial, all he could remember was positioning himself near the table of photographs and convincing himself just for a moment that she was still there.

His Vienna.

Especially when he saw the photograph, the one of her at the dinner table. For some reason in that picture Vienna seemed to be looking straight at him. *I love you, Daddy.* He could still hear her singsong voice. Still see her eyes just like that when she sat beside him on the way to school each morning.

The way Theo would always remember her.

And now . . . now she was gone. The memorials were behind them. Students had moved on with their lives and in an hour Theo and Alma would attend the dance recital. The one Vienna had been so excited about.

But then what?

He and Alma got ready for the performance quietly. In separate spaces, separate worlds. That was becoming more the norm now. They would wake up, say a few words and set about their days. All in silence. There wasn't anything to talk about, really. No reason to make dinner, no weekend to plan. No future to be excited for.

All of it had died when the drunk driver crossed the line.

On the drive to the school, Theo couldn't take the silence another minute. He turned on the radio. Love Songs & Oldies. The station was one of Vienna's favorites. They were a mile from the campus when Rod Stewart came on. "Have I Told You Lately?"

"Turn it off." Alma looked at him from the passenger seat. "Please, Theo. It's too much."

"No." Theo shook his head. He didn't want to argue with his wife, but moments like this didn't just happen. He turned up the volume, just enough to fill the car. "This is *her* song. On the way to *her* recital." He clenched his teeth. "That doesn't just happen."

Theo thought he'd cried all he could cry. At some point the healing had to begin. He couldn't get teary-eyed every hour—the way he'd been since the police officers walked up the driveway. But this time he couldn't stop himself.

The memory came back to him like it was yesterday. A month before she was killed, Vienna was in this very car with them and this song came on. Somehow, Vienna knew every word. He could hear her voice, feel her presence with them.

"Have I told you lately that I love you? . . . Have I told you there's no one else above you?"

She sang every line till the very end of the song. And when it ended she leaned up from the backseat, her hands on their shoulders. "That's exactly how I feel about both of you." She grinned at Theo and then at her mother. "Whenever you hear it, remember that!"

Alma dropped the fight. She looked out her passenger window, and when the song ended she reached over and turned off the radio. "Please, Theo. I need to think." She looked at him and her expression eased up. "I don't know how to do this."

"Me, either." He wanted to take her hand but this didn't seem like the time. None of this was her fault. But he knew something for sure. If they chose to grieve separately, in their own silent worlds, then in time it would hurt them. Their marriage.

One of the pastors who had talked to them after the accident told them to see a marriage counselor. Or a grief counselor. "Most marriages don't make it a year after a loss like this."

Most marriages. Theo had heard that before and he had scoffed at the possibility. No one would want to lose a child, but such a tragedy would surely make a couple closer. Not more distant.

Now, though, the tragedy was his and Alma's, and he understood. The silence was strangling the life from the two of them. Even when it was the last thing they wanted. As if the loss was too great to get around or over. Too deep and dark to walk through.

Like overnight they'd become blind to each other. All they could see was themselves, their own heartache and loss. Their separate memories of Vienna.

No wonder so many marriages didn't survive this.

Help us, God. Vienna wouldn't want us this way. We need You.

There was no immediate answer to his silent prayer. But halfway through the recital, Alma reached out and took his hand. Nothing about the action would've seemed unusual to anyone watching. But Theo knew differently. They hadn't held hands since they came home from the second memorial.

He took a sharp breath. Then he wrapped his hand around Alma's and held on tight. As if his next heartbeat depended on this one single connection. The whole time he kept his eyes on the stage. A girl in the front row was tall and thin, beautiful brown skin like Vienna. Theo watched her dance, watched her perform all the numbers Vienna had known by heart. Especially the last number. The encore.

The one Vienna had helped choreograph and had been so excited about minutes before . . .

Theo couldn't finish his thought. If he squinted just so, he wasn't watching someone else's daughter. He was watching his own. His precious baby girl. His Vienna.

Alma didn't let go of his hand after the recital, even when so many girls and their parents came up and hugged them. Jessie Taylor presented them with another framed picture, one of herself and Vienna taken at the last practice before the accident.

They were halfway home—not talking, but still holding hands—when Alma's phone rang. She answered it on the first ring. "Hello?"

No telling who was on the other end. Theo listened and kept his eyes on the road.

"Yes, this is she." She gasped under her breath. "Who . . . who gave you our information?" She looked at Theo. "The state? Okay, wait, so what's the situation?"

For a long time Alma listened. Then she took a deep breath and seemed to hold it. "Mr. Green." She exhaled. "I truly appreciate the call. Can I . . ." She paused, clearly bewildered. "Can I call you back tomorrow?"

A few more seconds and the conversation ended. Alma set her phone down and turned to him. "Theo. That was a private adoption attorney." She blinked, like the conversation was still hitting her. "Mr. Green. He said he usually didn't make these calls on a Sunday night, but he needed help."

"With what?" Theo had no idea where she was going with this. "What did he want?"

"The state gave him our names. Said we might do a short-term foster care of an infant. For two weeks." She leaned back in her seat for a few seconds and turned to him once more. "While the birth mother decides whether to go through with an adoption."

Foster care of a newborn? For two weeks? Tears blurred his eyes. He blinked a few times so he could still see the road. "Why would they call now? Of all things?"

"There's a girl. She keeps changing her mind about placing her child." Alma went on to explain the situation. "It's possible they won't even need us. He just wanted to know if we were open."

Theo wiped his hand across one cheek and then the other. Sure, their file was still active, their license to do foster care still valid. But a few years ago they had asked the state to stop calling until further notice. "How in the world?"

"Someone must've made a mistake." Alma searched his eyes. "The state never should've given him our name."

Theo was quiet, letting the reality wash over him. "It was all Vienna talked about before . . ."

Alma's voice filled with purpose for the first time since the accident. "We should tell him yes, right?"

"Absolutely." Theo heard the catch in his voice. "Only God could've done this, Alma. Only God."

"Definitely." Alma was crying now, too. They might've struggled to find each other this past week, and the road ahead was nothing but steep hills and sharp dropoffs. But right now they didn't need words to know what the other was thinking.

They were not alone. God was with them and He could see them. He cared. Because only He could've brought about this phone call from the adoption lawyer. A way of letting them know that Vienna was still living, safe with Him. Because this wasn't just a matter-of-fact call with a simple request.

It was their daughter's dream come true.

20

Some days Cole felt like he was carrying boulders in his backpack.

Elise had gone thirteen days without changing her mind. Thirteen days when all they talked about was the baby and whether they should stay in Bloomington for the summer or get settled in Louisiana and have the child there.

They talked about where Cole would work and how quickly he could start taking online classes. Elise had done the research. Liberty University had a crazy amount of online degrees. Hundreds of options.

All this made Elise happier every day. Her life was falling into place.

Not so much for Cole. His was falling apart. At least that's how he felt.

There were times when he would be sitting in his science class and just the sight of Elise made him work to catch his breath. Not the way she had affected him back in the beginning, when he couldn't take his eyes off her. But because the pressure piling up on him was too great to inhale under.

Like he was suffocating.

Here was the worst of it: He could only blame him-self.

Yes, he was in love with her. He still could barely think when her eyes caught his, or when he heard her laugh. And he was beyond blown away by her talent as an artist. He had found one of his mom's old easels and a box of paints she didn't use anymore. For the last few weeks Elise had come to his house a handful of times, and always she worked on a painting: Cole at bat in his Clear Creek uniform.

Yes, he loved everything about her.

But that didn't mean he was ready to change his life plan. Didn't mean he had it in him to move to Louisiana and start working full-time to provide for her. And it certainly didn't mean he was ready to be a father. He wasn't even nineteen.

Like always, his dad was right. But what was he supposed to do about his promise to Elise? Now she was counting on him. At different times, when the weight of it all built up and pressed in around his shoulders, he thought about finding a way to tell Elise. But then he'd look into her eyes and know that all he wanted was her.

Whatever the cost.

It was Easter Sunday and finally Elise was doing something she'd promised him weeks ago. He picked her up a few doors down from her aunt and uncle's. They still didn't know about him or the baby. Elise planned to tell them tomorrow. During his away baseball game.

"My mom says I have to explain everything to them. As soon as possible." She had shared this with him at lunch Friday. "I haven't been very social around them. They probably think I hate being at their house."

Cole hadn't paid a lot of attention to the details. Elise had talked about exactly how she should tell them, which words to use and what she should say. How they might react.

The whole time Cole kept shifting beneath the boulders in his backpack.

Didn't she see that he had more to deal with than whatever uncomfortable moments might come out of being honest with her aunt and uncle? Cole had so much to think about he was afraid his head might explode. Where was he going to work? And what if he'd mentioned marriage a little too soon? What if they ended up not getting married? Was he still supposed to work to support Elise and the baby? And for how long?

One boulder after another.

It was half an hour till the church service. Cole's parents and siblings were saving seats for Elise and him. Her coming to church was a step in the right direction, because until now Cole couldn't even answer the most obvious question: Did the girl he loved really care about following Jesus? As far back as he could remember that had been at the top of the list. His mom used to say, "Most important thing in life is figuring out what to do about Jesus." She would smile. "But second is finding a girl who believes in Him like you do."

Cole helped Elise into the car. She was five months pregnant and still not showing at all. She wore a flowery skirt and a fitted blouse. The perfect Easter outfit. "You look pretty." He still hadn't kissed her. Didn't want to until they had more of this figured out.

"Thanks." She settled into the seat beside him. "You didn't ask how my doctor appointment went."

That's right. Cole gripped the steering wheel. "Sorry." He'd had a home game. No question his hitting was off. The burden of life made it hard to see the ball the way he used to. That's what Cole had learned this season. He wasn't half the hitter he'd been last year.

And even still the Liberty coach wanted him to try out.

He tried to be interested in what Elise was saying. He still listened while she read the pregnancy app on her phone. How the baby had gone from the size of a pea to a grape to a cantaloupe. And how the infant's brain was developing, and the lungs and skin. The fact that the baby could hear now.

The details really were fascinating. But right now Cole only wanted to hit a home run, break out of his slump and turn a triple play at second base. He pulled into the church parking lot and found a spot. She was still waiting for him to ask about the doctor visit, her pretty hair spilling in waves over her slim shoulders. He remembered to smile. "How was your appointment?"

Her eyes sparkled. "I found out."

No telling what she was talking about. Sometimes Cole felt like they were moving in opposite directions.

She was obsessed with the baby growing inside her, and he . . . well, he wasn't. No matter how much he wanted to be. He turned toward her. They had to hurry. Church would start in fifteen minutes. "Found out what?"

Disappointment flashed in her expression. "Cole. You know!" She studied him for a few seconds. She must've seen that he clearly didn't know, because she let her head fall against her seat and she let out a loud breath. "Cole." Her eyes found his again. "I found out the sex of the baby."

That! Cole shifted in his seat. Of course! He took hold of her hand. "I thought you were going to wait."

"I was." She seemed to forgive him. Her tone was more relaxed again. "But they did an ultrasound. I guess that's normal at this point. Looking for stuff that might be wrong."

"Was everything okay?" There. That was better. More interested.

"It was." The corners of her lips lifted a little and her eyes danced. "The guy doing the ultrasound suddenly goes, 'Are you feeling her move a lot?'" She allowed a single laugh. "And I was like, 'Her?'" Elise lifted her free hand, as if she couldn't contain her excitement. "And just like that I had my answer."

"It's a girl?" Cole tried to sound as happy as Elise.

"Yes!" she squealed. "Cole, we're having a girl!"

We're having a girl? The suffocating feeling was back. What was he doing? He wanted to correct her that *they* weren't having a baby. They weren't married. He had no idea if they'd ever be married. Rather, *she* was having the baby.

But it didn't seem like the right time.

One thing was certain. As they walked toward the church building, their hands laced together, the idea of Elise's baby felt way more real. Since she still wasn't showing, it was easy sometimes to think of Elise as his girlfriend. The most captivating girl he'd ever met.

Here though, thinking about Elise having a little girl, the truth was much more tangible. With everything in him, Cole wanted to be like his dad. There for Elise, loving her through all that was ahead. But right now, even as they entered Clear Creek Community Church, Cole felt just one thing.

Overwhelmed.

They found their seats and Elise made her rounds from Cole's mom and dad to his brother and sister and cousin. They all liked her. Though only his parents knew about their plans to move to Louisiana.

The church band sang four worship songs, and when they were finished, Cole looked at Elise. She had tears in her eyes. Spilling onto her cheeks. His heart broke for her. All she'd been through on top of missing this deep connection with God . . . of course she was feeling it today. On Easter Sunday.

The sermon seemed written just for Cole. Or maybe for Elise, too.

"Sometimes life comes down to trusting God." The pastor looked around the congregation. "That's the story of Easter." He went on to talk about the fact that Jesus had told His friends He would rise from the dead. But still on Sunday morning they were shocked. Totally disbelieving that the tomb might actually be empty.

Cole let his mind drift. Was God trying to tell him to trust the situation with Elise? That somehow if he moved to Louisiana and spent the next few years—or even all his life—helping and loving Elise and her baby, then God would take care of things? Was that how he was supposed to trust?

He made eye contact with his dad and they both smiled. Maybe it was an entirely different spin. Maybe God wanted him to trust his parents on this and stick with his first plan. Going to Liberty. Trust that God would take care of Elise and that if it was meant to be, they would find a way to be together, later. When they were older. When Cole had his medical training.

As great as the message was, Cole was more confused than ever as the sermon wound down. If he were honest with himself, he didn't want to move to Louisiana. Didn't want to get a job and support Elise. He wanted to go to Liberty. His whole future was ahead of him.

What had he been thinking to make such a crazy promise to Elise? And now that she was counting on him, what was he supposed to do? The walls of the church seemed to be closing in, and once more he had to work to get a full breath. He lifted his eyes to the cross at the front of the church. *Jesus, I have no idea what to do. I feel like I'm drowning. Help me, please.*

That's when he noticed Elise still dabbing at her eyes, still crying. Why was she so upset? Was it just that good to be back in church, or something more? Had she heard from God?

Later, at his house after an early dinner, they walked to the stream that ran through his backyard. Like the first time he'd brought her here, he took her to the rock that anchored the edge of the water. Once they were seated she turned to him.

"I didn't want to talk about this before dinner." The sadness in her face was gone. Her eyes held a peace that hadn't been there before. "Cole, I think God was talking to me today. At church."

"Really?" He pulled one knee up and watched her, the way the breeze played with her hair. "What did He say?"

"The whole trust thing." She looked straight ahead. "I think He was saying I'm supposed to place my little girl up for adoption. With Aaron and Lucy—the couple I picked out."

Cole's heart started to pound. He couldn't sound too happy. What would that say about his desire to help her? That it was all an act? He exhaled and forced himself to be calm. Like when he came up to bat in the ninth inning, bases loaded. "So . . . what are you going to do?"

"I'm not sure."

"Okay." *Breathe,* he ordered himself. *You have to breathe.* He grabbed a quick bit of air through his nose. "I mean . . . do you really think that's what He was saying?"

"Maybe." She turned to him again. "I think it's me who's holding on. And now that I know she's a girl, she's so much more a part of me." Tears welled in her eyes again. "She's my baby."

Clouds gathered overhead and in the distance thunder rolled low and long. They had maybe ten minutes before the rain hit. Cole waited, listening.

"It's hard to explain, but I think I heard a voice. Not a real voice, but . . . I don't know." She hesitated. "It's like I could feel God telling me to trust Him. My baby girl would have the most amazing life with Aaron and Lucy."

Cole nodded. "What about you?" He wasn't sure he wanted to ask. "What do you want?"

She leaned closer and put her hand on his face. Then she stared into his eyes. "I want to be with you." Doubt flickered in her expression. "I'm not sure about raising a baby. That's the truth."

A flash of lightning lit up the sky not far from where they were sitting. "We need to go."

"I know." They stood but the rain came before they could make their first move toward the house. Like most Indiana springtime storms, the rain came in buckets. The rain simply released all at once right over them.

"Come on!" Cole shouted over the sound of the sudden downpour. "Run!"

They held hands and sprinted across the property. Thunder shook the ground and they moved even faster. By the time they reached the shelter of the porch they were drenched.

"Cole." She was out of breath, making a sound that was more laugh than cry. "Hold me."

And he did. He opened his arms and she fit right between them, up against his chest. "Elise." He brushed the rain from his face, still breathing hard. He whispered into her wet hair. "Sometimes . . . I'm so scared."

"Me, too." She held him tighter. Like she was only a child herself. "Why does life have to be so hard?"

Cole had no answers. Not for himself and certainly not for her. All he knew was that the idea of her placing the baby for adoption hadn't only eased the boulders. It had allowed him to breathe again.

And that had to mean something.

• • •

LONG AFTER ELISE was in bed that night, when sleep wouldn't come and the storm raged outside, Cole's words played over and over in her heart. *Sometimes . . . I'm so scared.*

So scared.

She had known for too long that Cole wasn't being completely honest with her. Yes, he loved her. She could tell by the way he looked at her. But he didn't really want to be with her. Not yet, when they were so young. That's what his eyes told her even if he didn't say the words.

What did either of them know about raising a baby? And how could they plan to be married when they'd hardly even dated? All because he wanted to be like his dad.

Elise rolled onto her side. As she did the baby moved. The feeling was more of a kick this time. The flutters were gone, since the baby was getting bigger. Her doctor told her she would probably be showing to the world by mid-June. At the latest.

Which meant she and Cole could go through graduation in love with each other. Spending their free time together. Cheering each other on through baseball games and paintings. But all of it was only pretend if Cole Blake was afraid.

How could she let him give up his dream of attending Liberty University and becoming a doctor if he was scared of what was ahead? And what about her dream of being an artist? Since she'd moved here she hadn't painted anything at all until Cole found the easel and paints from his mom.

But now that she was filling a canvas again, all she could think about was NYU. Her desire to become an artist had only grown stronger over the past weeks. Something she hadn't told Cole. Which meant neither of them was being fully honest, the type of honest they would need to be before they packed up for Louisiana. Before they even considered marriage.

She had talked to her mother today, told her she was having doubts again about the baby. About keeping her. This time her mom had seemed different, less willing to push Elise toward coming home and bringing Cole. Which all lined up with the way she felt God telling her to trust Him by placing her baby for adoption. Something she wouldn't have experienced if she hadn't gone to church with Cole's family. And today her mom had seemed to be on that same page.

"This is a decision that will change your life forever," her mama had said. "I'll stand by you, baby girl. Whatever you choose."

Her words brought Elise a feeling of relief. For a while there she had thought her mom might be disappointed if she placed the baby for adoption. But now things were completely back to what Mr. Green had told her. This was her choice. Completely hers.

And how much of her decision to keep the baby in the first place was because of Cole? Because she could picture him by her side, bringing the newborn home, feeding and changing her. All the little milestones were only beautiful in her mind because she had Cole right next to her. How could she even consider letting Cole pass up going away to college? It was beyond selfish of her. Agreeing with him that he'd be fine taking classes online? That was terrible.

Staying home to raise a baby or going away to college. There was nothing even a little similar between those two plans.

She rolled onto her other side. If Cole was the only reason she was excited about keeping her baby girl, what did that say about her desire to be a mother? Elise exhaled long and troubled. Tomorrow she would tell Aunt Carol and Uncle Ken about the baby. Everything was getting so real. So complicated.

No wonder Cole felt scared. They both should be terrified.

Her thoughts did spins and somersaults pulling her one way and then the other until finally she fell asleep. Suddenly she wasn't in her aunt and uncle's flowered little guest room. She was in her mama's house in Louisiana. And Cole was sitting on the couch working on a laptop.

But he looked older. Not as happy and carefree.

And then there was a loud noise at the door and someone kicked it open and Randy stepped in. Mean and big and screaming mad. "Elise, where's the baby?"

She didn't have to ask. She knew what he was talking about. "The baby's mine, Randy. Leave us alone."

"No. I changed my mind, Elise. I'm keeping her." Then he pulled out a gun and pointed it at Elise. At the last second he spun and aimed the weapon at Cole. "And I'm finished with you forever."

Randy pulled the trigger and Elise screamed. But before the bullet could tear into Cole, Elise sat straight up in bed. Her lungs gasping for air. "God, help me. Please . . . save Cole!"

She was still only half awake, and gradually the reality washed over her. Randy wasn't here. He hadn't burst through the door and he didn't just shoot Cole Blake.

It was a dream. The worst one Elise had ever had. But as she settled back into the pillow, as her heart found its regular rhythm again, she realized that one part of the dream was actually very possible.

The idea that Randy might come after her if she kept the baby. He had signed off his rights, but that didn't mean he'd leave her alone. Even if he moved away from Leesville, he could come back. And one day the kick at the door wouldn't be a nightmare. It would be real.

Suddenly the pieces started adding up. The fact that Cole deserved his own dreams and that she wasn't sure she even wanted to be a mother. The reality of Randy's temper and the way she longed to attend NYU. The truth that any day she would find out if she was accepted there, and she had the strongest sense she would be.

Elise put her hand on her stomach. It was still flat, but it was firm now. Getting hard as her uterus filled out. She ran her fingers over the area and felt something that hadn't been there before. A gentle rise between her hip bones.

"I'm sorry, little girl. I wish I could be what you need. I wish things were different." Her voice was barely a whisper. "I'm so sorry."

She cried herself to sleep and when she woke up she didn't have to ask God what the answer was. It was clear as the morning outside her window. And that afternoon a letter from NYU was waiting for her in the mailbox.

As fast as she could she tore into it and began to read.

Dear Ms. Walker,

We are pleased to inform you of your acceptance to New York University. We find your paintings to be of the highest

*caliber, and we look forward to the next four years of shaping
and refining your skills* . . .

Elise couldn't read another word. Not until she did
what she couldn't wait to do. She took a breath, trusted
God with all her heart, and made the call.

The call to Mr. Green.

21

With all the intensity of the situation with Elise, Ashley woke up on Cole's graduation day feeling a little cheated.

Years ago when he was little, as much as Cole delighted her more every day, she was often sad at how quickly he was growing up. That every few months he stood taller and talked more clearly.

Back then, when Cole was four, Ashley had taken a day to clean out his dresser drawers. Clothes Cole had outgrown she boxed up and gave to the Goodwill. All except a few special outfits. When she was done cleaning that day, she'd played the song "House at Pooh Corner" by Kenny Loggins and found her journal. Tears had filled her eyes as she opened it to a blank page. She could still remember what she wrote.

I grew up believing I could do anything. But today I realized there's something I'll never be able to do. I can't stop my Cole from growing up.

Then she had turned the page and done a little projecting. She wrote out the next fifteen years on so many lines and beside each date she wrote the grade Cole would be in. A minute later she was scribbling out the year 2019, and then the two saddest words she could imagine.

Cole graduates.

As far off as that year felt, Ashley had made a decision that day. She would savor every minute. Appreciate the seasons. Paint them. So that when 2019 had the nerve of rolling around and sweeping Cole from his little-boy bedroom to a whole new life, she would be ready.

But now here they were.

And Ashley felt like they'd wasted most of the semester helping Cole figure out what to do with Elise, how to navigate the situation, what decision to make. When he wasn't with the girl, he was talking about her, distracted by her.

Nothing about this past semester was how Ashley had seen it playing out.

Elise was a very kind girl, a free spirit and an artist. She'd been accepted to NYU and for the past month she seemed set once again on placing her baby up for adoption and heading to Manhattan for school. But she still had to give birth and hold her baby, still had to get through those last two weeks before the adoption would be final.

All those days before Ashley could be sure Cole wasn't going to throw away his dreams and follow Elise to Louisiana.

Ashley had studied the calendar, and depending on when Elise had her baby, there was a chance her two-week window could be the last two weeks Cole would have at home before leaving for Liberty. Which meant the final days before Cole moved might not turn out how she pictured them, either.

Whatever happened, Cole was going to be crushed when summer ended. He loved Elise that much.

It was early Saturday morning. Ashley had set her alarm for seven o'clock—way before the rest of the family would be awake. She wanted to finish Cole's graduation video, the one she'd been putting together since the start of his senior year. She had a few more edits to make and it would be good to go.

They'd play it tonight after the ceremony, when everyone in their extended family and many of Cole's friends gathered to celebrate. But before Ashley could work on the video, there was something she wanted to find.

At the top of her closet were two boxes filled with things that meant the world to her. Things she couldn't bear to throw away. Not ever. She pulled them down one at a time and took them to the living room. So she wouldn't wake anyone. She sat in the nearest chair and opened both of them.

At the bottom of the first one was the one outfit she'd kept from Cole's childhood. It was a pale blue sleeper covered with red choo-choo trains. Cole had worn it as often as he could the year he was three. Ashley lifted it from the box and ran her thumbs over the soft fabric.

"Cole, you were just this little. Where did the days

go?" She pressed the pajamas to her face and breathed in. They no longer smelled of him, of course. Over the years the outfit had picked up the smell of cardboard and dust and time.

Time most of all.

She rifled around the bottom of the container and found a small red and blue toy train, the colors worn off in spots. Much like the trains on Cole's well-worn pajamas. Ashley gave the wheels a gentle spin. The toy still looked the way it had all those years ago when Cole was a child.

How her oldest son loved this little train. Ashley smiled. Cole would make tracks with his blocks across the living room floor so he could take the train over water or snow or whatever his imagination came up with. And sometimes he would take the train airborne, when the ground was too limiting.

Ashley could still feel his little hand in hers on their walks through the neighborhood. She studied the toy. Cole had brought this train with him everywhere, especially to the park. So he could run it down the slide and take the tiny imaginary passengers for a ride on the swing. This train was part of his daytime routine until he was five.

When kindergarten interrupted his baby boy days.

Once more she held the pajamas and train to her face, then pressed them to the spot over her heart. If only she could have one more day back then. Back when these were everything to her little boy. The way they still were to Ashley. With tender care, she set the items back in the box. Souvenirs of Cole's childhood.

She would love them forever.

There was one more thing she wanted to find. She searched through the second box, sorting through stacks of papers and kids' artwork. What she wanted was the book of letters her mom had written to them before cancer took her. Not long after Ashley and Landon's wedding, her dad put the letters together and made a copy for each of the kids.

It took less than a minute to find it. She lifted the book from the box and set it on her lap. On one of the pages was a poem Ashley's mom had written for Luke the night before he married Reagan. Then, when her cancer returned, her mom had taken the poem and changed the ending. So it would be more fitting for the rest of the kids and grandkids.

Ashley didn't want to read it today. Didn't even want to open it. Finding it was enough. She set the book aside and closed up the boxes once more. After she returned them to the top shelf of her closet, she tucked the book of letters onto a shelf in the cupboard above the family computer. So that she could easily get it and read it to Cole at the end of the summer. In Cole's last hours at home.

Before he drove off to his new life—wherever that would be.

• • •

ALL SEMESTER ASHLEY had been charting the lasts. When they drove onto the school grounds, she checked off another. Last time they'd come to Clear Creek High School with Cole still a student.

Janessa skipped up beside her as they walked from the SUV to the football stadium. "Mama." She looked worried. As if her seven-year-old heart didn't like the idea of endings. Not where her big brother was concerned. "Does this mean Cole's grown up?"

Ashley felt her heart overflowing with emotions. Was it really 2019? Already? She took a full breath. There was no other way to answer Janessa's question. "I guess maybe it does."

"So soon?" Janessa furrowed her brow. "I thought he still had a few more years."

"I keep thinking that, too." Ashley loved her little girl. The two were so much alike. Janessa was still finishing second grade. But Ashley didn't dare tell herself they had forever. Cole's cap and gown told her the truth.

Children don't last.

They kept walking. Landon and Devin were a few yards ahead, and Cole had gotten here an hour ago. "Well." Janessa started skipping again. "I wish Cole had more time at home. I don't want him to move away."

"I don't, either." Ashley took hold of her little girl's hand. "Let's go get good seats."

"Yay!" Janessa dropped the sad conversation and ran with Ashley up the steps and into the stadium.

Everyone was coming to support Cole today, to cheer him on for reaching this milestone. He wasn't just graduating. He would walk with honors for his nearly perfect GPA. Even this past semester with everything going on Cole pulled off straight A's.

Ashley set out programs to save seats on two rows. Five for her brother Luke's family, and five for her brother Dayne and his wife and kids, all of whom had flown in from Los Angeles yesterday. Four for Brooke's family and four for Kari's, since Jessie was graduating also. Plus her dad and Elaine.

All together they needed twenty-five seats.

Landon had been talking to the parents of one of Cole's friends. When he jogged back over to her, he surveyed the blocked-off rows. He grinned at her. "Here we go."

Carolyn's parents approached them and for the next few minutes the four of them talked about Liberty University. The conversation helped take Ashley's mind off what was happening here, how in just an hour Cole would step onto the stage as a high school kid, and walk off the other side, a graduate.

A few minutes before the ceremony Elise came over. She wore a loose-fitting white blouse and dark jeans and her graduation cap. Her gown was hanging over her arm. Ashley watched how the girl's full dark hair fell in layers around her face and blew in the breeze. No one would've guessed she was pregnant. "Hi, Elise." Ashley turned to her. And for a few seconds it was like she was seeing a younger version of herself. The way she had looked when she left home for Paris.

"Mrs. Blake, I was wondering. Could my mom and

my aunt and uncle sit with you? They wanted to meet you."

Ashley didn't hesitate. "Of course." She stood and slid the extra programs down a bit, making room for three more. Then she faced Elise. "Will they be here soon?"

"Any minute. And thanks." Her smile looked untroubled, easy. With none of the doubt and shame that had plagued her much of the last few months. "For the seats. But also for taking me to church on Easter." She hesitated and looked straight at Ashley. "I have my faith back because of your family. That's everything to me."

"I'm glad." Ashley hugged the girl and then sat down again. "Congratulations. On NYU."

"Thank you." Her face lit up. "I can't wait to go." Elise hurried off to join her class on the grassy field.

Ashley watched her leave and a surge of hope filled her heart. Maybe Elise was going to go through with the adoption after all. Before Ashley could give the matter much thought, the rest of her family arrived. Cole's cousins Maddie and Hayley sat together. Ashley took the spot between Landon and Janessa. As she sat down a wave of guilt came over her. From the moment she'd found out Elise was pregnant, Ashley hadn't been a fan. Yes, she'd put on an understanding face around Cole. But deep down, this whole time, she hadn't wanted Cole tangled up with Elise's baggage, had definitely not wanted him feeling responsible to stay with her through the pregnancy.

Most of all she hadn't wanted Cole falling for a bad girl.

But twenty years ago that bad girl had been her. Ashley Baxter.

She lifted her eyes to the cloudy sky overhead. *I'm sorry, Lord. Why didn't I see this before?* No wonder Cole's last semester hadn't gone like she had hoped. Ashley had chosen not to enjoy it. Instead she had wasted far too much time being silently critical and judgmental of Elise. Wishing Cole had never met the girl. And now . . .

Lord, help me extend grace. The way it was given to me.

Like Landon had treated her, Cole had never judged Elise. He had only cared for her and stood by her and helped her through a difficult season. Yes, they were young. But Ashley had to believe Cole's actions were exactly what Landon would've done. *Thank You, God, for the summer. Let me make it up to Cole. And to Elise. To both of them.*

Ashley watched three people approach her, and immediately she knew who they were. One of the women definitely had Elise's eyes. Sure enough, the woman introduced herself as Elise's mom. The other two people were Elise's aunt and uncle. Ashley introduced herself and the three took their seats. They talked about how thankful they were for Cole. Elise's aunt mentioned that she had been shocked at the pregnancy news. "We only just found out." Regret seemed to come over the woman. "I wish I would've paid more attention."

"You couldn't have known." Ashley wasn't sure what to say. "Anyway, here we are. She's happy all of you are here."

After a few minutes, the conversation with Elise's family fizzled. Ashley looked around her at all the people she loved. A hush came over the crowd, and the band began to play "Pomp and Circumstance." Three notes in and Ashley felt the first sting of tears. Nothing about the song was a surprise. It was played at every graduation, every year all across the nation.

This time, though, the music swirled around her and pulled her in and as the graduating class of 2019 walked in two lines onto the field, tears slid down Ashley's cheeks. A few seats over she saw Kari going through the same thing. Because of the accident, this hadn't been an easy semester for Kari and her daughter Jessie, either.

Ashley found two tissues in her purse. She leaned over Landon to give one to her sister. Kari smiled at her, a look of gratitude and knowing. Once every few years, ever since their kids were babies, they had talked about 2019. How far off it was and how it would take a million years before Cole and Jessie were this old.

And now here they were.

Jessie entered with one of the first groups of graduates. Her pretty light brown hair hung past her shoulders, her posture straight and sure. Ashley shared a quick smile with Kari, even as they both dabbed at their tears.

Another few groups walked onto the field, but Cole would be among the last. That's what he had told them after the graduation rehearsal. They were being seated in reverse alphabetical order. Finally, Ashley spotted him.

"Landon!" She leaned closer and tugged his sleeve. "Look!"

Cole was easy to see, tall and blond. Not only did he act like Landon, he walked like him. He talked like him and acted like him. Strong and confident, with an air of kindness anyone could've felt all the way to the top of the bleachers. Ashley blinked away her tears so she could see him clearly. Throughout the procession, people would yell out the names of their graduates or stand and cheer extra loud.

So as Cole walked past them Devin jumped up and hooted, his fist in the air. "Go, Cole!" He looked at the people in the stands near them. "That's my brother!"

Several people laughed, everyone seeming to enjoy the fact that this was—after all—a celebration. Cole must've heard the shout-out, because he turned and saw them. Then he waved. Not just at the big group there supporting him, but at her. Ashley. And in his smile Ashley knew what he was telling her.

That it had been just the two of them from the beginning, and that they'd come a long way together since then. And something else. A deep gratitude because Ashley had stayed with him, raised him. In the beginning, doubt had told her that because of her choices, she and Cole would never have anyone, never be anything but alone.

But God and her family had other plans for Ashley

and Cole. They had loved her and embraced her and forgiven her. New tears slid down her face, tears of joy and
satisfaction, because they'd done it. She and Cole had
made it.

He was still watching her, still smiling and waving.
Ashley lifted her hand and did the same. And as she did
she caught a look at the family around her. All of them
were waving, too. And in a blur she wasn't seeing Cole in
his cap and gown. She was seeing him in his choo-choo
pajamas, the red and blue train in his hand.

And Landon was giving them a tour of his fire-
house and Cole was wearing Landon's helmet.
Wouldn't take it off. And she could see him, blond hair
combed neat, eyes wide as she dropped him off at first
grade and she could hear his little-boy voice, "Do I
have to stay all day, Mommy? What about our afternoon adventures?"

Ashley blinked and pressed her tissue to her face.
And she could see him running across a soccer field,
scoring his first goal as a nine-year-old and then making
the winning shot in his middle school basketball champi-
onship. And there he was sitting with her mother in the
rose garden outside the old Baxter house, the one they
lived in now. Her mom's head leaned close to his, Cole's
blue eyes looking at her, listening.

How Cole had loved his grandmother.

And she could see him standing next to her father at
the pond on their property, fishing and talking and
laughing. And she could hear Cole telling her that night,

"Papa told me fishing isn't really about the fish. It's about the people you fish with."

Another blink and Cole was getting out of her car and headed up to the entrance of Clear Creek High, waving and grinning, a lifetime of potential shining in his face. And the scene changed and he was a pallbearer after the accident that took Erin and Sam and three of their girls. And she could see him, strong and stoic in a suit that didn't quite fit, and hear him later that day. "Won't it be a party, Mom, when we're all together in heaven one day?"

Ashley dabbed the tissue against the river of tears again. And suddenly he was a sophomore, sitting in the car beside her, telling her about his school project. "I have to interview someone in my family. Tell their story." And for a series of weeks she could see Cole meeting with her dad. Interviewing his papa about Grandma Elizabeth. The grandmother he'd lost too soon. And they were sitting there and the sun was streaming through the window and Ashley's dad was wiping tears as he remembered the most beautiful love story.

And when the project was finished she could hear him asking about his own father. Ashley could feel again the panic that had seized her. She didn't want to talk about his birth father. There was nothing to say. He was a married artist in Paris who had wanted her to have an abortion.

She could hardly tell Cole that.

So she was hesitating and making small talk and trying to do anything but tell Cole the truth about his father, and suddenly Cole understood what she thought. And he was laughing and looking at her with curious eyes. "Mom, not that guy. I want to know about my dad. My real dad."

And it was Landon he'd been talking about all along and Ashley was realizing all over again that God had given them a miracle because Cole was fine. He was happy and whole and he never once missed "that guy" because he had a dad. He had Landon.

All of it flashed in front of her teary eyes in the time it took Cole to walk in cap and gown across the grass and take his seat with his class. A brief trailer of images that disappeared as quickly as the years they represented.

She lifted her eyes to heaven and smiled. *Lord, thank You for this life. Thank You for my oldest son, my Cole.* Once more she dried her tears and as the famous processional song ended, Ashley felt the breeze brush over her face. She could do this.

Landon took hold of her hand. He whispered near her face, "You okay?"

"I am." She sniffed and smiled at him. "We've had an amazing life, Landon."

His eyes looked damp, too, but his smile matched hers. "Yes, we have." He lifted her hand and kissed it. "This is only the beginning, Ash. Just another chapter."

She nodded and turned her attention to the graduation ceremony about to start. Enough reflecting on mo-

ments gone by. This was a time to remember, too, and
Ashley didn't want to miss a single second. After all,
she'd been dreaming about 2019 since she'd scribbled in
her journal that day, and now here it was.

Her oldest son was graduating.

• • •

NO MATTER HOW Ashley tried to hold on to the weeks
that followed graduation, they flew by like so many
hours. Elise remained sure about her adoption plans, and
she was still sure Cole should go to Liberty. No matter
what she decided about her baby. Cole had resisted at
first, but then he did something Ashley and Landon both
appreciated. He came to them each separately. Ashley
was first. He asked her one question.

"Mom, if you'd been a senior in high school when
you got pregnant with me, what would you have
done?"

It was a question Ashley had considered this past semester, especially in light of Elise's situation. Ashley
hated the answer, hated that if things had been different
she might not have made the same decision. She ached
to think of all she would've missed. How she never
would've known his baby face or the early years of his
life. But it was the truth and she had to tell him. "I really
think I would've placed you up for adoption." She
paused. "I'm sure I would've."

The two had hugged then and Cole had smiled at

her. "I'm glad you were older, Mom. I would've hated not knowing you."

Another time he went to the fire station and talked to Landon. Later Landon told her how the conversation had gone. Cole had asked what Landon would've done if he'd been in high school when he and Ashley reconnected. Landon's answer had been candid. He would've gotten his firefighting training and he would've waited a few years before even thinking about dating her.

Especially if she had a son.

Between Elise's insistence that Cole follow through with Liberty and his conversations with Landon and her, Cole finally seemed at peace. Convinced he was making the right decision. But once that much was clear, another issue rose to the surface. The fact that very soon Cole wouldn't only have to say goodbye to his family.

He'd have to say goodbye to Elise.

All of it seemed to push the days faster and faster toward August. Elise's due date wasn't until August 14, but on a sunny day the first of the month, Cole called home in a panic. He and Elise had been walking around Lake Monroe when her water broke.

"I'm taking her to the hospital." His words ran together. "Please pray, Mom. She doesn't look good. Come to the hospital as soon as you can."

Ashley's hands began to shake. This was really happening. Her son was about to stand beside his girlfriend while she gave birth. She contacted Landon and he was immediately on his way home to watch the kids. Cole had texted that Ashley could come to the delivery room. Elise wanted Ashley there so she could pray for her.

The whole way to the hospital and while she parked the car, on the elevator ride up to labor and delivery, Ashley told herself she could handle this. That Cole wasn't the father and she wasn't about to watch her own grandchild come into the world.

But nothing could've prepared her for what she saw when she walked into Elise's labor room. Cole was standing at her side, squeezing her hand, talking her through a contraction. "You've got this, Elise." He looked at the monitor. "Come on, you can do it. This one's almost done."

Ashley took a step back. Until the contraction passed, she just stood there, taking in the scene. Of the army of emotions surrounding Ashley, a few stood out. First, Cole was going to make a wonderful doctor someday. And second, when the time was right, Cole was going to be an incredible father.

She wouldn't let her other thoughts take hold. The idea that Elise could still change her mind, and Cole could, too. Instead, when the contraction was over, Ashley stepped in to do what she'd come to do. What everyone in the room desperately needed.

She joined Cole beside Elise's bed and they prayed.

22

It was almost time.

Cole and his mom had been at Elise's bedside for seven hours, the last ninety minutes of which she'd been pushing. The whole time he had stood near her head, looking away whenever a doctor or nurse came in to check her. Being here for her was one thing. But he had no intention of seeing her in such an intimate, vulnerable way. Because of the hospital sheet, all Cole could see were Elise's legs. He was grateful for that. And now, the moment was clearly getting close because three nurses and Elise's doctor had entered the room.

"Any minute," the doctor said. He helped position Elise's feet into the stirrups on either side of the table. "You're doing great, Elise. I can see your baby's head."

The room tipped, and Cole gripped the top of the hospital bed so he wouldn't look dizzy. The baby's head? This was really happening. It was more than Cole could believe.

His mother still stood across from him, and now she leaned in near Elise's face. "You okay?"

"I . . . think so." Elise squeezed her eyes shut. "I feel sick."

Cole didn't know what to do. "I can get you a cold cloth."

"Yes, please. Hurry." Elise's face was red. As Cole left, out of the corner of his eye he saw her lift up her legs and hold her knees. "I need to push!"

"Not yet, Elise." The doctor's voice was kind but urgent. "Not until I tell you to."

There was a sink in the room, so Cole took a clean cloth from the cupboard above it and got it wet. He was back at Elise's side in seconds.

"Thank you." She smiled at him through weary, anxious eyes.

Cole nodded. "Of course." He had read that sometimes girls could be mean during labor. Not sure what they wanted and snapping at everyone who tried to help.

Elise hadn't been like that at all. Cole laid the cool rag on her forehead just as the next contraction hit. This time the doctor moved into position. "Okay, I'll talk you through it, Elise. Here comes the head."

Cole shared a look with his mom. He had never known exactly what she'd gone through to bring him into the world until now. His mom squeezed Elise's hand. "You're doing it. She's almost here!"

This time Cole couldn't help but look. From his angle he could only see the baby's head. Wonder came over him. Here was the greatest miracle the Lord had given them, the miracle of life. To stand by and watch was as much proof of God as anything Cole could imagine.

"There you go, Elise." The doctor had hold of the infant's head now. "Okay, push again, just a little."

Elise grabbed her knees and pushed and then in a quick movement, the baby girl was out and the doctor laid her on Elise's stomach. At first the baby didn't cry. She was gray and slimy and covered in some kind of white cream. Also she was still attached to the umbilical cord.

Cole could never have imagined a moment like this. While he was trying to remember how to breathe, the tiny baby did a few gasps and began to wail. Loud and strong.

"She's perfect." Cole's mom put her hand on Elise's shoulder. "How are you feeling?"

Elise laughed but it was a mix of elation and relief. "I can't believe I did it." She seemed to instinctively know to put her hand on the infant's back. "It's okay, baby girl. It's okay. Mama's here."

Cole still hadn't said a word. But now, watching Elise with her newborn, he finally understood the full weight of the decision she faced. The one she thought she'd already made. After all this, placing her daughter with another family would be brutally hard.

"You did great, Elise." Cole still stayed near her head, allowing her a fraction of privacy as the doctor delivered the placenta. Cole took a deep breath. It was crazy that he even knew that a placenta had to be delivered. He'd learned so much because of Elise.

Again he watched her with her baby. This bonding

time was the attorney's idea. Mr. Green seemed intent on Elise not missing out on anything. If she could go through all this and still place the baby with the adoptive parents, then it was meant to be.

The attorney didn't want Elise having any regrets. Whatever happened after this, Cole was grateful Elise got to experience her child. After all, she was the baby's mother. Even if the best choice was for someone else to raise her.

Just then the doctor handed Cole a pair of scissors. "Would you like to cut the cord?"

He thinks I'm the baby's daddy, Cole thought. But it didn't matter. One day he hoped to make his future out of moments like this, maybe right here at Bloomington Hospital. He looked at his mom and she gave him the slightest nod. "Go ahead."

Cole put his hand on Elise's other shoulder. "You did it, Elise." He had to say this first. "God helped you. Your baby girl is beautiful."

"Because of you." She was crying now, happy tears falling onto her cheeks. "I couldn't have done it without God and you." She looked at Cole's mom. "And you, Mrs. Blake."

His mother smiled. "I'm glad you wanted me here."

Cole turned to the doctor. And—in the most surreal moment of his life—he took the strange-looking scissors from the man and cut the baby's cord. The whole time Cole could only think one thing.

How could Elise say goodbye to her baby girl after this?

• • •

LUCY WAS ON her way into work the second of August when she got the call. All along they had known that Elise's due date was August 14. Still a ways off but when Lucy checked caller ID and saw it was their attorney, she instantly pulled over and answered the phone.

"I tried to reach Aaron, but he didn't pick up. I wanted you to know," he sounded happy, but guarded. "Elise had her baby late last night. A healthy little girl."

"Dear God . . ." Lucy closed her eyes and gripped the steering wheel with her free hand. Was this really happening? They had learned months ago that the child was a girl. And they had given her the name Gracie Anne. Elise knew about the name, and apparently she loved it. Gracie Anne Williams.

If Elise didn't change her mind.

But until now all of this hadn't ever felt real. It was all legal documents and the temperament of a teenage mom. Now, though . . . now everything had changed. Was it possible they could have a child of their own in just fourteen days?

"Anyway," Mr. Green was going on. "I visited Elise this morning at the hospital." He paused. "She still wants to go through with the adoption."

Of course she does, Lucy wanted to tell him. She bounced up and down in her seat, her heart soaring within her. This was God's doing. Aaron had heard the

Lord tell him that they would have a baby soon. And now their little girl was here. Just hours old.

They'd been this close before, but this time was different. Lucy knew in her soul. Gracie Anne was theirs.

But before she could say any of that, Mr. Green added, "I must caution you, she still has the—"

"Two weeks." Lucy's voice had never sounded happier as she finished his sentence. "I know. Isn't that wonderful, Mr. Green? That means in just fourteen days that little girl will be ours." She refused to give in to fear, refused to let this day be anything but a party. "So is it okay if we don't worry about that today? Can we just celebrate?"

The attorney was quiet for a moment. "Yes." He sighed. "You can celebrate." His voice was hardly celebratory. "Just know that birth moms who have changed their minds before, often change them again. I don't want you and Aaron to get hurt by this."

"Too late." This time she didn't filter her thoughts. "Mr. Green, if we lose this baby, we will be hurt to the core. We'll remember it forever, just like every other baby we've lost these past ten years." She wasn't finished. "We bought a crib seven years ago, Mr. Green. We have baby animal sheets and Winnie-the-Pooh curtains and teddy bears just dying for little hands to play with them." She gathered herself. "So thank you for the warning. But it's too late."

"Okay." His voice fell a little. "Then yes, celebrate. You and Aaron certainly deserve that much."

Lucy barely felt the asphalt beneath her feet as she

hurried from her car to the hospital's administrative wing. The baby was here. She was born and she was right here in this building. She opened her husband's office door and their eyes met. He signaled that he was winding up a call and that he wanted her to stay. He didn't look away from her, as if he must've seen the joy in her face.

When he hung up he hurried to her and took her hands. "What is it?"

"She's here. The baby girl. Gracie Anne." Lucy felt the beginning of tears but she held them back. Today was a party. She wouldn't have it any other way. "She was born late last night."

Aaron blinked back tears, too, and he let his head fall lightly against hers. "This is it, Lucy. Our little girl."

There was no reason to warn Aaron the way Mr. Green had warned her earlier. They both knew the risks, the possibilities. But right now none of that mattered. Aaron looked at her again. "Can we see her?"

Lucy was wondering the same thing. Of course, she could easily see the baby, since she worked on the maternity floor. Elise knew that, which made the situation a little tricky. Technically they weren't supposed to see the baby until after the two weeks. If Elise still wanted to place the baby for adoption.

Should they stop by her room? Talk to her? Tell her how grateful they were that she'd chosen them? Aaron was the first to recall their agreement, the paperwork they'd signed at the beginning.

"If we visit Elise even once, she could take that as coercion." Aaron took a step back and leaned against his desk. "This whole situation needs to be by the book. For all of us."

Lucy remembered one more document, though. "The paperwork also says that I can't be prevented from seeing the baby." She felt a thrill of hope. "Because I work on the maternity ward. Remember?"

"True." Aaron's anxious expression eased a little.

Lucy's heart pounded at the thought. The other nurses in the unit didn't know Aaron and Lucy were in the process of adopting. It would be perfectly normal for her to check on the baby girl. Brooke was the only doctor aware of the situation. Brooke's nephew was dating Elise, after all. They had found that out a few weeks ago.

But Brooke was off today.

"I think we can see the baby." Lucy crossed her arms. Her heart had never beat so hard in all her life.

"I'm going to stay here." Aaron had clearly made up his mind. "But yes . . . it's okay for you. Based on everything we agreed to." He came to her and took her face in his hands. "When you see her, pray for her. And tell her Daddy's praying, too."

Lucy could hardly wait. The walk from Aaron's office to the nursing station in the maternity ward had never taken longer. Her heart was in her throat and every outbreath was a struggle. She signed in and said hello to her co-workers. Yes she was having a good morning. No she hadn't seen the new Tom Hanks movie.

Finally it was time to make her rounds. The baby was

healthy, so she wouldn't be in the NICU. With her knees and hands shaking, Lucy walked along the line of bassinets, the blue and pink blankets and the handwritten names on the fronts of the Plexiglas cribs.

Six babies lined the ward that day, and four of them were boys. Not until she reached the last baby in the row—a girl—did she know for sure. This was the baby, the one she and Aaron had prayed about and believed for and desperately wanted. Not just for the last five months.

For the last ten years.

Lucy stepped closer and looked at the tiny sleeping infant. She was perfect, her lips and cheeks and forehead more beautiful than any little baby's ever had been. Lucy could hear her heart pounding with every breath.

God, is she ours? Is this our little girl? Please, can she be our little girl?

And then she saw something that gave her the greatest possible hope. The most incredible moment in this journey. Because this baby wasn't just Elise's child or a nameless infant in limbo while her birth mother decided what to do. This baby had a name. The one written over her tiny crib.

Gracie Anne.

* * *

ELISE WAS ALONE in the hospital room for now. She was leaving soon. Cole had already gone to get the car. And so she had done something she was advised not to do. Not in cases of adoption. She had asked her nurse to get her baby girl for her.

One last time.

The woman was older, wisdom shone in her eyes. She hesitated at Elise's request. "Are you sure, honey?"

Every warning from Mr. Green came back to her. *Remember the reason you signed the papers, Elise. Don't put yourself through unnecessary pain, unless you are doubting your decision.*

She didn't care. Her smile came as easily as her next words. "Yes. I'm sure."

Sunshine streamed through the window and Elise lifted her eyes to the sliver of blue sky between the hospital buildings. She was sure about placing her baby with Aaron and Lucy. It was the right thing to do for all of them. She'd already gotten student loans lined up for NYU.

But right here, right now, the baby was still hers. And she wasn't going to leave without a proper goodbye. It was why she had sent Cole ahead. She didn't want him to be here for this. Cole wasn't the father of her baby. It had been wrong for her ever to pretend that was the case.

This newborn was hers alone. At least for another fifteen minutes.

The nurse returned with Elise's baby girl, sleeping in a small crib on wheels. She pulled it up next to Elise. "Here she is."

"Thank you." Elise was still very sore, but she was showered and dressed, sitting in the chair beside her hospital bed. "Would you please hand her to me?" She looked at the nurse. "And then could you give us a few minutes?"

Again the woman hesitated, but she did as Elise asked. She picked up the baby, swaddled in a white and pink hospital blanket, and she gently transferred her to Elise's arms. "I'll check on you in a bit."

"Okay." Elise nodded, but she wasn't listening. She was lost in the beauty of her firstborn, her tiny baby girl. When it was just the two of them, Elise nuzzled her face against the infant's. "I didn't have a plan for you, Gracie Anne." She kissed the child's cheek. "But God did." Tears must've filled her eyes because one fell on her baby's face. Elise dabbed it with the tip of her finger. "Yes, sweetie. God most certainly did."

She had read about newborns. Usually they slept most of the first few weeks, only opening their eyes in rare moments. But maybe because of the sound of her voice or the tear that had fallen on her baby face, Gracie Anne opened her eyes.

Opened them and looked right at Elise.

"Hello, there." Elise felt an ocean of pain building in her heart and throat. "I'm your mama, baby. I love you."

Gracie Anne blinked a few times. Maybe it was just Elise's desperate imagination, but for a few seconds her baby looked straight to Elise's heart. To the very center of her. As if to say she understood what was about to happen and she'd be fine with Aaron and Lucy. Better than fine. And that right here, while they still had the chance, she wanted Elise to know it was okay. That she would always love her for making this decision.

All of that seemed to come from the newborn in

the time it took Elise to breathe. And in that same instant Elise noticed something. How natural it felt to hold her baby. This was her baby, a part of her. She always would be.

"Your grandma wanted to be here, baby girl. She loves you, too." In the end she had decided it was best for her mom to stay back in Louisiana. If Elise changed her mind and kept the baby, her mother would see the child soon enough. If not, there was no point, no reason for her mom to be part of the heartache of this goodbye.

So she had done what Elise asked and stayed home. Elise was still looking into her baby girl's face, still taking in her soft newborn smell. Still feeling the gentle rise and fall of her tiny chest with every breath.

"Jesus loves you, Gracie Anne. Remember that." A soft sob caught in her throat. "And no one's ever going to hurt you."

Suddenly she knew just what she wanted to do. She opened her lips and began to sing. The same song her mama had sung to her. The one she carried with her even in her darkest days. And like her mother had done so many years ago, she changed the words just slightly. So that the song was directed straight to her baby girl. "Jesus loves you, this I know . . . for the Bible tells me so."

Another tear fell on her little girl's cheek. "Yes, Jesus loves you . . ."

The whole time, little Gracie Anne watched her, studied her. And so Elise memorized the moment, held on to it. This would be the only time she would ever sing over her daughter. Every single second was etching itself into her heart and soul.

When the song ended, a flash from her nightmare about Randy came to mind. She didn't want to worry about him ever being a threat to their baby girl's life. It was another reason the adoption made sense. She didn't want any connection with Randy. Not ever again.

Elise could hear the soft steps of the nurse as she approached her room. A final thought hit her as she held her baby close. Gracie Anne looked just like her, like the baby picture her mother had texted her a few weeks ago. Dark hair, high cheekbones. Elise ran her finger over her baby's forehead. "Little princess."

The nurse entered the room and came closer. Slowly. Like she didn't want to rush the moment for Elise. But Elise was ready.

She held her baby girl to her face, cheek to cheek once more, and whispered so only her daughter could hear. "I will never, ever forget you, Gracie Anne." She kissed her head, her velvet-soft face. "I love you, baby girl."

That was all she could take. She would collapse to the floor if the goodbye lasted any longer. "Please." She looked up at the nurse. "Take her."

There were no words from the nurse. What could either of them say? The older woman bent down and took the beautiful baby from her arms. Elise couldn't stand to watch her leave, so she closed her eyes. Squeezed them shut as tight as she could.

Though she had known this moment would be hard, she'd wanted it anyway. Wanted to talk to her daughter and tell her goodbye. Sing to her. But she hadn't expected this ache, this very deep hurt that came from her heart and radiated down her empty arms. The only reason she could keep breathing was because she knew the truth. Her decision to say goodbye wasn't yet final.

Not for two weeks.

• • •

THEO SET THE car seat down in the private office on the first floor of the hospital and took the chair next to his wife.

"I still can't believe this." Alma looked wide-eyed, like everything about the moment might only be a dream.

"That Vienna would push us to take in foster babies the hour before she went to heaven." Theo shook his head. "And now . . . here we are."

"You're sure, right?" She looked at him. "You can handle this? Knowing that she has to leave us so soon."

Theo didn't blink, didn't look away. He could feel the heartache in his eyes, the one that would be with him as long as he lived. "Sometimes little girls leave too soon." He smiled. "No one knows that like us."

Tears filled Alma's eyes and she nodded. "Yes." She took a tissue from the desk and dabbed at her face. "I won't cry. Hold me to that, Theo. I won't cry. This is foster care. Help me remember."

"Yes. I'll help you." He put his arm around her. "But some days we'll have to help each other."

Foster care came with certain rules and understandings. Loving a child was encouraged. Attachment was not. Most foster children were only placed in a home short-term. Always the goal was reunification with the parent.

But this case was so different. Theo's voice fell. "I wonder if Mr. Green would've called us. If he'd known about Vienna."

"Probably not." Alma sniffed. She was finding her composure. Theo could see her making the effort. "But there're no foster parents in all the state who will love this little girl like we will. Even for two weeks."

"That's right."

As Theo finished speaking, the door opened and Mr. Green entered the room. He was with a nurse, who was pushing a tiny bassinet. Inside was a fair-skinned little girl swaddled in a white and pink blanket.

The attorney smiled. "This is Gracie Anne."

Theo and Alma were on their feet. They moved slowly to the little bed and stared at the baby. Her precious face and eyes. The way the newborn girl was wrapped up tight brought back a million memories for Theo. Vienna had been born with dark skin and a full head of hair. So of course his own daughter had never looked like this white infant. But the familiarity of the moment tripped up Theo's heart. He could feel it was the same way for Alma.

And for a moment he was back in 2004 and the baby in the bassinet was their daughter. Their Vienna.

They went over the details with the nurse, how much formula and how often. When to change the baby's diaper and what to look for if jaundice developed. Theo and Alma had fostered more babies than he could count. They knew the routine.

Finally they were given permission to move the baby girl to the car seat. After she was strapped in, Theo pulled his car around and like that they were headed home. The two of them with the infant in the backseat. Theo glanced at Alma and then checked the rearview mirror. And he was consumed by a single thought.

Somewhere in heaven, Vienna was celebrating.

23

Ashley was going through the T-shirts in Cole's middle drawer, enjoying the quiet, the way every item in his room reminded her of his growing-up years. Summer was almost over. The plan hadn't changed, at least not yet. Cole was headed to Liberty in a couple days. It had been two weeks since Elise had her baby and so far she was still on board with the adoption.

One more folded shirt and Ashley heard Cole run up the stairs looking for her.

"Mom." He stopped short, his eyes full of gratitude. "You didn't have to do this. I told you I'd take care of it tomorrow."

"Tomorrow, I'd rather have you spend time with the family. Your dad is grilling and we can play games. Just be together." She let her eyes hold his a few beats longer. "In no time you'll be gone."

"I know." His exhale sounded heavy. He came up beside her and looked through a stack of shirts. "I don't wear any of these."

"Exactly." She smiled at him. "I figured I could put

them in a box in your closet. You'd have an easier time packing and later—next summer—you could give the boxed ones away."

He nodded. "I like that." His tone held a certain depth, his countenance heavy.

Ashley understood. "You're going to Elise's?"

"Yes." He hesitated. "Her aunt and uncle are out for the night. I told her I'd stay with her till midnight."

"Right." Ashley couldn't imagine what Elise was going through. "The two weeks?"

"It's officially up then. At that exact minute." Cole folded his arms and looked at her. "All I know is I wouldn't want to be her."

Ashley set down another shirt and turned to him. "Do you think she'll change her mind?"

"I don't." He clenched his jaw. "We've talked about it. She's afraid the guy would still come around and try to be part of the baby's life, even though he terminated his rights. So it's a few things. The fact that she's not ready to be a mom, the way she really wants to go to NYU and start her life. And the reality that she doesn't want her baby anywhere near the father."

Relief and heartache mixed in equal amounts in Ashley's soul. She had come to really embrace Elise these last few months. Extending the same grace to the teenager that eighteen years ago had been extended to her. Her heart broke for Elise Walker.

But Ashley was beyond grateful that Cole wasn't

moving to Louisiana, wasn't going to soldier through keeping a promise he hadn't been mature enough to make in the first place.

Ashley didn't have many more of these moments with her oldest son. But she had this. She held out her hands to Cole. "Let's pray. For tonight. For Elise." She hesitated. "For the two of you."

Tears gathered in Cole's eyes. "I can't believe she's flying to New York tomorrow morning." He shrugged. "I'm not sure when I'll see her again."

It was that, too, of course. Tonight was goodbye for Cole and Elise. "Come on." She took hold of her son's hands. Then she prayed over the night, that Elise would know what to do, and that she would follow God's leading. And that Cole would have the words to say as they parted ways. That God would hold both of them in His caring hands. And that whatever His plans for Elise and Cole, they would hear God's voice tonight.

When she was done, Cole hugged her, the way he used to hug her when he was a little boy. As if in her arms he was still safe and young and without a care in the world.

Even if that was no longer true.

Ashley watched him go and she looked at the time on her phone. Thirty-eight hours. That's all they had left. From the first moment she held Cole in her arms as a baby through a lifetime of loving him, to this very day . . . in just thirty-eight hours he would pack up his Explorer and drive away. Ashley put her hand to her face and breathed in. *Please, God, help me get through this.*

Please. There was still one thing Ashley wanted to do that morning. Something she planned to read to Cole before he drove off.

Her mother's poem about the lasts.

If only Ashley could survive it.

• • •

THEY WERE FINISHING the best parts of Elise's burned lasagna, and she was doing everything she could to keep things light.

"So, I guess art majors get a whole locker full of supplies. Right from the first day." She picked through the charred noodles on her plate. "I'll be painting every minute of the day. It'll be hard to stop to eat."

Cole raised a blackened bite in her direction. He grinned. "Especially if you make this."

Elise laughed and the feeling washed over her like the summer sun. She was so tired of being sad. But she still had this day to get through. No doubt the hardest part was just ahead.

"How exactly did you get it this color?" Cole wore his Clear Creek baseball shirt and faded blue jeans. His face was tan from taking batting practice with his dad this past week. He dragged his fork through the casserole and a laugh slipped from his lips. "I mean, this is about as bad as I've seen."

"I told you." She shrugged, still laughing. Still loving how it felt. "I cooked it at four-fifty for three hours. Instead of three-fifty for one hour."

"An easy mistake." He chuckled harder. "I'm just glad you're an art student."

"Me, too."

The conversation went on that way through dessert and cleanup. It was ten o'clock when they sat down in the living room and faced each other. She wanted to laugh with Cole tonight. It was the reason she had decided to make him dinner. Her cooking skills weren't the best, so she knew they'd share a little humor over that. And they had.

Her aunt and uncle were out for the evening and Elise wanted to do something that would make tonight feel normal. Light and happy, the way she'd felt when she first met Cole. But now all the teasing about her dinner was as far in the past as every other beautiful moment she and Cole had ever shared.

The laughter had long since died.

"So." Cole took her hand. He worked his fingers through hers. "How are you feeling?"

How was she supposed to answer him? She looked down at the place where their hands were joined. They should've said their goodbyes yesterday. Today was the end of the two weeks, of course. Such a sad day, already. And on top of that, now she would have to let go of Cole Blake.

She reached out and touched the dark key that hung around Cole's neck. "I never asked you about this. It says 'Blake.'" Her eyes found his again. "Why do you wear it?"

Cole sat up straighter. He took hold of the key and

ran his thumb over his name. "It's for my future wife."
His eyes had never looked sadder. "A gift for her."

The truth hit Elise like a truck. She blinked a few
times and nodded. With every breath, she fought to
avoid crying. The key would never belong to her. It was
one more thing she had lost in all this.

He was still looking at her, still waiting for an answer.
How did she feel? She glanced up, stared into his beauti-
ful pure blue eyes. "I could never put it into words, Cole.
I feel . . . so much."

He nodded. They took their time. As if the hour
hand on the clock next to the TV wasn't racing toward
eleven. "I mean . . . about the baby." He checked the time
then turned back to her. "Are you having doubts?"

"Every minute." It was the truth. As often as Elise
drew a breath she was mindful that the decision was still
hers. That she could change her mind. A heartbeat didn't
happen without her feeling her tiny daughter in her
arms again.

"So . . . you might call Mr. Green?" Cole looked surprised. But his expression couldn't have been more sup-
portive. If she wanted to keep her baby, he would be first
in line to congratulate her, to tell her she could do it.

Her mama would be second. Elise was sure of that.

"I don't know, Cole." Her doubts had nothing to do
with keeping her baby or going through with the adoption. They weren't because she didn't feel supported by
the people she loved. It was hard to explain.

"Take your time." Cole's words came as a whisper. His

tan face and blond hair. The way his shoulders flexed with her hand in his. He had never looked more handsome.

She nodded. He was so kind to her. Even now. "I guess I'll always wonder if I made the right choice. I mean . . . to see her." She shifted her gaze to the ceiling, gathering her thoughts. Then she found his face again. "I held her. I looked into her eyes and kissed her cheek." She paused. "After you went to get your car that day." She kept her tears at bay again. "I'll never forget that."

Patience exuded from Cole. But she could see from his expression that he still didn't get it. "So you're not going to change your mind?"

"No." She smiled. "I want Gracie Anne to have what I never had. Two parents from the beginning. A mama and daddy ready for a baby." Nothing about this was easy. "No amount of support from my mom or you would change the one fact. I'm just not ready."

Cole looked like he was processing that. After all, his mother had raised him without a father for his first few years. And Elise's mother had done the same. All her life as a single parent. "Elise . . ." Cole's voice was almost a whisper. "Are you sure?"

"I am." Elise pressed her teeth together. "It's still so hard."

Something flickered in Cole's eyes. Understanding. Like in light of all she'd just said, the idea of her going through with the adoption made more sense. He squeezed her hand. "But it's what you want." It wasn't a question this time.

"Right." She sniffed. "Gracie Anne deserves a better story than I can give her." She let herself get lost in Cole's eyes. "I believe that with all my heart."

They were quiet for a while. Then they talked about Cole and his next few weeks at Liberty. He was going to try out for the baseball team, and based on the way he'd been hitting in his summer league games he felt good about his chances.

Elise understood. Cole was a different player than he'd been this past spring. When he was thinking he might be a father come August. The pressure wasn't something he'd ever complained about. But it was there. That much was obvious.

"Maybe . . . you can come watch one of my games." He faced her and took her other hand. "You know . . . if I make the team."

"Yeah. Maybe." Elise had expected him to say things like this. But she knew the truth. At Liberty, Cole would find someone like him. Someone good and true and pure, without the baggage Elise carried.

"I know what you're thinking." He leaned closer and put his hand alongside her face. "You think I'll meet someone else and forget about you."

No one had been able to read her the way he could. "It's okay if you do."

"I'm not planning on it." He seemed careful not to make any promises. "It's just . . . college, you know?"

Elise nodded. "I'll be in New York and you'll be in Virginia." She remembered something. "Did I tell you they asked me to stay for the summer next year? I'll work three art camps and make enough money to pay for one semester when my sophomore year starts."

"Elise! That's amazing!" A smile filled his face. "That's my girl."

Later when Elise looked back she knew she wouldn't remember everything they'd talked about tonight or how the time went from ten o'clock to 11:55 so quickly. But she would remember forever the way Cole looked at her. The feel of his fingers between hers. The compassion in his voice.

Elise took a slow breath and glanced at the clock. "Five minutes."

"Yes." Cole kept his eyes on her. "You okay? You sure?"

"I am." Elise had known every day for the past two weeks how she would spend these final minutes. She stood. "Can you hold me, Cole? Please?"

He was on his feet immediately. He took her in his strong arms and rocked her ever so slightly. The way they were standing, Elise could still see the clock. 11:56. The second hand raced past the three and on down to the six.

The way Elise wanted to spend these minutes was by simply remembering her, one more time. In the chair in the hospital room, her baby girl cradled in her arms, close to her heart. Her baby was still hers. Four more minutes. And once more she could feel the warm weight of her daughter, smell her skin and her infant breath.

Another glance. 11:58.

She was making the right decision. What she'd told Cole was the truth. Gracie Anne deserved a better life. Two parents who wanted a baby more than their next breath. And maybe one day decades from now she'd meet Aaron and Lucy, and she'd thank them. And she could tell Gracie Anne to her face how she had made this decision for one reason.

Out of the greatest love Elise had ever known.

11:59.

She could see it all again. Her baby girl opening her eyes, looking into Elise's as if to tell her it was okay, this was the best decision. This was all going to be okay. Better than okay. And she was lifting her daughter to her face, brushing her cheek against her baby's velvet-smooth skin. And the nurse was coming to get her and she was kissing the tiny infant's face and her cheek.

She and Cole turned and watched the clock together as the second hand made the climb past nine and ten and eleven. And just like that it happened.

Midnight.

Elise closed her eyes and let her forehead fall against Cole's chest. But instead of tears, she felt the most beautiful peace. As if God Himself was standing beside her, cheering her on, holding her up. She pictured Aaron and Lucy—the couple who had given her little girl the most beautiful name. Gracie Anne.

And Elise smiled. Because from this minute on Elise's baby wouldn't only be a child Aaron and Lucy got to name.

She would be theirs.

Forever and ever and ever more.

• • •

COLE HAD NEVER known anyone braver than Elise Walker, the way she had handled this night. Everything from her humor earlier to these last five minutes. Watching the clock forever erase any chance of Elise being able to change her mind.

Watching her let her tiny daughter go. For always.

It was a few minutes after midnight, and he needed to leave. Elise had to finish packing and Cole had to do the same. Their futures were waiting for them.

"You okay?" Cole felt like he'd been asking her that all night. But he wanted to know. Especially now. With the two weeks behind them.

"Yes." Tears welled in her eyes. She blinked and shook her head a little. "I promised myself I wouldn't cry."

He chuckled. "Me, too."

"Crazy, right?" She laughed even as two tears made their way down her face. "I'm so happy, Cole. Really. There's no reason to cry."

It was one of those moments when the best thing he could do was listen. He searched her eyes. "Mmmm."

"I mean it." She released him and did a spin in her aunt and uncle's living room. "My baby girl's going to have the best life." She raised her brow, her eyes bright. "Can you imagine how happy she's going to be? Aaron and Lucy will tell her about Jesus and about how I loved her enough to let her go."

She was celebrating the moment, and Cole thought the world of her for it. But tears streamed down her face even while her voice filled with joy. Rivers of tears.

"Gracie Anne has parents now! It's official." Elise raised her hands in the air and a few sobs slipped from her lips. "Cole. Gracie Anne has parents!" The wind in her happiness seemed to fade. She came to him again and fell into his arms. "Maybe someday, right?"

He wasn't sure what she meant so he eased back and searched her eyes. "Maybe someday?"

"You and me." Her tears wouldn't stop. "When you have your medical degree and I'm a famous artist in SoHo or Chelsea."

Tears blurred his eyes now, but he smiled. With his thumb he pushed her dark hair off her forehead and stared into her eyes. "Yeah, Elise." He wanted her, wanted her to know that he loved her more than a friend. "Maybe someday."

"Will you do something for me, Cole? Before you go?" She was shaking, clearly dreading the goodbye ahead as much as he was.

He took a step closer and framed her face with his hand. Her skin was soft beneath his touch. The attraction between them had never been stronger. "Will you kiss me, Cole? Just once?"

Long before this moment, Cole had made up his

mind. He wouldn't kiss her. No matter how bad he wanted to, he couldn't. It wasn't fair to either of them. Not when their futures were taking them in such different directions. But that plan was out the window now. There were only the two of them in this empty house, Elise looking like a vision and wanting just one thing from him. "Elise . . ." His resolve was wearing thin, his breath soft against her face. "We shouldn't."

"I don't mean like that." She closed the distance between them, her eyes never leaving his. "A kiss goodbye." Her smile was the saddest he'd ever seen. "God would be okay with that. Don't you think?"

Cole didn't need any more convincing. He took gentle hold of her face with his other hand and brought his lips to hers. The kiss lasted longer than he intended, a handful of seconds when there was only Elise and him and a life and love that had almost been.

But would almost certainly never be.

He drew back, the feeling of her lips fresh on his, the heat in his cheeks something he had never known before. He was more sure than ever that he needed to leave. Now. Before he kissed her again.

She walked him to the door and they hugged once more. She wasn't crying now and he wasn't, either. As if—in the end—they both had agreed to this goodbye. Because it was the best decision.

Just like Elise's choice to let Gracie Anne go to the adoptive couple.

"I love you, Elise." He touched his lips to hers one

more time. Not the hot kiss from a minute ago. But the final way he wanted her to remember him. As someone who had always liked her more than a friend. Someone who loved her.

"I love you, too." She touched his face, and the feel of her fingertips lasted long after she took a step back.

They both waved and he walked to his car. As he climbed in and drove away, Cole thought about the kiss, his first kiss. Their last kiss. And he felt something grab hold of him, something he'd never felt before. He didn't have to wonder what it was. He would remember this feeling forever.

The feeling of a broken heart.

24

They decided to hand off little Gracie Anne at the local social services office. Mr. Green had set up the meeting for ten that morning. The two weeks had ended, just hours before, at midnight.

Gracie Anne belonged to her adoptive parents now.

Theo and Alma had taken shifts holding her since she woke up that morning. It was Theo's turn now. He cradled her against his heart and closed his eyes. For one more minute the baby wasn't a foster child headed to her forever home.

It was his Vienna. The way it felt to hold her when she first came into their lives. He steadied himself and looked at the baby. Her eyes were open. Pretty, and full of light and love and hope. She was almost smiling at him.

"You know what you did, little one?" He nuzzled his face against hers. "You changed our lives."

Alma walked up. She was ready, her purse over her shoulder. "You tell her, honey." She leaned over the infant and smiled. "Uncle Theo is right, baby girl. God knew we needed this time with you."

Together they loaded her in the car seat and set out

for the state office. Theo still couldn't believe all that had happened these past two weeks. From the first night, having Gracie Anne was perfect proof that Vienna was right.

They were supposed to get back into foster care.

But with Vienna gone, they had taken the idea a step further. Alma gave her notice at work. She wouldn't return in the fall. Not only that, but there was a For Sale sign in the front yard.

Vienna wouldn't want them drifting around this house like a couple of ghosts, lost in memories of yesterday. Aching for her, missing her. Seeing her in the kitchen getting an apple from the refrigerator or in her bedroom doing homework on her bed. Dancing across the foyer and grinning at them from the dining room table.

What sort of life would that be? How would it honor everything Vienna stood for?

So three days after they brought Gracie Anne home, Theo had made a call. He'd heard about a Christian children's ministry a few miles away, not far from Clear Creek High. The campus was made up of fifty acres and six houses. Each house needed parents willing to make a full-time job out of caring for teenage foster kids. The ministry was in dire need, actually.

Theo grinned at the memory. He took Alma's hand and looked at her. "First of September."

"Yes." Alma's smile started in her eyes and filled her face. "I can't wait."

The house they would run had an office so Theo

could carry on his job, doing sales from home. And Alma would work full-time with the teens. The ones who didn't have parents.

All because of Gracie Anne and these last two weeks.

"God is good, Alma." The Spirit of the Lord was all around them. Theo could feel Him. "Vienna would be so happy."

"She *is* so happy." Alma looked back at the baby in the mirror on her visor. Then she turned to Theo again. "He knew exactly what we needed."

"A little baby girl who helped us remember how to love again." Theo blinked back happy tears. "Even if only for two weeks."

● ● ●

ON THE WAY into the social services office, Lucy stopped and stared at the door. Just stared at it. "I . . . I can't believe it."

Aaron stood beside her. He glanced at the knob and then at her, clearly anxious. Their baby girl was waiting on the other side. "Honey . . . can we, you know, talk about this later?"

Lucy uttered the softest laugh. "I mean, I can't believe it." She looked into his eyes. In all their marriage she'd never felt more in love with him. "Thank you, Aaron. For trusting God. For never giving up."

"You're welcome." He gave her a quick kiss and put his arm around her. "We don't want to be late, Lucy. Come on."

She laughed again. "You do realize our entire life is going to change when we walk into that room, right?"

"Yes." He looked ready to explode with happiness. "Please. This isn't the time."

He was right. Lucy followed behind as they approached the door and stepped into the office.

A kind-looking couple in maybe their late forties sat in a pair of chairs. The man was holding Gracie Anne.

Lucy wondered if she might collapse here on the floor. Her heart would stop and she'd never get the chance to hold her daughter. *God, please, give me the strength.* Ten years had led to this moment.

But there was no script on how it would play out.

The man stood and shifted the baby to one arm. Then with his free hand, he shook Aaron's. "Theo Brown."

"Aaron Williams."

Lucy introduced herself to the man's wife and as they finished their hellos, Theo looked into Gracie Anne's eyes. "God used this little girl to save us. In more ways than anyone will ever know." He smiled at Aaron and then Lucy. "She's a miracle baby, for sure."

You have no idea, Lucy wanted to tell him. And for a moment she thought about the way this couple must feel. It wasn't only Elise who had to give up her beautiful baby girl. But this couple, too. She looked from the man to his wife. "Thank you. For stepping in. For helping us this way."

"The pleasure was ours." Alma put her arm around her husband. "Honey." She smiled. "I think they'd like their daughter now."

Mr. Green stepped into the office. "You're here!" He grinned at Aaron and then Lucy. "I have to tell you, I really wasn't sure about this one."

"I was." Aaron looked at their daughter and then at the attorney. "God told me we were going to have a baby. He just waited till now so we'd have the *right* one." Aaron turned to little Gracie Anne again. She was still in Theo Brown's arms. Aaron touched her cheek then turned to Lucy. "You take her first, honey."

Lucy stepped up and held out her arms. She wasn't shaking or trembling. She didn't feel cold or sick to her stomach. She felt perfect. Whole and content and like she was standing smack in the middle of the happiest moment in all her life.

"Bye, little one." Theo handed her to Lucy and eased back. "Someday, my wife and I would love to get dinner with you. So we can tell you our story."

The feel of their daughter in her arms was like nothing Lucy had ever known. Like she'd been given permission to breathe fully for the first time. Lucy couldn't take her eyes off the infant. *She's Yours, God. And You gave her to us. How can I ever thank You?*

Aaron was talking to Theo, telling him that yes, of course, they'd love to get together, love to hear the couple's story, and he was saying how their Gracie Anne could never have enough aunts and uncles. But all Lucy could think about was the infant in her arms. And that no one could ever take her away from them.

She was still consumed by that single thought when

Aaron came alongside her, one arm around her shoulders, the other under Gracie Anne. Their baby. Their daughter.

The Browns said goodbye, and Mr. Green had final papers for them to sign. But the moment didn't last long, and in a rush of joy and gratitude and disbelief, they were snapping Gracie Anne's car seat into their SUV and heading home.

The three of them.

Everything about the morning was about to be full of firsts. Gracie Anne's first car ride home, her first time inside their house. Her first bottle with the two of them. First nap in the nursery. All of it was just ahead.

Through every minute of the ride home, Lucy couldn't stop smiling. Aaron, too. They were like a couple of kids whose every wish had finally come true. Most moments Lucy didn't believe it was really happening. Yesterday they were at work and wondering if Elise would change her mind.

And today they were parents.

The day after Gracie Anne was born, Lucy had talked to her supervisor. She wanted to give a tentative two weeks' notice. If the birth mother didn't change her mind, she would be done on August 14 and she wouldn't be back. Not for the foreseeable future.

She was a mother now. There wouldn't be enough time in the day for her new job. Not enough moments to rock her daughter and feed her and sing to her. Aaron had already been given permission to work one day a week from home. This was where their happily ever after would begin.

Page one in the best chapter of their lives.

They arrived at their house, walked inside with Gracie Anne and looked at each other. Aaron couldn't stop smiling. "There's something I want to do first, before anything else."

Not for a moment did Lucy have to ask what. She already knew. And with Gracie Anne in her arms, she followed Aaron upstairs to the nursery. The room that had for years caused Lucy so much pain.

The room where Aaron sought the heart of God day after day. Never once giving up.

"This place will always be sacred to me." Aaron's voice fell to a whisper. Gracie Anne was sleeping. They would tell her later about the day they brought her home, and how they could do nothing but come here first.

"For me, too." Not because Lucy had always believed God would come through. Most of the time she was racked with doubt. But because this room was where she watched her husband fight for their family. Where his faith grew stronger with every passing season.

And because of that, in time so had hers.

Aaron lowered himself to his knees and he helped Lucy do the same thing. And there, with their baby daughter nestled between them, they whispered the words that mattered most. They thanked God for His faithfulness and for working out every detail of this adoption, and they praised Him for the fact that all along, Aaron had never given up.

They whispered thanks to God for helping Elise make the decision that adoption was best for both her and her baby girl. And they prayed for Elise, that in the years ahead she would know this was the right decision and that God would comfort her whenever she doubted.

Finally they thanked the Lord for every wonderful day ahead and the privilege of raising their very own daughter. Gracie Anne. Through all the seasons to come, the learning to walk and talk and ride a bike and the school days. The teaching and singing and playing together. They thanked God for all of it. From now till her high school graduation.

A million years from now.

25

Ashley could remember what it was like, being a young mother and feeling sure the day Cole would move off to college was still a million years away. At least a million.

But now, as she watched Landon and Cole pack the last of his things into his SUV, it didn't feel like that at all.

A blink. That's all it was on the journey of raising a child. Just a blink.

All the kids had taken turns moving things to Cole's Explorer and now they were gathered around the dining room table. One final breakfast with Cole before he left. That was the plan.

Ashley didn't want to spend Cole's last hour making food. So Amy was cooking instead. Scrambled eggs and sausage and sliced oranges. Janessa and Devin were in charge of the toast.

And Ashley, well, she was doing what she had planned to do this morning. She was leaning against the doorframe watching Cole and Landon pack. Watching the easy way they had with each other, and the smiles that came more readily for guys on a day like this.

She wasn't crying. Not yet. She'd had this date circled on the calendar since Cole had been accepted to Liberty. Along the way there were whole months when she wondered if Cole might really move to Louisiana with Elise. But God had heard her prayers and Landon's. Cole's and Elise's.

Things had worked out in the best possible way. Not that it was easy. The night Cole said goodbye to Elise, he'd come home and broken down in her arms. Ashley didn't have any clever sayings or easy answers. Heartbreak was hard.

It broke her own heart to see Cole so upset.

But the next morning he had found her and Landon again. His eyes were clear and he smiled at them. "Elise landed safely in New York. She had an early flight."

Ashley had waited, not sure how Cole was handling all this.

"How do you feel, Son?" Landon had spoken up first.

Cole nodded and thought for a moment. Then his smile fell off a little. "Sad." He shrugged. "That's just honest. This whole thing has been sad." He paused for a few seconds. "But I feel good, too. This is the right thing. For both of us."

That had been yesterday, and now here they were living out the moment Ashley had dreaded since she'd brought Cole home from the hospital. Back when she thought she had forever.

Cole and Landon came up the walkway, laughing about something. When they reached the door Landon nudged Cole. "Tell your mother."

"Girls." He shook his head, still laughing. "Carolyn Everly texted me. Her car broke down. Like completely."

"Her dad thinks it's the transmission." Landon chuckled. "So good thing Cole's SUV isn't totally full."

The situation finally made sense. "You're taking Carolyn to Liberty?"

"Looks like it." Cole shook his head, a silly dazed look on his face. "We'll be packed to the roof, but her dad says he'll make sure we're safe."

Landon checked his watch. "We better get this breakfast going. It'll take you nine hours to get to Lynchburg once you and Carolyn hit the road."

Ashley's head was spinning. Carolyn Everly? How had she missed the fact that Carolyn was going to Liberty? She had been one of Cole's friends all through school. This new development filled Ashley's heart with possibilities, but she didn't voice them. There were years for God to shape things with Cole and Carolyn, or whomever He might bring into Cole's life.

Even possibly Elise somewhere down the road.

They gathered around the dining room table and Cole hugged Amy first. "Look at this! It's a feast. Thank you, Amy." Next he gave Devin a hug and Janessa. "Thanks, you two. I'll always remember this."

Their three youngest basked in the warmth of Cole's compliments, as Ashley shared a look with Landon. This was why they were going to miss Cole so much. He was the best big brother, and such a wonderful son. As the others took their seats, Ashley walked to the cupboard

over the computer and pulled out the book of letters
from her mother.

"I have something I want to share with you, Cole."
She sat at the table and opened the book to the page
that held her mother's poem. "A long time ago, your
grandma Elizabeth wrote these letters for me and my
siblings."

The kids were listening.

Landon put his hand on her shoulder. Ashley was
grateful. He always knew when she needed his support.
This was one of those times. She looked at Cole. "Before
she died, your grandma took a poem she had written for
your uncle Luke the night before his wedding . . . and
she rewrote it. She wanted me to read it to you kids the
day you drove away to college."

"That's today for Cole!" Janessa didn't look happy
about the reality. She gave Cole a sad smile. "Unless you
change your mind, Coley."

A light round of laughter came from each of them.
"So . . . before we pray, before we eat, I want to read this
from your grandma Elizabeth. It's a poem that speaks to
a truth we all need to remember. The importance of
every day."

Tears sprang to Ashley's eyes before she read the first
line. *Please, God, help me do this. Give me my voice.* She
took a slow breath and gradually her control returned.
"Long ago you came to me a miracle of firsts. First smiles
and teeth and baby steps, a sunbeam on the burst."

Ashley looked around the table at Devin and Amy

and Janessa and finally Cole. Then she kept reading. "But one day you will move away and leave to me your past. And I will be left thinking of a lifetime of your lasts."

The next part of the poem spoke of those very lasts. It was all Ashley could do to get through it. "The last night when you woke up crying, needing to be walked, when last you crawled up with your blanket wanting to be rocked." Ashley lifted her eyes to Cole and then back to the poem. "Precious simple moments and bright flashes from your past. Would I have held on longer if I'd known they were your last?"

Line after line, the poem walked through the life of a child. The very life Ashley had lived with Cole. The last at-bat in Little League, last soccer goal, last piano lesson. Last vacation to the lake.

"The last time that you need my help with details of a dance. Last time that you ask me for advice about romance." Ashley could feel the sadness in her smile as she looked at Cole. "The last time that you talk to me about your hopes and dreams." She hesitated. "Last time that you wear a jersey for your high school team."

Landon put his arm around her. Ashley glanced at the other kids, as she pictured the moments her mother had written about. Almost as if she'd been there to see them lived out.

The final part was the hardest. *Help me, Lord. This is important. Please.*

She took a deep breath. "For come some bright fall morning you'll be going far away. College life will beckon in a brilliant sort of way. One last hug, one last goodbye, one quick and hurried kiss. One last time to understand just how much you'll be missed." She held her breath. "I'll watch you go and think how fast our time together passed. So let me hold on longer, God, to every . . . precious last."

She closed the book and returned it to the spot in the cupboard. When she faced the table again, everyone was standing. "Mom." Cole held out his arms. "Breakfast can wait."

And with that, they formed a group hug and Cole led them in prayer. "Father, You know how much I'm going to miss this." He had his arms around Ashley and Landon, his siblings tucked into the middle of the circle. A smile filled Cole's voice. "But You also know that this family always has held on longer. Every precious last was something we appreciated. Because that's what love does." He took a breath. "So thank You, God, for this family. And thank You for the good times ahead. This isn't an ending. It's a beginning. In Jesus' name, amen."

Ashley replayed Cole's words through breakfast and as they walked him out to his SUV. How wise was her son? And how faithful was God to let this be how this chapter of Cole's childhood came to a close?

Landon was beside her again, his arm around her. Strong, reassuring. Always there for her. He smiled at Cole. "We're all coming for family weekend."

"That's right!" Devin punched his fist in the air. "We get to see a football game!"

Amy laughed. "We get to see Cole. That's all that matters."

"Right." Janessa stood by Amy. She still looked a little confused. Like Cole couldn't really be moving away. "And you'll be back every Sunday for church, right, Coley?"

"No, sweetie." Cole bent down and kissed her cheek. "But I'll be home for breaks. Thanksgiving and Christmas. And a really long one every summer."

Janessa relaxed a little. "Okay." She didn't sound quite sure.

It was time for goodbyes. Cole started with Devin and then Amy, Janessa and Landon. He saved his goodbye for Ashley till last. "Mom." He searched her eyes. "It's going to be okay. I can FaceTime you."

"True." Ashley ordered herself not to cry. Not now. "I'm happy, honey. You know that, right? Liberty is the best place for you." She smiled at Landon. "Your dad and I have always thought that."

Cole nodded. "It is. I can't wait." He pulled her gently into his arms, her tall son, and for a long time he held her. The way she had held him when he was a baby or when he skinned his knee when he was a toddler or a hundred other times.

"Bye, Mom. I love you." He looked at her once more.

"I love you, too." She stepped back and held up her hand. "Call us when you get there."

"I will." He climbed into his Explorer and gave them all a final wave.

Then he drove off.

Ashley waited until Landon and the kids had gone in the house before finding her favorite chair on the porch and letting the tears come. She wasn't crying because she was sad this part of Cole's life was over. The two of them—all of them—had enjoyed every single day. There was nothing to be sad about. Rather, they were happy tears. Yes, that's what they were. Happy tears because she'd been blessed to ever have Cole at all.

Because God had spared him and because in all His goodness, the Lord had allowed her the privilege of being his mother. Ashley Baxter, of all people. And because even this morning her son had showed all of them his maturity and confidence. He was ready for this, ready for all that was ahead. And most of all her tears were happy because like Cole said this wasn't an ending. It truly was a beginning.

The most beautiful beginning ever.

• • •

COLE HADN'T SPENT much time thinking about what this moment would be like, watching his home fade away in the rearview mirror. But now that he was living it, he could understand what his mother was feeling.

What his grandma Elizabeth must've felt when she wrote the poem about the lasts. He understood a little better now. Tears stung his eyes, but he didn't cry. He was too excited to be sad.

He didn't want to think about the past as he drove to

Lynchburg today. He wanted to think about the future. The new beginning. Classes he was going to take and the tryout next week with the baseball team. And catching up with Carolyn Everly, a friend he'd nearly lost track of this year.

Yes, he would miss his family every day, and he would look forward to the time in the not so distant future when he would come home again on break. But things would be different. Because he would never be a kid again, never have that first day of middle school or the years when he'd played baseball for Clear Creek High.

Those were gone.

And so were the days of his final semester and the weeks of this past summer. Cole leaned back and kept his eyes on the road. The radio was tuned to a love song channel. Something he'd listened to for the last few days. And as Cole turned right on the highway on the way to Carolyn's house, a pretty melody began.

He glanced at the console. Barbra Streisand's "The Way We Were." The tune was familiar, so Cole turned it up.

Memories . . . light the corners of my mind . . .

The song continued, every line speaking to the hurting places in Cole's soul.

As the music played on, a thousand beautiful moments filled his heart. Beautiful and tragic and deep. The bowling and bike rides and ice cream. And other crazy intense moments. Times that had taken him to possibilities he never would've considered otherwise. Marriage. Being a father to another guy's baby. Giving up Liberty.

Every moment anchored around the first girl he'd ever loved.

A breathtaking girl with long dark hair and piercing blue eyes and a laugh that sounded like summer and sunshine all mixed together. Even on the coldest winter day. A girl with a song on her voice and a heartbreaking past. The girl who would forever be his first love, his first crush. His first kiss. The girl he would never forget as long as he lived.

Elise Walker.

ACKNOWLEDGMENTS

No book comes together without a great deal of teamwork, passion and determination. That was definitely true for *Two Weeks!* Weeks of debate were spent over whether the title worked, and if it would resonate with you. Same with the cover image. We knew something great was going to happen with this book because it took so long to pull together what you now hold in your hands.

On that note, I can't leave *Two Weeks* and the tearful, beautiful experience it has been for me without thanking the people who made it possible.

First, a special thanks to my amazing publisher, Beth Adams, Becky Nesbitt, and the team at Howard Books. Also to the team at Simon & Schuster—Carolyn Reidy and the rest of her gifted team who bring my books to you! I think often of our times together in New York and the way your collective creative brilliance always becomes a game changer. You clearly desire to raise the bar at every turn. Thank you for that. It's an honor to work with you!

This book is one of my favorites ever because of the talent and passion of my editor, Becky Nesbitt. Becky, you have known me since our kids were little. Since the

Baxters began. How many authors actually look forward to the editing process? With you, it's a dream. And always you find ways to make my book better. Over and over and over again. Thank you for that! I am the most blessed author for the privilege of working with you.

Also, thanks to my design team—Kyle and Kelsey Kupecky—whose unmatched talent in the industry is recognized from Los Angeles to New York. Very simply you are the best in the business! My website, social media, video trailers, and newsletter along with so many other aspects of my touring and writing are top of the book business because of you two. Thank you for working your own dreams around mine. I love you and I thank God for you every single day.

A huge thanks to my sisters, Tricia and Susan, along with my mom, who give their whole hearts to helping me love my readers. Tricia as my executive assistant for the past decade, and Susan, for many years, as the president of my Facebook Online Book Club and Team KK. And, Mom, thank you for being Queen of the Readers. Anyone who has ever sent me an email and received a response from you is blessed indeed. All three of you are making a tremendous impact in changing this world for the better. I love you and I thank God for each of you!

Thanks also to Tyler for joining with me to write screenplays and books like *Best Family Ever*, a Baxter Family Children Story. You are a gifted writer, Ty. I can't wait to see your work on the shelves and on the big screen. Maybe one day soon! Love you so much!

Also, thank you to my office assistant, Aurora Galvin. You create space for me to write! This storytelling wouldn't be possible without you.

I'm grateful to my Team KK members, who use social media to tell the world about my upcoming releases and who hang out on my Facebook page answering reader questions. I appreciate each of you so much. May God bless you for your service to the work of Life-Changing Fiction™.

There is a final stage in writing a book. The galley pages come to me, and I send them to a team of my most dedicated reader friends. This team volunteers to read my books first and fast, catching typos or other glitches that still remain. A big thank-you to the test team— Hope, Donna, Renette, Zac, Sheila, my sister Sue, and my nieces Shannon, Melissa and Kristen. Thank you for loving my work, and thanks for your availability to help out down the stretch!

Also, my books only happen with the help of my family, especially my amazing husband, Donald. Honey, thank you for your spiritual wisdom and leadership in our home, and thanks for talking through books like this one from the outline to the editing. The countless ways you help me when I'm on deadline make all the difference. I love you!

And over all this, thanks to a man who has believed in my career for two decades, my amazing agent, Rick Christian of Alive Literary Agency. From the beginning, Rick, you've told me to dream big, set my sights high. Movies, TV series, worldwide reach. All for God and through Him. You imagined it all, believed it, and prayed for it alongside me and my family. You believed. While I write, you work behind the scenes on film projects and my work with Liberty University, the Baxter family TV series, and details regarding every book I've ever written. You are brilliant and driven, compassionate and dedicated. I used to dream of having you as my agent. Now I'm the only author who does. God is amazing. Thank you, Rick, and thank you for praying for me and my family. That most of all.

Finally, my greatest thanks to God Almighty, who is First and Last and all things in between. I write for You, through You, and because of You. Thank You with my whole being.

Dear Reader Friend,

I dreamed up the idea of *Two Weeks* when my youngest son, Austin, was heading off to Liberty University. When we were on the verge of being empty nesters. It occurred to me—what if Cole met a beautiful, deeply troubled girl, a girl in a situation similar to the one Cole's mom was in before she had him?

Not long after, I was on the road at a book signing, and a reader friend stepped up and told me that we had helped inspire her family to adopt an infant. "But," she told me, "it was a struggle because we couldn't bring him home for two weeks. In my state, that's how long the birth mother has to change her mind."

Suddenly all I could do was think of those words: *two weeks.*

My heart raced at the emotions of those fourteen days and the lives that hung in the balance on a single teenager's decision. It was from that place that the story took root and grew. Before long it simply had to be told. And what a perfect way to show Cole as the guy giving Elise support during that time.

A wonderful way to share in Cole's final semester of high school before moving to college. I tell you, I cried when I wrote this book and through every stage of editing. It's deep. It holds pieces of my soul.

You may wonder about the poem Ashley read to Cole as he left for college. The poem is actually a picture book I wrote years ago called *Let Me Hold You Longer.* It's available online and in bookstores. Tyndale Publishers brought it to life when it was only a poem I had written for *my* kids. And they graciously allowed me to use it here, for Ashley and Cole.

As you close the cover on this book, think about who you can share it with. A friend whose child is grown and heading off to school? A sister who can't seem to have the baby she's always prayed for? Someone struggling to make sense of a loss? Or just that person who loves to read.

A book dies if it's left on the shelf. So please share it.

As with many of my other books, this novel gave you the chance to spend a little time with our favorite family—the Baxters. And now you are about to have the chance to watch the first season of *The Baxters* on TV. Something I only dreamed about back when God gave me these very special characters. The series is expected to become one of the most beloved of all time. I know you'll be watching.

You won't find the Baxters in my upcoming book—*Someone Like You*. It's a stand-alone love story that is perhaps the most unique, breathtaking story I've written yet. I can't wait to tell you more!

Visit my website, KarenKingsbury.com, to find out more about *The Baxters* on TV and about my other books. At my website, you can sign up for my free weekly newsletter. These emails come straight to you and offer pieces of my writing you will not find anywhere else. Sign up today! You can also stay encouraged by following me on social media.

Remember, the Baxter family isn't just my family. It's yours. And with them at the middle of our lives, we are all connected. Until next time . . . I'm praying for you.

Thanks for being part of the family.

Love you all!

THE BAXTER FAMILY:
YESTERDAY AND TODAY

F or some of you, this is your first time with the Baxter family. Please know you don't have to read any other Baxter books to read this one. Like my other recent titles, *Two Weeks* stands alone! But if you read this and want to start at the beginning, the starting place is *Redemption*.

That's where the adventure of the Baxters begins.

Whether you've known the Baxters for years or are just meeting them now, here's a quick summary of the family, their kids and their ages. Also, because these characters are fictional, I've taken some liberty with their ages. Let's just assume these are their current ages.

Now, let me introduce you to—or remind you of—the Baxter family:

• • •

THE BAXTERS BEGAN in Bloomington, Indiana, and most of the family still lives there today.

The Baxter house is on ten acres outside of town, with a winding creek that runs through the backyard. It has a wraparound porch and a pretty view and the memories of a lifetime. The house was one John and Elizabeth Baxter moved into when their children were young. They raised their family here. Today it is owned by one of their daughters—Ashley—and her husband, Landon Blake. It is still the place where the extended Baxter family gathers for special celebrations.

· · ·

JOHN BAXTER: JOHN is the patriarch of the Baxter family. Formerly an emergency room doctor and professor of medicine at Indiana University, he's now retired. John's first wife, Elizabeth, died long ago from a recurrence of cancer. Years later, John married Elaine, and the two live in Bloomington.

· · ·

DAYNE MATTHEWS, 44: Dayne is the oldest son of John and Elizabeth. Dayne was born out of wedlock and given up for adoption at birth. His adoptive parents died in a small plane crash when he was 18. Years later, Dayne became a very visible and popular movie star. At age 30, he hired an attorney to find his birth parents—John and Elizabeth Baxter. He had a moment with Elizabeth in the hospital before she died, and years later he connected with the rest of his biological family. Dayne is married to Katy, 42. The couple has three children: Sophie, 9; Egan, 7; and Blaise, 5. They are very much part of the Baxter family, and they split time between Los Angeles and Bloomington.

● ● ●

BROOKE BAXTER WEST, 42: Brooke is a pediatrician in Bloomington, married to Peter West, 42, also a doctor. The couple has two daughters: Maddie, 21, and Hayley, 18. The family experienced a tragedy when Hayley suffered a drowning accident at age 4. She recovered miraculously, but still has disabilities caused by the incident.

● ● ●

KARI BAXTER TAYLOR, 40: Kari is a designer, married to Ryan Taylor, 42, football coach at Clear Creek High School. The couple has three children: Jessie, 18; RJ, 12; and Annie, 9. Kari had a crush on Ryan when the two were in middle school. They dated through college, and then broke up over a misunderstanding. Kari married a man she met in college, Tim Jacobs, but some years into their marriage he had an affair. The infidelity resulted in his murder at the hands of a stalker. The tragedy devastated Kari, who was pregnant at the time with their first child, Jessie. Ryan came back into her life around the same time, and years later he and Kari married. They live in Bloomington.

● ● ●

ASHLEY BAXTER BLAKE, 38: Ashley is the former black sheep of the Baxter family, married to Landon Blake, 38, who works for the Bloomington Fire Department. The couple has four children: Cole, 18; Amy, 13; Devin, 11; and Janessa, 7. As a young single mom, Ashley was jaded against God and her family when she reconnected with her firefighter friend Landon, who had secretly always loved her. Eventually Ashley and Landon married and Landon adopted Cole. Together, the couple had two children—Devin and Janessa. Between those children, they lost a baby girl, Sarah Marie, at birth to anencephaly. Amy, Ashley's niece, came to live with them a few years ago after Amy's parents, Erin Baxter Hogan and Sam Hogan, and Amy's three sisters, were killed in a horrific car accident. Amy was the only survivor. Ashley and Landon and their family live in Bloomington, in the old Baxter house, where Ashley and her siblings were raised. Ashley still paints and is successful in selling her work in local boutiques.

• • •

LUKE BAXTER, 36: Luke is a lawyer, married to Reagan Baxter, 36, a blogger. The couple has three children: Tommy, 16; Malin, 11; and Johnny, 7. Luke met Reagan in college. They experienced a major separation early on, after getting pregnant with Tommy while they were dating. Eventually Luke and Reagan married, though they could not have more children. Malin and Johnny are both adopted.

ONE CHANCE
FOUNDATION

The Kingsbury family is passionate about seeing orphans all over the world brought home to their forever families. As a result, Karen created a charitable group called the One Chance Foundation.

This foundation was inspired by the memory of her father, Ted C. Kingsbury. Ted always said, "Life is not a dress rehearsal. We have one chance to love, one chance to truly live!"

Karen often tells her reader friends, "You have one chance to write the story of your life!"™ Now, with Karen's One Chance Foundation, readers can join her in the belief that all of us have one chance to make a difference in the lives of orphans.

In the Bible, James 1:27 says people with pure and faultless religion look after orphans. The One Chance Foundation was created with that truth in mind.

If you are interested in giving to Karen's One Chance Foundation and having your dedication printed in one of

Karen's upcoming novels, visit www.KarenKingsbury .com. Below are dedications from some of Karen's reader friends who have contributed to the One Chance Foundation:

- To my twin sister, Jeanice. She passed away in 2008. I will miss her forever and talk to her all the time and know she hears me in heaven. Janice Nelson

- In memory of Allison Holt, our brave CF warrior who fought the good fight & finished the race. How you loved reading these books. You're forever in our hearts! Mom, Dad & Sister (Sharon, Bill & Kristen)

- Alyssa Mae—You are my Greatest Joy and I am so proud of you. I love you Forever and Always, Mom (Rebecca Lentz)

- To our dear Addisson, May you continue to be blessed by the message of love. Grandma and Grandpap

- In honor of my husband, Gary Q. Geist. 30 years in the US Navy & retired as a Captain (06). Battling Alzheimer's for the last 8 years, I would like him to be remembered as the great Father & Husband he is. Love, Brenda

- To an Amazing Wife and Mother, Thank you for everything you do! We love you! —Caitlin and Patrick

- To my two gifts from China—Tiffany & Rachel. I'm so thankful that the Lord blessed us with you. You have both grown up to be beautiful young ladies.

- In memory of Ray & Nina Dammar—Karen's books so blessed Dad as he cared for Mom! Love, Sherry Lynn

- Landon, you are my greatest joy. Remember to have courage and be kind. All my love, sweet boy, Mama

- In honor of our son and brother, Luke. We miss you every single day. Love, Mom, Dad, Lynsey & Lacey

- Happy Birthday to my granddaughter Emma Nelson of Bloomington, IN! Love you 4ever! Grammy Dena Patrick

- Dorothy Peltomaki, I love you very much, Mom! You are strong & courageous. Love & Prayers, Denise

- Mom & Dad/Grandma & PopPop, We love you very much! Joe, Sheri, Jackie, Joey, Seth & Nora

- To my Beautiful Mother and Mother-in-Love, who left us too soon, we will always love you!! —Gayle Clayton

- Thank you, Mom, for cheering me through college! I finished because of your love! Love always, Hannah

- To my grandmothers, Linda and Alma, for always being there for us and loving us. —Heidi

- In memory of Dustin Kyle Fowler. Brother and best friend. Forever missed. Love, Candace and family

- Karen Hammond—My Beautiful 4 Granddaughters, Jaycee Baca, Mila Vonschoech, Samantha Peters & Lu Lu Peters

- Remembering Jacob & Joey. See you at our Heavenly Reunion one day! Love, Mom Karen & Sister Katie

- The Barretts are like Baxters: Faith, Family, FFF! Love You, Lori! Hugs, Ken

- I love you, momma! I will always be here for you. Your Loving Daughter, Kim

- Thank you to the Kingsbury family for changing so many lives with His love! Lots of love, Kristen Sullivan

- With gratitude to my KK Prayer Warriors . . . Blessed that Life-Changing Fiction connected us! Love, Sheila Holman

- Dottie (Mom)—Thanks for sharing your love, talents and wisdom with Lori & me. You model the Proverbs 31 woman with such grace. Love you, Linda

- My dear beloved Robert, Thanks for praying with me & for sharing 16 years of your life with me.

Thank you, Jesus, for 2nd chances & for answering the prayer of a lonely father. In my heart, Robert, I will always love you more. Your precious, Lou

- To Marcia Schibi: the nonfictional Elizabeth Baxter of our family. Yellow7, Mom!

- In honor of Debbie Everhart: a true and faithful woman of God. Love, Lee

- In Memory of my beautiful daughter, Marci Taylor Strebin. I will always love you & I will miss you until we are reunited in Heaven. Until then, we will love & watch over your boys. Love always! Mom

- Daughters of my heart: Shannon, Stacie, Nicole, Sarah & Samantha, may God's Word lead you home. Love, Mom

- To my wonderful, beautiful Mama, Patricia K. Conoly. Thank you for EVERYTHING that you do. We love you very much. Love, Rachel & Jason ♥

- To my loving husband, Howard. Our 8 children: Danielle, Christopher, Travis, Jorrdon, Jaeydon, Sara, Shiarah & Sherese. I love you with all my heart! Mom (Lori Sunkler)

- Julie & Samantha: Beautiful mothers, sisters, daughters. Forever loved, forever missed. Ron and Carol

- In loving memory of Ronda Sue Prentzas. Your loving heart & consistent faith will never be forgotten. Love & miss you —All of us

- To my first grandchild—Baby Boy Dearman! Happy 2nd Anniversary to my kids!! Love, Tammy Atarian Brooks

- Mom, Thank you for being the Mom you didn't have to be! I love you! Love, Tara

- Audrey—When you need a little loving from home, just press your hand to your cheek ♥ Luv ya & Miss ya —Mum

- To Sandy, the bravest God-fearing woman I know! I count it a blessing to call you friend. Vickie

- In memory of Frank, Sadie, Ernest & Juanita. You are forever in our hearts. Your legacy lives on in the lives of your children, grand- & great-grand-children. In love, Joel, Sheron, Keith & Sonya

- Elizabeth, have strength & courage for the Lord your God is with you wherever you go. Love, Mom & Dad

- We met in 1960. We married as 87-year-olds. Love you, Dr. (Pastor) Jim Conrod. —Lois Brudi-Conrod

TWO WEEKS

KAREN KINGSBURY

1. Share about a time when you were in a difficult situation. In what ways could you relate to Elise?

2. Tell of a situation when you helped or rescued someone in trouble. How did that work out? Why?

3. Why do you think Cole was so quick to stand by Elise—even forever?

4. Elise changed her mind often. What decision would you make if you were in her spot?

5. Do you agree with Elise's decision? Why or why not?

6. What are your feelings about adoption? Explain.

7. Ashley was quick to think Cole might've been the father of Elise's baby. Tell of a time when you jumped to conclusions. What did you learn from that?

8. Ashley goes through all the emotions of seeing Cole off to college. Have you or has someone you know gone through this type of goodbye? Tell about that experience.

9. Do you know anyone who has struggled with infertility? Talk about their journey.

10. In general, do you relate more to Aaron or Lucy? Explain.

11. Have you prayed for something that didn't happen the way you hoped? Talk about it.

12. How is it possible to have faith in God, even when your prayers don't get answered the way you like?

13. Vienna's accident happened without warning. Tell of a tragedy in your life or the life of someone you know. How do you get through a personal nightmare?

14. How can faith in God help you survive a tragedy? Give practical examples.

15. Read John 16:33 in the Bible. What do these words mean to you? Are they comforting? Why or why not?

16. Cole was a true friend till the end with Elise. Talk about a friend like that in your life. What sets that person apart?

17. Cole is a giver, kind to those in need. What can you do to spread kindness in your family, neighborhood or workplace?

18. The goodbye between Cole and Elise was difficult. Tragic almost. When has a goodbye deeply affected you? Talk about it.

19. As Cole sets off for college and a life of new beginnings, he feels sad. But also hopeful. What new experiences are up ahead for you? Have you ever thought of finding fresh opportunities and possibilities at your local church?

20. How did God help Theo and Alma because of their decision to care for a baby girl during those two weeks? What does the phrase "beauty from ashes" mean to you?

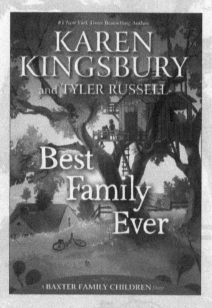

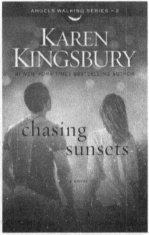

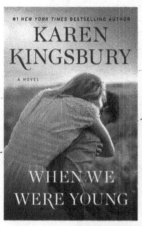

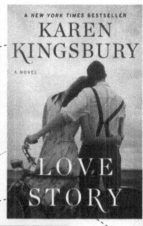

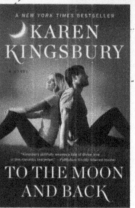